When the War is Over

Anja May

© 2018 Anja May

When the War is Over
First edition, June 2018
Original title: Am Ende dieses Jahres

Translated from German by Linda Gaus

Editor: Isabel Gross
Cover: Dominika Hlinková
Published by Bauermeister, Moltkestr. 26, 47058 Duisburg

ISBN: 978-1983259449

For Grandpa

Chapter 1

If only we weren't at war. It could be the most beautiful summer's day. The sun warms my calves as I grip the second-to-last rung of the ladder with my bare feet, trying to reach the branches higher up. There, cherries dangle in thick clusters, tempting me. As I slip one of the fruits into my mouth, its sweet juice running down my throat, I almost believe I'm on summer vacation, just like during my school days. Since I started my apprenticeship last year, I've had little time off. But today it's too hot to work, so my master's wife gave me the afternoon off to pick cherries for her.

I can hear the Brahms violin concerto playing softly through the open kitchen window, mingling with the song of the blackbirds. The aroma of fried onions drifts out into the garden. Already, my mouth is watering.

Suddenly the music stops, and the voice of a newscaster breaks in. It sounds distorted, tinny. I can only make out scattered phrases and don't bother to listen any further. But then one word catches my attention.

I look at the window as if this could help me hear better. Did I get that right? Or am I imagining things? Maybe I've been out in the sun too long?

Frau Pollack, the master's wife, throws the window all the way open and leans her head out. Her round cheeks are redder than usual, like the baked apples that we make at home for Christmas. She fixes me with a puzzled gaze and glassy eyes.

"Anton," she gasps, while the newscaster's voice buzzes on in the background. She pauses briefly like she's out of breath. "There has been an attack on our *Führer*."

So I did understand correctly.

I freeze on the ladder. The only thought running through my head is: did they succeed this time? The answer to this question will determine everything: what will happen to Germany, to my brother Helmut, Uncle Emil, and all of the other soldiers on the front. It will decide about winning or losing, about the end of the war.

I draw in a breath. My heart is thundering in my ears, so I nearly miss the next words.

"The *Führer* is alive! He's alive!" shrieks the newscaster hysterically.

What? My fingers and toes slip on the rung, and I fall blustering and crashing down the ladder. With a dull thump, I land on the ground, hardly noticing that I've skinned my knees. I have to keep listening.

"I repeat. Our *Führer*, Adolf Hitler, is alive. By the grace of God he has survived another cowardly attempt on his life and sustained only slight injuries. Immediately after the attack, the *Führer* resumed his mission to bring peace and prosperity to the German people. Later tonight, he himself will address all citizens in a radio broadcast."

"By the grace of God"? By witchcraft, more like! It's practically a miracle. This bastard has as many lives as a cat; he always escapes death at the last second. Or is the fact that he has survived so many previous assassination attempts really a sign that he's "destined to lead us Germans"?

But lead us where?

Frau Pollack beams at me from the window. Her face has returned to its normal color. She disappears into the kitchen and turns the radio down. I look at my bloody knees and pull a few blades of grass from the scrapes. My holiday mood has vanished.

At dinner, the attack is the number one topic of conversation.

"Boy oh boy, that was quite the news, wasn't it! Enough to make your blood freeze in your veins," says Master Pollack. He sounds indignant, but at the same time excited, like a small child who has witnessed an air battle on the weekly news for the first time.

"Heavens, I almost burned the onions," *Frau* Pollack chimes in. "And the boy fell straight off the ladder, that's how hard it hit him. Right, Anton?"

"This miraculous rescue, all of the Party members agree: it's an omen! A sign that the *Endsieg*, the ultimate victory, will come soon. With a *Führer* who's invulnerable, immortal—what could possibly happen to us?"

"Oh, Hermann, I'd like to believe that, I really would. One always hears such awful things. But if the *Führer*...I can't even say it. If we'd lost him, we'd be finished. Over and done with. Just like that."

"Come now, you must have more faith in him, Hilda!"

"Aren't you hungry, Anton?"

I startle at the sound of my name and notice that, up until now, I've just been pushing the food around on my plate. The mountain of mashed potatoes has hardly shrunk, and I'm cutting the bratwurst into smaller and smaller pieces.

I shake my head. "It's delicious, *Frau* Pollack."

If only Mother were here. Or Gerhard. Someone I could talk to.

"What's the matter, boy? Frog in your throat?"

The master laughs so hard that his gray walrus-mustache trembles and bits of mashed potato fly through the air. He wipes his mouth with a checkered napkin.

Master Pollack likes to laugh and laughs a lot. He also likes to eat and eats a lot. I'm always amazed at the skill of his sausage-like fingers when he changes the tiny gears of pocket-watch mechanisms. Only his eyes have been growing weaker over the years.

"I'm happy that I have a pair of young eyes to help me," he always says, thumping me on the shoulder.

I started my apprenticeship as a watchmaker about a year ago, after the death of my father, who was also a watchmaker. He and Pollack knew each other from their apprenticeship days. I'm pretty good at it; my hands are steady and clever, and my eyes are sharp. But staring through a magnifying glass all day long, looking at the insides of watches, bores me to death.

"Come now, what's going on, boy?" the master presses, his voice laden with good-natured concern.

"I just..." I can't think of an answer. I stare at the portrait on the opposite wall, which covers the blue flower pattern of the wallpaper. From his dark wooden frame, the *Führer* glares down at me, almost life-sized, with a stern gaze and hair parted just as strictly. The square mustache on his upper lip lends his features a hard and unforgiving quality.

"The boy is probably still a bit shocked about today's news," suggests *Frau* Pollack.

I nod. That's almost true.

"No wonder," booms the master. "Even full-grown men who've seen a whole lot more than you, boy, had their hearts in their mouths. I felt the same way myself! And you should have seen old Petzold—he was white as a sheet. But everything turned out alright, didn't it? The *Führer* will catch these traitors and put them to death."

"Tonight, my boy, you may stay up until after the *Führer* has delivered his address," *Herr* Pollack adds.

Oh, wonderful! I can hardly wait to hear his blabbering. I force a grateful smile, but I'm still not able to eat very much.

After dinner, we all sit down on the sofa in the parlor, more or less spellbound by the radio on the table in front of us. As it does every evening, the *Wehrmacht* bulletin reports on our brave soldiers' victories and some "alterations" of the front line—that's what they call it when we're forced to withdraw. Apparently, our troops on the western front have continued to retreat since the Americans started their offensive about a month ago. And in the east, not far from Breslau, the Russians are already stepping on our toes. I ask myself again and again whether things would be different if the attack on Hitler had succeeded. Would Germany now have a new government? Would there be a cease-fire?

As the evening wears on, special messages and urgent reports—none of which provide any new information—are interspersed with irritating march music to bolster the spirit. I'm considering whether I should fake a headache and retreat to my room when the telephone rings.

Master Pollack lifts himself laboriously from his armchair, grumbling. "That will be *Frau* Fegerlein. Old gossip."

He shuffles over to where the telephone hangs on the corridor wall and puts the receiver to his ear.

"Yes?" He shouts into the mouthpiece as if he still doesn't understand that the telephone bridges long distances between people *without* them having to scream at each other.

"Oh, it's you, *Frau* Köhler! Yes, he's here…ah…yes, of course…Anton! Your mother would like to speak to you."

A call from Mother? At this hour? We don't have a telephone at home. To call me, she has to go to the town post office. This can't mean anything good.

"Are you okay?" I ask as soon as I reach the phone.

"Yes."

"And the kids?"

My seven younger siblings are a lot of work for Mother, especially now that I'm not there to help her. Maybe Max and Fritz, the twins, have been up to trouble again?

"Don't worry, Anton."

"Helmut?" I croak.

"According to his last letter, he's arrived in the anti-aircraft barracks in Aachen."

Relieved, I let my shoulders slump forward.

"And how are you, Anton?" she asks.

I hesitate for a moment. With the master and his wife in the next room, I can't say what's really bothering me. "I'm doing fine. Why are you calling?"

"It's Uncle Emil. Martha sent me a telegram. He was badly wounded in the east, and they've put him in a military hospital in Breslau. He'll be released soon, but he needs help to get back to Leipzig."

Mother pauses for a few seconds, and all I hear is buzzing on the line.

"They say he's been blinded, in both eyes."

I swallow hard. Blinded. "Permanently?"

"I don't know exactly. But I promised Martha that we would take care of him." She sounds resolute. "Unfortunately I can't leave here, but if Master Pollack agrees to give you a few days' leave, you could accompany Uncle Emil on the train to Leipzig and deliver him safely to your aunt's."

"Of course." It's a sensible solution. I'm already in Breslau, very close to Uncle Emil.

"You will have to go to the transport office at City Hall and get special permission for the trip."

"Okay," I say, although my head is swirling.

I have so many questions, but here in the hall, under the watchful eyes of the Pollacks, I cannot ask them.

"I'll bring him home in one piece," I say, by way of conclusion.

When I explain the situation to *Herr* Pollack, he immediately understands and agrees to let me go for a few days. Then I excuse myself before Hitler has spoken, and thankfully, nobody stops me. I climb the creaky wooden stairs to my tiny attic room, which has just enough space for a narrow bed and a chest of drawers. At least there's a window. I throw it wide open to admit the mild night air. Outside, the wind has died down, and the crickets chirp their song as though the world were still in order.

I throw myself onto the bed stomach-first, ignoring the loud creaking, and pull out my small leather suitcase from underneath. Since I go home every weekend, it's not worth it to unpack the few things that I take along each time. *Frau* Pollack has given up lecturing me about it. I open the suitcase and slide my hand into the side pocket, where I keep all of my personal treasures: soccer trading cards, sheet music, postcards depicting city scenes, tattered adventure novels, and a small leather folder with photographs.

I pull out the photos. They show me with my brothers and sisters in our garden and on walks in the forest. In Mother's favorite picture, all eight children—including me—are arranged by size in front of our house, like the pipes of an organ. That was two years ago, when father was still alive. Back then little Erich wasn't born yet, and Helmut wasn't at the front. I'm standing between Helmut and Fritz. My hair is parted and smoothed for Sunday. Like the twins Max and Fritz, I have inherited father's chestnut-brown shimmer in my hair and Mother's hazel eyes.

And then there are the pictures of my summer vacation. Back when I was in school, I spent two weeks in Leipzig with Uncle Emil and Aunt Martha nearly every summer.

Though the occasion is not a pleasant one, I find myself growing increasingly excited. I will see Gert and Walter again, my cousins. In the picture, we're standing in front of the swing in the neighbors' garden. Next to me is a girl, her thick braids hanging over her shoulders. Her eyes are as blue as cornflowers, although the black and white picture doesn't show it. Luise Hofmann. My stomach turns a few flips when I think about how I might see her again quite soon.

Chapter 2

The hospital sits on the bank of the Oder River, near the center of Breslau. Rather than get off there, however, I hop off the streetcar in the center so I can have a look around: I don't get into the city very often. Luckily, Breslau hasn't been touched by the war. The old city center, with its Gothic city hall and church spires stretching high into the sky, never fails to impress me. It's all so different from my hometown. The marketplace, edged by medieval patricians' houses, transports me to a time I've only read about in my father's history books. I wish they'd taught us more history in school, and not just about the Germanic conquests and the Jewish infiltration of Germany.

In the market square, farmers have set up colorful stands with canvas awnings. People have formed long lines, eager to snatch up fresh tomatoes and cucumbers, ripe plums and apricots. These are not rationed, but they're difficult to come by in the city.

Frau Pollack has given me a food parcel containing two pounds of the cherries I picked, among other things, so I'm not tempted to stop and look at the produce.

At the hospital, I ask one of the nurses where I can find Emil Schmidt. She directs me to Room 114, in the right-hand wing, where the convalescing soldiers are housed. The facility is now serving as a reserve hospital for soldiers from the front lines who are no longer in critical condition and are stable enough to be transferred. I peek into one of the rooms as I pass. More than a dozen cots have been set up next to one another, but the men in them are all wrapped in clean white bandages. I skirt around a nurse who hurries by, dressed in a neat white coat and a little hat marked with a red cross. A one-legged man hobbles down the hall on crutches, his eyes dull.

When I arrive at Room 114, my courage deserts me. I don't know what to expect when I meet Uncle Emil, can't imagine how it must feel for him to have lost his eyesight forever.

But the cry of "come in!" that answers my knock doesn't sound dismissive or harsh. Uncle Emil occupies a double room, a privilege reserved for officers. In a bed by the window lies a gray-haired man with a pale face and one arm and leg in plaster casts. He stares out of the wide-open window, seemingly unaware of my presence. Uncle Emil sits on the other bed, wearing his uniform, upright and clean-shaven. His brown hair is trimmed and neatly parted, just as I remember him. But one thing is different: a black blindfold has been wrapped around his head, and a long scar mars his left cheek, still red and horribly ragged along the edges. It runs from below the bandage to the corner of his mouth.

"Uncle Emil," I say, then add, "It's me, Anton."

He smiles. "Anton! It's nice to…" he falls silent, but reaches out a hand to grope the air in front of him, searching. I grip it with both of my hands and squeeze hard.

"So you've come to take me out of here, yes?"

I nod, before remembering that he can't see me.

"Yes. Aunt Martha will be so happy to have you back."

Uncle Emil's hand finds my cheek and lingers there.

"Should I pack anything else?" I ask, my gaze sweeping the room.

"The nurse already took care of that. I just have to sign out, then they'll give me my medical discharge papers. That way no one can say I've bound up my eyes for fun, just to shirk my duty."

I peer at the gray-haired man in the other bed. Though he doesn't seem to hear us, I don't dare speak openly in front of him. I want to ask Uncle Emil whether the rumors I've heard are true—those rumors about soldiers in Russia, especially those caught in the battles around Stalingrad, who wounded themselves to escape the front. But nobody can accuse Uncle Emil of cowardice under fire, I'm sure of that.

I grip Uncle Emil's right arm and take his suitcase in my free hand. Just as we reach the door, he motions for me to stop.

"The flowers," he says, gesturing at the bed with a tilt of his head.

On the nightstand sits a small bouquet of violets. I'm confused: why would he want the flowers if he can't see them? But then I realize he can smell them. I lift the bouquet out of the water, let it drip dry, and hand it to Uncle Emil. He places it in the breast pocket of his uniform, and we leave the hospital room.

Wheels must roll for victory, announces an enormous propaganda poster over the entrance to the central train station. Next to it hangs the red swastika flag, so large that it covers almost half of the old building's façade. Once we're inside, Uncle Emil stops and tilts his head, apparently listening. In the vaulting station hall, the echo of clicking heels on the stone floor intermingles with the indistinct murmuring of dozens of voices. The stationmaster's announcements resound above the clamor. In the distance, trains wheeze and clatter, their wheels squealing on the tracks.

"Our train leaves from platform three," I say, after studying the display board. We have a strenuous trip ahead of us: nearly seven hours' ride, and we have to change trains twice. Once we cross the Neisse River to Saxony, passenger trains are only allowed to run at night because of the danger of air raids.

As I lead Uncle Emil to the track, I notice a host of armed men in uniform patrolling the train station with German shepherds on short leashes. Some of the men are standing next to the trains, guarding the doors. The uniforms tell me they're SS and Gestapo. What are *they* doing here? Though we aren't scheduled to leave for another half hour, our train is already waiting on the track. It too is being watched. All of the doors are still closed, except for the first one, in the carriage directly behind the engine. A knot of people has gathered there: passengers with luggage, like us, clearly eager to board.

"What's happening?" asks Uncle Emil.

"They're checking passengers' papers individually," I say quietly. "We have to wait in line. This might take a while."

"It's because of the assassination attempt," Uncle Emil says, speaking still more softly.

"Are they looking for the conspirators?"

My uncle places his forefinger on his lips, and I'm forced to accept that I'll have to wait for answers. I help him light a cigarette. Then we wait until the line thins out and it's our turn to be inspected.

"Papers!" the officer says gruffly, and, after studying us carefully, "Where are you headed?"

"To Leipzig. *Oberleutnant* Emil Schmidt has been released to his family after sustaining severe wounds in service of the Fatherland," I answer.

The officer glances at Uncle Emil's bound eyes before scrutinizing our travel documents once more. "And you, boy?"

"I'm just accompanying him."

Apparently, the officer can't find anything to object to. He waves us through, and I release a breath I didn't know I was holding.

"*Herr* Schmidt!" he calls back to us as we move toward the train. "Have a good trip. *Heil Hitler!*"

Uncle Emil freezes for a moment, then nods in the officer's direction. I help him board. Uncle Emil is a war hero, now. He'll have to get used to this.

The walls of the train carriage are plastered with wanted posters depicting the heads of the "high traitors," with their names listed below. Some of them look familiar. When I tell Uncle Emil that Carl Friedrich Goerdeler, Leipzig's former mayor, is among the wanted, he just nods slowly. Without looking into his eyes, I can't tell what he is thinking.

I find us a compartment occupied only by a woman and her young daughter. The little girl stares anxiously at my uncle, but the woman greets us amicably. I guide Uncle Emil to a seat by the window and help him get settled. A few minutes later, I pull the bag of cherries out of my suitcase and let him reach in. I also offer some to the little girl and her mother. We nibble silently on the fruits as the train gains speed.

We travel westward, passing fields and small towns. From time to time, heavily armed men patrol the corridor outside our compartment. After our first stop at a small train station in a town just outside of Breslau, the SS combs the entire train, and we have to show our papers again. The little girl hides behind her mother, probably frightened by the machine guns that the officers carry slung over their shoulders.

They repeat the procedure at every stop. I would really like to ask Uncle Emil some questions, but the presence of the woman and her daughter prevents me.

Suddenly, there's a commotion in the corridor. The door from the adjacent car opens with a squeak. I hear the footfalls of heavy boots at a run. "Hey, stop!" somebody bellows. A dog barks.

I rush to the compartment door to peer through the glass, just as a man in a gray jacket hustles by through the corridor.

In a few seconds, he reaches the end of the car and realizes he's trapped as it's the last one. He looks around frantically, and for a brief moment, I can see his face, distorted by fear. Now his pursuers come into view, wearing black coats. One of them is holding a sheepdog, which strains against its short leash, stretching it almost to breaking. The man they're chasing tears open the rear door of the car and throws himself out of the moving train with an anguished cry.

My heart is hammering. Though I don't know the man, I'm on his side; I want him to escape. Is he one of the men on the posters? Could he have survived the plunge?

"Stop the train!" the SS men roar as they storm by. For a mad, fleeting moment, I imagine myself opening the compartment door and sticking my leg out into the aisle to trip them up. But of course, I don't. The officers pull up short at the door the man just jumped out and point their Mausers outside. The rattling of the gunshots drowns out even the clattering of the train. The little girl screams and presses close to her mother.

"Don't be afraid, sweetie. They won't hurt you," Uncle Emil tries to comfort her.

The train comes to a stop, squealing and puffing.

"All passengers must stay where they are," the announcement blares through the loudspeaker.

I sigh and sit back down next to Uncle Emil, who is talking quietly to the woman. He seems to know what's happening, even though he can't see any of it. After what feels like an eternity, the train starts up again. We don't find out who the fugitive was and whether he got away. I hope so.

Our companions disembark in Liegnitz. Now we're alone, finally. I sit across from Uncle Emil at the window. Slowly he undoes the knot of the blindfold at the back of his head. As he removes the black cloth, I see that there's a gauze bandage underneath. He unwinds this as well until the only things covering his eyes are two round cotton pads. Carefully, he pulls off one, then the other.

I stare at what's hidden underneath. His eyes are closed, his lids and lashes stuck together with white goo. The deep scar that runs over his left cheek continues across his swollen eyelid, dividing it in two.

"Anton, can you please get the salve from my bag, and some fresh cotton pads? It itches really badly."

I rummage in the bag and hand him what he asked for. My hand trembles as I grasp the jar of ointment. "Do you…need help?"

"No, it's okay, son."

Uncle Emil carefully wipes away the old, greasy cream with the cotton pads and applies a new layer. I wonder whether there are even still eyes underneath those bruised lids. If not—what then? Empty sockets? I shudder.

"Uncle?" I begin.

He pauses in re-winding the bandage around his head. "Yes, son?"

I gather my courage. "How did it happen?"

Uncle Emil nods as if he was expecting this question. Then, without a word, he resumes tying the bandage, appearing completely immersed in the activity. He's silent for such a long time that I'm afraid I've asked the wrong thing. I look out the window, fearing that he'd know if I stared at him—but of course, that's stupid.

"It was about a month ago," he finally says, his voice flat. "The Red Army began an offensive to drive us out of their territories. A clever move after the Americans had just landed in Western France. We'd been waiting for the Russians to advance, but the attack still hit us harder than we expected. My division received the command to close a gap in our defenses at Ludsen. But the Russians had much better equipment—tanks, airplanes, weapons—and many more soldiers. Every day we fought for our lives, and we were constantly in retreat."

Uncle Emil seems to look right at me through his bandage.

"It was one of our own mines. We'd laid it to keep the Bolsheviks in check. As we were retreating, one of my comrades set it off. I was just hit by a few splinters. After that, they promoted me to *Oberleutnant* and awarded me the Iron Cross." Uncle Emil laughs bitterly.

I stare at the small silver pin on his uniform jacket. Just a piece of metal that won't replace his eyesight.

"How are things where you're living, Anton? Have you been hit as well?"

"Up until now, the bombers have left Breslau alone."

"That's why they call it the Reich's bomb shelter. It's true, then. I just wouldn't bet that things will stay that way forever."

I shake my head.

"When will you be sixteen?" he asks suddenly.

"In March."

"Let's hope the war is over by then."

"Do you believe…?" I falter when one of the SS men comes running down the aisle of our car, passing our compartment. Only when he's gone, I begin again. "Do you believe we still have a chance?" I whisper.

"A chance?"

"At winning the war."

Once again, Uncle Emil is silent for a long time. He pulls a cigarette out of his case, and I light it for him. Uncle Emil blows a fine plume of smoke out from between his lips. I watch as it curls and puffs in the air, almost giving up hope that he'll answer. Then he leans in closer.

"In my opinion, the war has been lost for a long time," he says in a clear voice. "But our *Führer*"—it sounds as if he's spitting out the word—"will never capitulate until the last German soldier has fallen in his name."

Chapter 3

Aunt Martha greets her husband with tears and kisses. Even though it's six in the morning, the whole family is awake when we reach the Schmidts' house. If my aunt and cousins are shocked by the blindfold, they hide it well.

Aunt Martha serves us cake. She must have saved extra sugar and flour coupons for it. Now we sit in the spacious living room, Uncle Emil surrounded by his sons and holding little Mathilde on his lap. We talk about everything under the sun, except the war and Uncle Emil's injury.

The doorbell rings. I jump to answer it so the family can stay together. Who could be visiting so early in the morning? I open the door, and an army of butterflies flutters up in my stomach.

It's Luise.

"Oh my God, Anton, is it really you?"

My voice fails me. All I can do is raise my hand feebly, but I lower it again when I see that Luise is clutching the handle of a wicker basket with both hands. How long we stand there, staring at each other, I don't know. I'd forgotten how bright her hair is, like ripe fields of wheat shining in the sun.

"Did *you* bring *Herr* Schmidt home?" she asks, finally.

I can only nod.

"So…may I come in?"

She holds her basket up higher; I can see the neck of a bottle protruding from underneath a checkered cloth.

"Oh, of course!" I croak and take a step to the side. In my hurry to let her through, my right shoulder bumps against the door, which hits the wall with a loud thump. We both cringe, startled. Then our eyes meet, and we begin to laugh. Even me. *Smooth, Anton, really smooth!* as my best friend Gerhard would say.

Luise passes me cautiously, holding the basket protectively in front of her as if I were a watchdog that might bare its teeth and charge her at any moment. I follow her back into the living room.

"I hope I'm not interrupting," she says. "I just wanted to bring you a little something, *Herr* Schmidt. A welcome present from Mother and the rest of us."

Smiling, Aunt Martha accepts the basket and pulls out a bottle of Cognac from its bed of juicy, blue-black plums.

"Thank you, Luise!" Uncle Emil says earnestly. "Send your mother my best. When I have a chance, I'll come over and thank her in person."

Luise grasps Uncle Emil's hand. "*Herr* Schmidt, I wanted to tell you how much I admire your service. You are a true German hero. If we didn't have soldiers such as you and my father, who are prepared to make such sacrifices for the Fatherland…"

Suddenly the room falls quiet. Luise falters, perhaps sensing the change in mood. Uncle Emil's expression is wooden, mask-like.

"That's really a lot of plums," says Aunt Martha into the silence. "If I'd known, I would have baked a plum cake…" She rushes into the kitchen.

Luise glances at me, but I look down at my feet.

"Have you heard anything from your father?" Uncle Emil asks her.

"Oh, yes! We get news in the mail almost every day. He's still in the military hospital in Lemberg, behind the Ukrainian lines, convalescing."

"Is he badly hurt?"

"His arms and legs were hit by grenade shrapnel. The fragments are still moving around, but he says he's healing well. Maybe he'll have home leave soon. And once his leg is better, he'll be deployed again, I'm sure. Are you also headed back to the front?"

"What would they want with a blind soldier?"

Luise looks sheepishly at the floor, then quickly says goodbye because she has service with the BDM, the League of German Girls. I'm a little disappointed as I'm leaving again tomorrow. If I don't see her again before then, she will always remember me as the guy who mumbles nonsense and bumps into doors. Just great!

"Hello, Anton!"

I've spent the entire afternoon outdoors, playing soccer with Gert and Walter, or sitting on the grass with little Mathilde and reading to her from *Der Struwwelpeter*. I even made an effort to comb my hair to the side with water, though usually I hardly pay any attention to my looks. Smoothed this way, my hair gleams like ripe chestnuts. I'm just about to head back into the house because Aunt Martha shouted from the kitchen window to say that dinner is almost ready when Luise appears at the fence that separates her garden from the Schmidts'.

She's wearing her BDM uniform, a knee-length skirt of coarse dark blue cotton and a bright white blouse with a black neckerchief. Even in that plain getup she looks like an angel. I wish Gerhard were here now, to be my wingman. What would he do?

Oh, come on! he'd say. *You managed just fine before.* I see myself sitting side by side with Luise on the wide wooden swing that hangs from the apple tree in her garden. Back then we laughed and talked effortlessly, the way children do. The memory gives me back my voice.

"How was service?" I ask, ambling over to the green wooden fence.

"Just some clearing-up work. We helped remove the rubble from the streets," she says, studying me. I can sense her forget-me-not-blue gaze traveling up and down my body, and I suddenly feel very hot.

"Wow, Anton, it's been a long time!"

"Nearly two years," I confirm.

"You look really different. But at the same time, you don't. I recognized you right away," she says with a smile.

I realize that I'm now almost a head taller than she is—that didn't use to be the case. But she has changed, too. I don't remember her being so…curvy. I clear my throat and hope that she won't notice my red ears in the sunlight.

"Everything looks the same here. Your house is still there, that's good…" Man, what am I babbling on about? "I mean, if you look at the rest of Leipzig…when we drove through the streets this morning…there's debris everywhere, holes in the pavement…even the main train station took a hit."

"Yeah, that happened last December. But at least it's still standing. The Allied terrorists can't blow it away that easily! Our part of the city hasn't been hit so hard because we're so far away from the center. Only a few emergency bomb drops. It's just a little annoying that we have to run to the cellar whenever there's an alarm." She says this as if it were the most natural thing in the world, as if all the citizens of Leipzig were already accustomed to the constant air raids.

"Do they come during the day, too?"

"They do now. And usually right in the middle of my favorite subjects. Of course, Oskar is happy when there's no school. But normally they're on their way somewhere else, to Dresden or the industrial part of Leuna, places like that. They look like a cloud of locusts, the way they darken the sky. And then the thundering starts, when our flak shoots back at them. At night they drop those parachute flares to illuminate their targets—Christmas trees, we call them—and the whole city is lit up bright as day. I guess that could be useful if it weren't so scary: saving electricity, you know. During the December fourth attack, when they hit the main station, even the walls of our house shook. And afterward, the sky above the whole city center was fiery red. But we won't let that intimidate us." She takes a breath. "What about you? What have you been up to?"

I tell her haltingly that I started an apprenticeship after Father's death. Her bright eyebrows draw together slightly, causing a tiny wrinkle to appear on her forehead.

"So you're going to be a watchmaker." She sounds almost disappointed.

"It looks that way," I say a bit uncertainly.

"What happened…with your music? Our dream. Do you remember?"

Of course I remember. We wanted to become a famous duo and learn to play Schumann's *Träumerei* together, me on the violin, Luise on the piano. But that was just a childish fantasy.

I shake my head. "I can't even play an instrument."

"You could still learn," she says with conviction.

"And who will earn money in the meantime?"

Luise opens her mouth, but says nothing.

I wrap my hands around the fence pickets and stare at the worn-out toes of my shoes. It's not just the fence that separates us. Luise doesn't have to worry about money. Her family owns the house she lives in; they rent it out to other people, too. Her father is a teacher, and she's brilliant herself. She goes to the *Gymnasium*, while I only attended a country school through the eighth grade because my parents couldn't afford more. It's clear that I'm not good enough for her.

That didn't matter when we were children, but now it suddenly does. She's so pretty, a true German girl with her flashing blue eyes, her dimples and golden hair; and so slender, too. Suddenly, I can no longer imagine the two of us side by side.

"I..." she hesitates, "I learned a new Mozart sonata. Father gave me the music last time he visited. Would you like to hear it?"

I nod, and forget everything I was just thinking. In one fluid motion I jump over the low fence. As we walk toward the house, she asks, "Did you see *The Punch Bowl* at the movies, with Heinz Rühmann? It was a blast, wasn't it?"

"Yeah. *Pfeiffer* with three *f*s. One before and two after the *ei*," I quote.

"Sit down," Luise mimics one of the movie-teachers and pretends to inspect me over an imaginary pince-nez. "Too bad my teachers aren't that funny."

"At my school we had a teacher who actually talked like that," I say. "Old Monse. Once I was daydreaming in German class, and all of a sudden I heard him say my name. I nearly jumped out of my seat—I was scrambling to figure out what he'd asked me. But he just looked at me like I'd grown three heads. The whole class stared."

Luise opens the door to the house and turns to me. "And what *was* he asking?"

I grin. "Nothing. He just said *the weather's getting Köhler*. He meant cooler, get it?"

Luise bursts into laughter. I'm a little proud that I can make her laugh.

We enter the living room, where the grand piano, made of shiny dark wood, still stands against one wall. On the opposite wall is a bay window crowded with flower pots. Through it, I can see the apple tree with the swing in the garden. It smells fresh and flowery, and everything is immaculately clean.

Luise sits down on the piano bench and, for a moment, places her hands gently on the keys without pressing them. Then her slim fingers begin to fly across the piano, climbing up and down and taking on a life of their own. She plays from memory, without so much as a glance at the music, keeping her eyes closed for most of the time, while the tones tumble forth from beneath her nimble hands. I watch her and listen spellbound, wanting to remember as much of her as possible.

When the final chord sounds, I can barely keep myself from bursting into applause.

She turns to me with shining eyes.

"Would you like to try?" she asks, and slides over on the bench, which is wide enough for two.

I stare at the polished wood floor, unable to look her in the eye. "But I can't play."

"I can teach you." Her voice sounds strange, shy and inviting at the same time.

At that moment, her mother emerges from the kitchen. "Oh, *hallo* Anton, it's nice to see you again."

She has pinned her hair up in the latest fashionable style, and even in her apron she looks smart. A "*fan*-tastic" woman, Gerhard would say. I think she could be an actress.

"Do you mind if I turn on the radio? It's time for the *Wehrmacht* report" her mother says.

Luise looks down at her hands. I shake my head, but inside I'm kicking myself. Why didn't I just sit down next to her?

Now both of us act as if we're listening intently to the news. Everything is as usual: losses on all fronts—which are played down, of course. Then the newscaster rambles on about how the German soldiers are bravely putting themselves in the line of fire to keep the enemy from advancing. In the end, he urges all Germans, especially the women on the home front, to make sacrifices for the total war, for the *Führer* and the soldiers.

"As if we aren't already doing that," cries Luise, after the report is over. "Every week, my BDM group helps the refugees that arrive at the train station. We serve them bread and tea, you know. Those people are so thankful! We Germans have to stick together at a time like this. My BDM leader, Gertrud, always says that as long as the *Führer* has young people like us, and soldiers like Father and your uncle, Germany cannot perish. And then there's the *Wunderwaffe*."

"The *Wunderwaffe*?" I ask contemptuously, before I can stop myself.

"Yes, it's supposed to be ready soon."

I snort. Does she actually believe that some miracle weapon will save us? It's all just propaganda, anyway. I'm a bit disappointed in Luise. I thought she was smart enough not to believe everything we're told. Hasn't she ever listened to an enemy radio station?

She looks at me, astonished. "Don't you think so?"

"Oh, yes, I'm sure the *Wunderwaffe* exists." *In fairy tales!* I add mentally.

For an instant, our eyes meet. There is so much desperate hope in her gaze that I can't hold it against her. Still, I'm sad that I can't speak openly with Luise. Mother and Father drilled into me that I shouldn't trust anyone with my true thoughts unless I'm absolutely certain that they feel the same way. That's what things have come to in Germany!

Luise's mother turns off the radio. I can see that it's time to take my leave when she begins to set the table.

"I have to go," I stammer, suddenly feeling awkward again. Luise gets up slowly and faces me, her hands playing with the folds of her skirt.

"When are you going back?"

"Tomorrow morning."

Her eyes seem to dim. Then she nods. "Travel safe, Anton! I hope your train gets back without any trouble. And take care of yourself in Silesia."

"Yeah, you too," I reply. I realize that I probably won't see Luise again for a long time.

Chapter 4

Winter has descended upon us, and that's not all: since October, bombs have been falling on Breslau, too. We are not the "Reich's bomb shelter" anymore. Now the trains only travel at night, and after sunset, you have to take special care to pull down the blackout blinds on all windows.

But today we're not thinking about that. It's Christmas, the sixth wartime Christmas. It has snowed and outside everything is still. Beyond the blinds, the white coat glistens in the pale moonlight, illuminating the night. No lanterns burn, no candlelight gleams through the windows of the neighbors' houses. But in our living room, the Christmas tree glows.

Earlier today, I went to the woods with the twins, Max and Fritz, to cut down a cute little fir, which we dragged home. Mother and the girls have hung straw stars on its branches and lighted a few candles. We can't burn them for long, because wax is in short supply, like everything else. Still, my siblings are delighted by the sight. When they're finally allowed into the room, they clap their hands, and little Erich coos with enthusiasm. We all sing "Silent Night" and then "Ring, Little Bell." Mother has put the framed photo of Father on the table next to the sofa so he can be with us.

"Why isn't Helmut here?" asks Lieschen when the last note fades. She must be thinking about how he used to accompany us on the violin. Helmut, my older brother, was drafted to an anti-aircraft unit. They sent him to Western Germany a while ago to defend us against air raids.

"He's indispensable to the war," I say.

"What's 'indispensable' mean?" asks Max.

"It means that he's too important and they can't do without him." When I see my sister's face fall, I add, "But that's why Gerhard is here."

"Yayyyy," Lieschen clings to Gerhard's leg.

Gerhard is basically part of the family. He's the same age as I am, and we went to school together. Back when he still lived in the orphanage at the edge of town, he visited us nearly every day. Mother and Father probably thought, privately, that one more child didn't really make a difference. Now Gerhard is working for farmer Moltke, who gave him the day off.

With a gesture at the presents under the tree, I distract my sisters from asking any more questions. The little ones pounce on the packages. I watch them from Father's worn-out leather armchair, amazed at what Mother has scrounged up. Even if it's just a handful of hazelnuts or a crocheted woolen hat, there's something for everyone. Fritz is pleased with the whittling knife I've given him.

I'm not expecting any presents, so I'm even more surprised when Lotta comes running toward Gerhard and me, her face shining, and hands us a package wrapped in brown paper and tied with a simple hemp cord. Gerhard and I exchange glances. From the shape and softness, I can already guess that it contains something knitted. Gerhard is the first to unwrap his gift: a pair of thick socks made of coarse gray wool. He beams like he's just received the nicest present in the world.

"*Fan*-tastic, *Frau* Köhler!"

Mother smiles. "Farmer Moltke gave me the wool. Please thank him for me. I thought that you two could really use thick socks. *Frau* Weber is predicting a long, hard winter. And her aches and pains are almost always right, as you know."

I unpack my own pair and unfold them. In the process, I notice something glimmering from where it's been tucked between the socks. Curious, I pull the object out.

It's a pocket watch, about the size of a walnut, with a thin casing of matte gold. I open the cover and examine the faded Roman numerals on the face, the delicate hands, which have frozen in place. I know it well: the watch belonged to Father. On the cover is an etched inscription. The lettering is tiny, already partially scratched off, and it's hard to decipher. But I know exactly what it says:

> *When heart and conscience are aligned,*
> *The right path you'll always find.*
> *J.W.v. Goethe*

I smile. That's what Father always said to Helmut and me: "In the end, a man answers only to his conscience." He wholeheartedly believed that, and he acted accordingly. Once, when Father and I were secretly listening to enemy broadcasts, he said, "If you want to get an accurate read on a situation, you can't listen to just one side. One side can always lie. But if you listen to several lies, perhaps you can find the truth somewhere in between."

Suddenly, Mother is standing beside me, her hand resting on my shoulder. "Ernst would have wanted you to have it," she says quietly.

Me! Not Helmut. Not the eldest son, this time. I turn the little wheel to wind the watch and hear its satisfying ticking sound as the hands resume their work. Then I close the cover and put it in my pocket so that I will always have it with me.

Fritz and Max come tumbling over to show me the model airplane that Gerhard has built for them. The short wings and tail are made of cardboard, and the body is constructed out of tiny sticks, with a propeller on the nose. He's even fastened a pair of wheels underneath, made of hard paper wads.

"Is it a dive-bomber?" asks Fritz.

"Exactly! It's the Junkers Ju 87. A little out of date, but wow, could it do some damage," says Gerhard, taking the model from his hand. "They call it a dive-bomber because it dives on its prey, like a hawk." Gerhard makes the plane swish vertically downward. "And just before it reaches its target, it drops the bomb. It almost always hits its mark. Then the pilot brings the plane out of the dive...and *vrooom*...he pulls the machine back up, into the air."

Max and Fritz listen, wide-eyed. "Do the enemies have planes like that too?" Max asks.

"Of course. The Tommies have Barracudas, the Yankees have Apaches..."

I leave Gerhard behind, as he rambles on about various countries' airplanes, and go to give Mother a hand in the kitchen. A fire crackles in the old iron stove. It already smells like baked apples. Tonight we're having potato pancakes with applesauce because there's not much else. Not that I mind; I love Mother's potato pancakes. The ingredients come from our own garden. I even helped preserve the apples in the fall, though I can't help Mother much otherwise, what with my apprenticeship. But she believes the money I bring home each week is support enough.

Mother smiles at me and presses the grater into my hand. She hands me the peeled potatoes, and I grate them into a bowl, to which she adds eggs, onions, salt, and pepper. While we're doing this, we listen silently to radio broadcasts: the *Wehrmacht* report and Goebbels' speech.

"In this hour of celebration, our people will stand before the *Führer* like a wall," he roars.

"That's exactly right," says Mother. "We're supposed to form a wall of bodies. Become human shields—just so the people in Berlin can live a little longer."

I stop grating and look at her. Mother hardly ever speaks this way.

"How many soldiers have given their lives for nothing because of that stupid order that says they can't surrender territory under any circumstances, even when it's already lost? And now it's the civilians' turn. The *Volkssturm* will have to make it right: old men, teenage boys, and women. And then the last sacrifice, the children."

I notice with a start that Mother has stopped peeling potatoes and is wiping her eyes on her forearm. I've never seen her cry before. Her eyes have sunk deep into their sockets, and the gray strands in her hair have multiplied. Today she is showing her worry for the first time.

"I can't stop thinking about Helmut," she says, resuming her work. "How he's doing on the front. It won't be long now. If he can just stick it out! I almost wish he'd be taken prisoner, by the Americans or the English. Just not by the Russians. Anyone but them." She looks at me, concern etched into her face. "What are we going to do if the Russians keep advancing?"

The Russians. Everybody here is afraid of them. In recent months they've gained more and more ground, crossed the borders of the Reich in the east, and now they're at the Vistula River, just two hundred miles from Breslau. In East Prussia, they've already forced thousands of people to flee. It's rumored that they've laid waste to whole towns, assaulting women and girls, killing children and the elderly…and supposedly, German POWs have been taken to work camps in Siberia, where they're treated like animals and left to starve or freeze.

I don't know how much of what I've heard is true. But I do know one thing: the Russians have good reason to hate us. Didn't we do the same thing to their villages in '41 and '42? I heard Father say that often enough.

If the Red Army breaks through our defenses—and it's just a matter of time—what will happen to my family?

I don't know how to answer that question. But I'm determined to protect Mother and my younger siblings as best I can.

After dinner, I slip out of the living room, where Mother is playing a game of *Mensch ärgere dich nicht* with the children. I walk down the long hallway, with its creaking floorboards, to the last door, which leads into a small workroom: Father's old shop.

I haven't been in there in a long time, but today I feel drawn to it, somehow. Perhaps because it's Christmas and Father isn't with us. I open the door carefully and flick on the light. The weak ceiling lamp illuminates the long wooden table where Father sat hunched over for hours, working with pincers on the tiny screws and wheels of watch mechanisms.

And that's also where I found him: slumped over his last project. That was nearly a year and a half ago. The endless work was too much for his heart, Mother says. I stroke the unfinished wood of the workbench, leaving a stripe the width of my finger in the dust. In the far corner, there's an old grandfather clock whose pendulum hasn't been wound for a long time. And next to that…Father's violin in its case.

I take a quick peek over my shoulder before I open the well-worn black leather case. There it is, lying on a bed of midnight-blue velvet. Its amber body glistens as if freshly polished. I can almost hear Helmut's voice, rebuking me for having picked up his violin. *His* violin! He was the one who skipped music class as often as possible. Of course Mother and Father knew nothing about that; otherwise, they might've spent the money for his lessons on me instead.

But Helmut isn't here anymore.

Suddenly I remember my last conversation with Luise. *What happened with your music? Our dream.*

My heart pounding, I stretch out my hand and, gingerly, wrap my fingers around the slim neck; the raw metal strings bite into my fingertips. I lift the violin from its case and place it on my left shoulder. My fingers tentatively strum across the fingerboard. Then I take the bow in my right hand and touch it to the strings, ever so gently. The note's vibrations run through my hand and into my arm, spreading from there throughout my body. I don't just hear the tone, I feel it. The hairs on my arm stand up. I imagine myself playing not just a few shaky notes, but whole songs, concertos, symphonies. If only I could play like the great violinists, like George Boulanger and Yehudi Menuhin, who I've heard on the radio…if only I could excite other people with my music, make them dream….

"Oh, so that's where you've gone off to."

I cringe so violently that the bow skitters over the metal strings, making a screeching noise that gives me goosebumps. Guiltily, I lower the violin and turn around. Gerhard is leaning on the door, his lanky figure almost as tall as the frame.

He makes a face. "Ouch! Looks like you could use some practice."

I redden and clear my throat, putting the violin back in its case. "I was just…"

"I get it. You've always looked at the violin like it was a pretty girl, all dreamy-eyed."

"No, I didn't!" I say, hurrying towards the door.

He gives me a crooked grin. "Sorry I disturbed you two. I can leave if you want…"

"Just let me through!" I punch him lightly in the ribs. He bends over theatrically and takes a step back so I can pass.

After Gerhard has left the workshop, I pull the door closed behind us with a bang. "Do *I* laugh at you because you want to be an aerospace engineer—*farmhand*?"

"Hey, why so sensitive all of a sudden?"

"It's nothing!" Knowing that my ears are still red, I storm back down the hall to the living room. He runs after me and grabs my arm before I can open the door.

"Sorry, man."

I turn to him. "Forget it. I was being stupid."

"I won't tell anyone," he whispers conspiratorially, winking. I can't help but laugh.

Chapter 5

The holidays and the days after pass much too quickly. We have snowball fights, sled down the cemetery hill, and skate on the frozen town pond. The only unusual thing is that Mother has started to pack bags and suitcases with our most important possessions, in case we have to leave in a hurry.

On New Year's Day, notice arrives that all boys born in 1929 should report to the Hitler Youth center in my town. The command surprises me and leaves me feeling uneasy. Since I began my apprenticeship in Breslau, I have been going to the HY center there. Why are they calling us here now?

When I arrive in the courtyard of the old weaving mill, I see Gerhard and many of my other former groupmates already gathered. I went to school with some of them. Unfortunately, Wilhelm Braun is also there.

"Hey Anton, how's it going?" Herbert slaps me on the back in a friendly fashion. He was the captain of our soccer team. "Do you know what all this is about?"

"Maybe they want us to shovel snow," I answer hopefully.

Wilhelm raises his eyebrows. He looks smug, like he knows more than we do. I don't do him the favor of letting on how curious I am. We never liked each other much back at school because I couldn't stand him bullying weaker kids.

But since his father held such a high position in the SS, nobody could say anything.

Wilhelm saunters over. He stops in front of me and regards me like I'm an obnoxious insect. "So, Köhler, you're back, are you?"

"I'm on vacation," I mumble.

He is at least a head taller than I am. With his blond crew-cut and penetrating gray eyes, he looks as if he's sprung directly from the pages of one of those Nazi magazines. Gerhard stands next to me. He's as tall as Braun is, but thin and lanky, while Wilhelm acquired his muscles from boxing. I'm neither as tall as Gerhard nor as muscular as Wilhelm. "Wiry as a wildcat," is what Mother always says—meaning that my build comes from having spent a lot of time in the forest climbing trees when I was growing up.

"Oh yeah, now you're a *watchmaker*. Like your old man."

"What's that supposed to mean?" I squeeze out between my teeth.

Gerhard puts a hand on my arm and shoots me a warning glance.

"Work that's truly essential for the war," scoffs Wilhelm. "But perhaps you'll do something useful soon."

"Without watches, the *Wehrmacht* wouldn't be able to function," says a thin voice behind me. "Military precision. Punctuality."

I turn around and smile at August. In the past he wouldn't have stood up to Wilhelm—he was always the one who suffered the most under Braun. Once, when Wilhelm filled in for our corps leader, he drilled August so hard that the smaller boy nearly broke down in the summer heat. August was never much of an athlete, but he was the best student in the class.

"Who asked you?" Wilhelm snarls at him.

I ignore him. "How are you, August?"

"Doing well. I'm going to the *Gymnasium* now."

Like Luise, I think wistfully. "Do you know what they're going to do with us?"

August shakes his curly head. "Maybe we're going to be drafted," he whispers wide-eyed.

"I don't think so. We're not even sixteen yet."

"Why are you grinning like that?" Gerhard snaps at Wilhelm.

Wilhelm shrugs nonchalantly. "What if they do enlist us? Do you soil yourself at the thought?"

"I'm ready to do my duty," says Herbert, the officer's son, with his head held high. "I won't just sit around while the Russians advance on us."

"I wouldn't mind finally doing something either," adds Gustav. "That's what we were trained for."

Trained? I guess he means the boot camp where we were tormented for a few weeks at age fourteen, and the drills with the air defense force...but my groupmates are shooting their mouths off.

The clock in the church tower chimes one. At that moment, a tall man in a long black coat rounds the corner into the courtyard.

"Form a line," bellows Wilhelm.

Though the command catches us by surprise, we obey. We can do drills in our sleep.

"Stand still. Eyes forward. Count off!" he calls as the man approaches. Now I recognize him. It's Wilhelm's father, SS-*Hauptsturmführer* Braun.

We quickly count to twelve.

"Köhler, where are your feet?" Wilhelm barks at me.

"Heels in line with everyone else's! Didn't they teach you anything?"

I clench my teeth and slide a few inches forward.

Herr Braun stands next to Wilhelm, surveying us. He is just as tall, with the same blond, parted hair and the same unforgiving steel-gray eyes. Around his upper arm, he wears the red swastika band, and I can see the two silver lightning-bolt-shaped insignia on the lapels of his uniform. The iron eagle standing on a skull gleams on his cap. I've always thought the skull was a fitting symbol for the SS, Himmler's band of thugs.

"Father," says Wilhelm, sounding suddenly less sure of himself.

His father shoots him a sharp glance.

"I mean…SS-*Hauptsturmführer* Braun! I dutifully report that twelve Hitler Youth appeared as ordered." He salutes, and so do we.

"*Heil* Hitler!" cries *Hauptsturmführer* Braun, eying each of us like a falcon about to dive on his prey.

My whole body begins to tingle as though I were covered in ants. The longer the *Hauptsturmführer* is silent, the worse it gets.

"I've come to see for myself what a fine group of young men you are."

There's a general scraping of feet on the swept cobblestones. Nobody was expecting this. Braun generously ignores the disturbance.

"My son Wilhelm has already reported back to me. Some here are in good shape. Others…less so." His eyes rest on August, who shrinks by another head. "But each of you, I'm sure, will greet the message I'm about to convey with joy."

He pauses and strides back and forth in front of us, his hands folded behind him. With each word, a little cloud of steam issues from his lips.

"I don't have to tell you how things are looking on the front. Despite some setbacks, the *Wehrmacht* still stands like a rock in the face of the Bolsheviks. There is no doubt that we will stem the red tide and strike back with twice the force. But for this, we'll need every man who is willing to fight. We have arrived at a crucial point. From here we can only go forward. To victory—or defeat."

He stops, turns to us again, and seems to hold all of our gazes at once. "Which will you choose?"

"Victory!" we bellow. All of us—even me. There is no other answer.

He nods with satisfaction. "You're not yet sixteen, and therefore you're not entitled to enlist. But you don't have to sit at home uselessly and watch your mothers and siblings, your grandparents and aunts fall into Ivan's hands. *You* will have the opportunity to do your part. To propel us to victory! Effective immediately, you're all *Wehrmacht* helpers."

Everybody stares at him, dumbfounded. *Wehrmacht* helpers? I try to figure out what that means.

"Boys," bellows *Hauptsturmführer* Braun suddenly. I flinch. "Are you willing to leverage your youthful strength and vigor for the health and well-being of your fellow citizens? Are you willing to sacrifice yourselves for our *Führer*? Are you willing to contribute to the victory of the Thousand-Year German Reich?"

"Yes, sir!" resounds around me. The words pound in my ears, pulse in my arteries. I say them too, almost involuntarily.

"Good!" cries Braun. "I expected nothing less. At eight a.m. on Tuesday you will report to the Breslau-Rosenthal barracks, where you'll receive your orders. You may bring your winter clothes."

Again, the *Hauptsturmführer* bores into the group with his falcon-like eyes. I feel numb.

"*Sieg Heil,*" he cries, his right arm flashing upwards. Then he turns on his heel and leaves.

Chapter 6

Mother cries when I tell her the news. I don't know how to comfort her. How can I look after her and the kids now? We are leaving tomorrow. I only have one very short afternoon at home.

Before the sun has disappeared, I tell Max and Fritz that I need to talk to them, man-to-man. Together we head down to the banks of the Oder River. The two are quieter than usual; they walk almost solemnly next to me through the snow, their thick woolen hats protecting them from the biting wind that whips around the corners of the houses.

When we reach the riverbank, I wipe the snow off a fallen tree trunk and sit down. Max and Fritz sit on either side of me. There we are, perched like birds with their feathers fluffed out, pressed close together on the trunk. I gaze silently out over the river, now invisible under its untouched layer of snow and ice. Spruces laden with snow stand on the opposite bank. Against the glowing red sky, they seem a fairy-tale landscape.

"Do you remember your brother Frank?" I ask.

They didn't expect this question. Max shrugs, but Fritz nods slowly.

"He died of pneumonia, didn't he?" he asks, wrinkling his brow.

I nod and gaze across the river again. "Five years ago, when I was as old as you are now, I came here with Frank in the wintertime. The Oder was frozen over, so we skated a bit."

The memory creeps back to me like the cold crept into my thin shoes that day. "The ice looked darker in some places than others. River ice freezes unevenly, see, because of the currents. I told Frank he should stay close to the bank, where the ice is thicker and stronger. But Frank kept skating further and further out toward the middle. Suddenly, there was a huge noise. The ice underneath him split apart."

Fritz and Max look at me breathlessly.

"Frank fell into the water, but he managed to hold onto the edge of the ice. I lay down flat on my belly and held a thick branch out to him. He was able to grab it and pull himself out, but he was soaked to the bone. Of course, we should have gone home right away...but we didn't."

"Why not?"

"Because we were dumb. Frank was afraid that Father would yell at him. So we walked up and down the bank until his clothes dried out. It was bitter cold, and he shivered like an aspen tree."

I unbundle my scarf and sniff to keep my nose from running. I should have taken better care of Frank, even if I was only eleven—I was the older brother.

"And then?" asks Fritz.

"Three days later he came down with pneumonia."

I stand and turn toward my little brothers, staring directly into their faces, with their red noses and gleaming brown eyes, so very like my own.

"Alright, fellows, listen to me very carefully now. You know that I'm going away tomorrow to do my duty as a

Wehrmacht helper. That means, starting now, you're the men in the house! You're old enough to be helping Mother. Listen to her and take good care of your little sisters and Erich. And don't be stupid like Frank and I were. Promise?"

"Scout's honor," they say, their faces deadly serious.

We shake on it. Then we go home.

That night, I can hardly sleep. I wake up shortly after five and am not surprised to find Mother already up. She throws an egg in the pan, using the last of our butter. When I protest, she says, "You need to keep up your strength. Who knows what grunt work they're going to have you do."

"But you need your strength, too," I say.

She shrugs. "We'll muddle through, somehow."

I get up, walk around the table, and stand in front of Mother. I'm amazed that I have to look down at her. Just a little while ago, it was the other way around.

"Mother?" I say, and catch her eyes, dark and unreadable in the light of the kerosene lamp. "If you hear so much as a rumor that the Russians have crossed the Vistula and are advancing toward Breslau, grab your things and run. Go to Aunt Martha's," I say urgently.

"What about you?"

"I'll come as soon as I can. We'll see each other again, I promise."

She looks at me pensively, her eyes shining. "You've really grown up in the last year," she says, shaking her head.

Finally, I stand in the morning cold with my little suitcase, wearing a long wool coat that keeps me nice and warm. In the inside pocket, I've put father's watch and a few photos. Those are all the personal items I can take with me. Wiebke, Lieschen, Anna, and Lotta hug me. Then I stroke Erich's soft hair and shake hands with Max and Fritz.

Saying goodbye isn't as hard as I imagined. I've been going to Breslau every week before this. Today could be just another one of those days. The beginning of a new week at the master's. And I'll be back again Saturday afternoon....

I trudge through the snowy garden, turning around at the fence to wave. They stand huddled together in front of the house, their arms crossed against the cold, shivering. Still, they remain there until I've rounded the corner onto Breslau Street.

I meet Gerhard along the way. He's wearing his worn-out coat, which is already five years old. Its sleeves are much too short.

"It's a little chilly," he says, noticing my glance. "But I have a feeling we'll be warmer soon—they'll build a fire under us."

"I'm afraid they will."

We walk side-by-side to the train station in silence. The sky is dark and overcast, and the sun hasn't managed to push through the clouds. A few people are already waiting on the platform: all of our former groupmates from the HY, as well as a few boys from nearby towns. Some of them have come with their parents.

A plump woman in a bright red coat is pushing a boy in front of her, toward Gerhard and me.

"Ow, Mama, I can walk by myself," he objects softly. It's August's voice.

With the oversized pompom hat and a scarf covering everything but the tip of his nose, I would never have recognized him.

"*Herr* Köhler!" his mother booms at me. Her voice is as large and imposing as she is. "My boy has told me so much about you!"

I blink, surprised that *Frau* Hubrich knows my name, and even more so that she uses the formal address.

"I have an urgent request to make of you," she thunders on, placing her leather-gloved hands possessively on August's shoulder.

"My August here, he's not done growing yet. He was always scrawny and a bit sickly. And now, in the middle of winter, he's supposed to toil away like a plow horse! I don't even know if they'll feed you properly. Keep an eye on him, will you? Make sure he doesn't overexert himself. And don't let him forget to apply his nose drops in the evenings. He needs them for his chronic sinusitis."

Everybody in the circle is staring at us, even Wilhelm Braun, the corners of his mouth curled upwards in a gleeful smirk. August buries himself even deeper in his scarf.

I nod, confused. *Frau* Hubrich is lifting August's suitcase. "I packed you two pairs of long underwear and thick socks," she tells her son in a voice that cannot be overheard. "And don't forget…"

"I know, Mama!"

When it's time to board, *Frau* Hubrich pulls out a big checkered handkerchief and blows her nose. It sounds like an infantry division trumpeting the command to march.

"Sorry," says August sheepishly, sitting down on the wooden bench across from Gerhard and me in our compartment. "My mother doesn't have a tactful bone in her body."

As the passenger train chugs off, he waves halfheartedly out the window to his mother.

"Oh, she's just worried," says Gerhard. "That's how mothers are." Says the boy who's never had one himself.

"But most mothers don't tell their sons to wear their long underwear in front of everyone," August says, his face contorting painfully.

I struggle to suppress a smile. "Never mind," I try to reassure him. "It'll all be forgotten once we arrive at the barracks."

Around us, the mood is almost festive. The boys talk and laugh loudly like we're going on summer vacation. Just like on those yearly HY camping trips that we did when we were little, with campfires and outdoor games. Then somebody starts singing, and soon the whole train is singing along.

> *"The young are the soldiers of the future,*
> *The doers of future deeds.*
> *Germany, you will shine brightly on*
> *Even if we perish.*
>
> *Our flag flies before us,*
> *Our flag is the new era,*
> *Our flag leads us into eternity.*
> *Yes, the flag is greater than death."*

Chapter 7

The barracks look dismal even from afar: gray plastered walls with identical rows of dark windows, surrounded by a high barbed-wire fence. Guards are stationed at the entrance; they don't so much as acknowledge us as we jump from the military truck and stream into the inner courtyard. Here we find still more boys our age—I'm guessing a few hundred in total. They glance around uneasily, their faces tense. Some of them whisper to one another and laugh uncertainly. Everything here seems cold and foreign.

"Line up! Rows of five!" cries a full voice in a thick Silesian accent, even as the last boys are pushing through the gate.

We've practiced formations a thousand times, but never with such a haphazard troop. I stand in the third row next to Gerhard and peer between the heads in front of us, trying to get a glimpse of the man who issued the command.

He reminds me a little of my master: tall and strong like a bear, with a round face and, beneath his uniform jacket, a belly that's just as round. I can sooner imagine him in a beer garden eating sausages and potato dumplings than in a *Wehrmacht* uniform. He scans the crowd with a good-natured twinkle in his eyes.

"Everything okay, boys?" His deep voice carries across the length of the courtyard.

"*Jawohl, Herr Unteroffizier*," we echo back, despite his unusually casual form of address. The words sound as if they were spoken by a single mouth.

"Excellent. I can see that someone has already taught you manners. I won't have to work so hard then, right?" He laughs a full-throated laugh, which makes his belly jiggle. Then, suddenly, he turns serious.

"So, boys, I am *Unteroffizier* Swarowski. You all know why you're here. The Soviets are nearly upon us, but we can't let our beautiful Breslau fall into their hands just yet, can we? We're going to transform the Oder into a fortress that neither the Russians nor their tanks can cross. You all are going to dig anti-tank ditches, string razor wire, and stack shells for the artillery and flak units so they're never without munitions in a pinch. But don't worry, we won't be doing any sharpshooting. Unless it's with chocolates."

Once again he laughs his full-throated laugh, unperturbed by our confused silence.

"I'm not going to sugarcoat this," he continues seriously. "This isn't going to be a walk in the park. You'd better be ready for aching bones and torn muscles. But you're young! And at least you'll be able to say you've done your part after a good day's work, right? Now a few small things: reveille's at six a.m. The early bird catches the egg—er, how does the saying go? Something like that. Breakfast is at seven o'clock sharp in the canteen, and after that everybody heads out to the work site. There's enough food for everyone, so you won't starve! We need you nice and strong. Lunch is served on-site, dinner back in the canteen at seven p.m. With me so far?"

"*Jawohl, Herr Unteroffizier!*"

"Good. Now, we're going to read off your names, and then you'll go find yourselves a place in the barracks. Each room should choose a room leader: he's in charge and answers to the acting petty officer. After that, you'll report to the equipment room, where you'll receive your cadet uniforms. I hope you little weeds fit into them. Any questions?"

"Yes, *Herr Unteroffizier*." Somebody in the first row is courageous enough to raise his hand. "Can the boys that know each other from Hitler Youth room together?"

Swarowski nods amicably. "Of course—no objections here, my boy. It raises morale."

Just great! Gerhard and I exchange glances. That means we're going to have to share a dorm with Wilhelm!

Swarowski reads off our names in alphabetical order. When I hear mine, I step toward him to show him my Hitler Youth ID. He waves me on and I trot to the barracks to find Gerhard and the other boys from our HY cell who've already been called.

"There are twelve bunks in each room," announces Herbert, who's been listening to the chatter.

"Who's going to be our room leader?" asks Wilhelm.

"Let's vote," I suggest, and add immediately, "I nominate Herbert." Herbert's father is a highly-decorated officer, so he's always enjoyed a certain respect, even from Wilhelm.

"And I nominate Anton," Herbert replies.

"Me too," squeaks August.

I'm less than enthused when more and more boys call out my name. Gerhard, who knows me well, votes for Herbert. Wilhelm receives only his own vote, plus Gustav's and Heiner's.

"So, by a majority of votes, Anton is our new room leader," concludes Herbert. Wilhelm's upper lip curls disdainfully. Great! This is going to be fun!

I sigh. "I'll go look for a room, then…"

A little later, we move into a dorm on the second floor of the barracks. There's only one tiny window with a view of the courtyard and a tattered, red-checkered curtain in front of it. The unheated room is hardly warmer than the air outside. At least, we have a pot-belly stove in the corner closest to the door. Six bunk beds with straw mattresses and coarse army blankets are arranged in tight rows against a bare wall.

"Okay, so they aren't exactly canopy beds, but they're not terrible," says Gerhard. He claims a bed for us near the stove. Across from the beds is a long row of wooden lockers. I tell everyone to put their things in there.

"Swarowski is a weirdo," Gerhard comments as he unpacks his clothes. "But in a good way, I guess."

"Yeah, he's alright," I say. "But I'm not crazy about this 'room leader' business. Now I have to take the rap whenever one of us does something stupid."

"Hey, I didn't vote for you, buddy."

I clap him on the shoulder. "I can always count on you."

He leans in close and whispers, "Anyway, now you can spit in Braun's eye instead of the other way round."

I raise my eyebrows I doubt I'm tall enough for that.

Just then, I hear Wilhelm's strident voice and turn around. Speak of the devil....

"What's up, mama's boy? Have you put your long johns away properly?"

Braun is looming over August and peering into his locker. "This is a mess! What kind of garbage do you have in here, anyway?"

He pulls out the blue pompom hat that August was wearing on the train. "You put this on your *head*? It's good you're too thick to notice if you have trash on your noggin."

In a rush of heroic courage, August tries to get his hat back. He lunges for it, but Wilhelm whips it over his head, out of August's reach.

I knew this room leader position would get me in trouble....

"Give it back," I say, standing next to August. I take a quick glance at his locker. It looks alright to me: his winter coat is hanging up, his other clothes are neatly folded in the compartments, and his suitcase lies down below.

"What's it to you?" Wilhelm growls.

"I'm responsible for maintaining order."

"Then pay attention to the order in your own locker! You all have no idea how to put your clothes away properly."

"And *you're* the expert on that?"

"My father showed me how to do it."

"I don't care. Now give back the hat."

Wilhelm doesn't react. He still holds his arm stretched up high.

"Oh well, I don't really need the hat," mumbles August.

I feel all of my groupmates' eyes on me. They expect me to do something, something to prove my authority as room leader. I'm half a head shorter than Braun. If I try to reach the hat, I'll just make a fool of myself. I'm not much of a fighter, and I've always hated getting into a brawl. But I can't show any weakness now, or I'll lose all credibility. And August's mother did ask me to look after her son.

Wilhelm leers, and I do the first thing that pops into my head: I bring my boot-heel down forcefully on Wilhelm's left foot. When the pain hits him, he lowers his arm. This is what I was betting on. I grab the hat and shove it into August's hand as Braun hops around on one leg.

The boys hoot and jeer. August looks admiringly at me and Gerhard nods, grinning.

Then everything happens so fast that I don't have time to react. Braun pulls back. I see his arm flying towards me. The next second, his fist drills into my gut, knocking the wind out of me. I bend over like a folding chair, gasping for air, before I straighten with difficulty, just in time to see a second blow coming my way. But he won't land this one! I throw myself at Wilhelm's massive upper body and knock him off-balance.

Everything spins out of control. I hardly know what I'm doing, only hear the cries of the others ringing around us. I barely feel the blows raining down on me or notice that I'm dealing them out.

"Show him!" someone cries.

Suddenly the door is yanked open and a blast of cold air sweeps in from the hall. Wilhelm pushes me away, and I slam back against the lockers. Aside from my own wheezing, the room has gone completely silent.

Chapter 8

A soldier looms in the doorframe. I'm alarmed that he's just an enormous blur in my vision. He enters the room, stooping low so he doesn't bump his head. When my gaze clears a bit, I can make out the trappings on his uniform, identifying him as the acting petty officer. He is broad-shouldered and has rough farmer's hands that look like they could grab a bull by the horns.

"What's going on here?" he bellows, taking a good look around.

We're jolted out of our staring and stand up straight.

"Who's the room leader?" he snarls in a coarse voice.

Just great! I run my tongue quickly over my lower lip, which feels swollen. Taking a deep breath, I step forward.

"Anton Köhler, sir…?"

"Stoss. *Unteroffizier* Stoss." He studies me from head to foot. "What happened to you?"

"I fell," I mumble through my thick lip.

"Right on your face, ey? You look like shit." His gaze wanders across the room again. "What else have you been up to? Don't you have anything to do? Do you think this is a vacation resort?"

Nobody responds.

"I asked you a question, room leader!" Stoss roars in my face.

"No, nobody thinks that."

"What kind of answer is that supposed to be? It's 'No, *Herr Unteroffizier!*' You have your orders! Aren't you supposed to report downstairs to get your uniforms?"

"Yes, *Herr Unteroffizier.* We were waiting until the line was a bit shorter."

Stoss squints and wrinkles his nose like he smells something foul. "Have you at least used the time to organize your room? Let's see your lockers!"

Now comes the hour of truth. I try my best not to hobble as Stoss opens the lockers one by one. He peers into some with disgust and pulls the contents out of others, throwing it in a messy pile on the floor.

"This is a pigsty!"

Now it is.

My underwear goes flying onto the floor, which has been transformed into a muddy brown mess by our wet boots. Stoss continues like this for a while. The others stand perfectly still, but a glance at their faces reveals growing despair and, in some, anger.

"Clean up!" cries *Unteroffizier* Stoss when he finishes his inspection. "Then go and get your uniforms. If this place isn't tip-top in half an hour, you won't be getting lunch. Understood?"

"*Jawohl, Herr Unteroffizier.*" I make sure to click my heels together.

As soon as the officer's footsteps fade down the hall, there is a flurry of activity. I don't even have to give instructions—nobody wants to miss a meal.

"Told you," Wilhelm mopes, reluctantly picking up his clothes from the floor.

"Shut up," I say.

"Bastard," Gerhard grumbles.

"Who, Braun or Stoss?" I ask.

"Both. I like Swarowski a thousand times better."

I try to beat the dirt from my clothes before I fold them neatly the way Mother showed me. Then I help August with his things. Finally, I go through all of the lockers again. Here and there I have to tell someone to fix something.

When Stoss returns, he is greeted by exceptionally tidy lockers. Because he can't find anything to complain about there, he points at the floor instead, grumbling that it still looks "like a pigsty." But he sends us down to get our uniforms anyway.

It looks as if we're the last ones to line up. The storeroom is crammed with uniforms, weapons, duffel bags, shovels, flashlights, and other equipment, hanging on hooks on the walls or arranged on shelves. Three soldiers eyeball each boy's size and hand him one of the cadet uniforms.

When it's August's turn, the soldier in charge searches through the piles of clothing for a long time.

"Sorry, but we're out of smalls. This is the best I've got. You'll have to roll up the arms and legs a bit. The shoes might be more difficult."

"I can stuff them with newspaper."

The soldier nods and piles everything into August's arms until he disappears behind a mountain of cloth.

My uniform is a bit too big as well. I pull on my pants and jacket, feeling the rough gray-green material. Since we're helpers, not true recruits, the uniform isn't decorated. But the boots are made of real leather despite the leather shortage. I'm glad because that means Gerhard can get rid of his old shoes that are much too thin and worn for the winter still ahead of us.

As we cross the courtyard on our way to the canteen, the heavy grey clouds finally release their load and it starts to snow. Gerhard is walking next to me, the uniform sagging on his figure. Although he is tall enough, he can hardly fill it out.

"You look sharp. Like a real officer," he says when he notices my gaze. "Except for the fat lip, maybe. If only the girls could see you now—they'd be all over you. Too bad there aren't any around. I wouldn't mind having a few young female *Luftwaffe* helpers around."

I smile to myself.

The canteen food is warm and tasty. We dig in, stuffing ourselves with pot roast, potatoes, and carrots until we're fit to burst.

"Man, Anton, that was great! The way you stomped on his foot!" August whispers to me, eyes gleaming.

I shrug. "I wasn't planning to get into a fistfight."

"He deserved it, though," Herbert says.

My groupmates' praises almost make the fat lip worth it.

We spend the whole afternoon, as long as it's still light out, carrying shells for the flak units. I don't think my groupmates imagined their illustrious careers as *Wehrmacht* helpers playing out like this. It's monotonous drudgery. We go from the munitions storage to the gun emplacements, then back again. The shells for the four-inch cannons weigh twenty pounds apiece. Now I'm even more annoyed that I let Braun provoke me into fighting. My bones already ache, and every time I bend and straighten, I feel like a sixty-year-old with creaky joints. We stack the shells next to the guns so that they are readily available when the canons have to fire.

Time passes slowly. I can't see the sun, so I can't guess how late it is from its position. Every now and then I pull the watch out of the breast pocket of my coat and check the time. When it's finally dusk, we stumble on wobbly legs back toward the barracks. The exhilarated pack of Hitler Youth that arrived in the early afternoon has become a heap of shaky snowmen who can barely put one foot in front of the other. Swarowski waddles next to us in his thick fur hat and laughs good-naturedly at our ineptitude. When August stumbles and falls face-first into the snow, he pulls him up by his coat-collar, saying, "Come on, boy!"

"Hopefully we'll get some proper food, at least," says Gerhard, and thumps August on the shoulder to shake off the snow.

We've barely sat down in the canteen with our loaded trays when we hear the long, ebbing and swelling howl of the air raid alarm. Immediately after, the flak starts thundering.

"We're under attack!" someone cries. All of us rush to the windows; some people even run outside. In the northeast, where we were stacking shells this afternoon, searchlights pierce the night sky. Bright sparks flare up and die. There's thunder and lightning, like during a storm. The flashes illuminate a gruesome image—an enemy plane was shot down!

"Man, that must have been a Russian *Rata*, I'm sure of it! The rat's dropping from the sky," cries Gerhard. The others rejoice.

I can't help but feel the excitement as well. It's the first time that I've been this close to an attack.

"Into the bunker, now!" Swarowski bellows.

But we've barely made it halfway across the courtyard when the all-clear sounds and Swarowski calls us back. I wonder if this is going to happen often.

After dinner, we head back to our bunks. The fire in the stove has gone out, and I ask Gerhard to build it up again. It's so cold in the room that my breath puffs out in little clouds in front of my mouth.

"Shine your shoes, guys," I call, "otherwise old Stoss will fly off the handle again during inspection."

Though lights-out isn't for another hour, many boys crawl straight into their bunks. Herbert spreads a card game out on one of the lower beds and announces, "I'll lend the winner my collection of *Faith and Beauty* girls."

Immediately some boys crowd around him. "Where did you get those?" "C'mon, let us have a look!"

"Only if you win," smiles Herbert.

Gerhard joins the group. He obviously doesn't want to miss seeing the girls, in their sporty poses and short white gymnast suits.

I turn down the offer and retreat to August, who is sitting cross-legged on his bed and gazing into space, glassy-eyed. He has wrapped a blanket around his shoulders, but he's still shivering. I perch on the edge of the bed.

"Is everything alright?" I ask softly. He's unnaturally pale. August shrugs.

"We'll get used to the workload," I say.

"I'm not worried about the work. Mother tells me not to overexert myself, but I can work just as hard as anyone here."

"Of course you can!"

"How's your lip?"

I note that it's still swollen and puckering slightly. "Healing fast. The snow kept it cool."

We stare silently at the floor for a while. The firelight from the open pot-belly stove flickers and dances on the wooden boards. The room smells a little smoky, reminding me of home, of Christmas. That was just a few days ago, yet it seems so far away.

"Hey, Anton? What do you think, how long will we have to stay here?" The lenses of August's glasses reflect the firelight, concealing his eyes.

"I'm guessing a few more weeks, until the work is done. Or until the Russians come."

He shivers even more.

"Will you show me your cigarette trading card collection?" I ask, trying to distract him.

His face lights up and he pulls a book out from under his pillow. August is an avid collector. Back in school, we used to trade cards, but I haven't looked at mine for ages now.

"So I have almost the entire flag and uniform collection," he starts in, flipping through the book. I'm only half-listening. The other boys are laughing softly, bent over Herbert's photos. I don't need to look at those pictures—I have something better: a photo of Luise in my coat pocket. I'm glad that she's not a part of the *Faith and Beauty Society*. If other boys looked at her doing gymnastics, wearing little more than her underwear…the thought makes my ears heat up.

"…my favorite collection. Right, Anton?"

I startle and look guiltily at August's book. Where's a bucket of cold water when you need one? He points to a page with pictures of airships and seems not to notice that I was far away, immersed in my thoughts.

"Oh yeah, they're awesome. You'll have to show Gerhard sometime. He loves anything that flies." I yawn.

"Time for bed," I announce.

It's strange, giving orders. But Gerhard makes sure that everyone obeys.

My first night in jail, I think. That's how it feels, anyway.

Chapter 9

Swarowski greets us with a "*Heil* Hitler." When he says it, though, it sounds like a throw-away remark, which makes me like him even more. During morning roll-call, he paces along the rows of boys, winking encouragingly at a couple of them, even doling out a clap on the shoulder here and there.

"You've done good work for the past ten days."

We've been here for ten days already? Thanks to the monotonous work, the hours pass in a blur without my noticing. Now, I'd actually be happy to take up my apprenticeship with Master Pollack again. But who knows if I'll ever have the chance to do that.

"If you keep this up, you'll have a free afternoon on Sunday. How does that sound?" He stops right in front of me, grinning broadly. I smile back. Swarowski really is a good guy.

After stacking shells for the past ten days, today we're scheduled for the trenches. I climb up onto the truck behind Gerhard and prepare myself for a hard day's work. It snowed again last night, but this morning, the sun is shining and the whole landscape has disappeared under a blinding, spotless blanket that swallows up all sound. Here and there an alder or a birch pokes its naked branches up out of the sea of white. Where cars have already driven, the snow has been compacted into a hard, gray sheet that winds like a dirty ribbon through the landscape. Each breath stings my lungs, for the day is clear and the sky crystal blue.

The truck stops and we jump down, shovels in hand. The trench must be ten to fifteen feet deep so no tanks can cross it. Together with the frozen Oder, it will be the last line of defense around Breslau. But is it enough?

Despite the cold, I'm soon warm under my uniform. Gerhard next to me has beads of sweat on his forehead. I scoop one load of earth after the other onto the blade of my shovel and throw it over the edge of the trench, where a high wall has formed; even standing up, I can hardly see over it. My muscles are getting tired.

August, who's working on my other side, can hardly lift his arms high enough to throw the loads of his shovel out of the trench. Under the cap, his face is pale, despite the exertion. He coughs slightly, but when I stop and scrutinize him with furrowed brow, he waves me off.

"I'm okay, Anton."

At noon, we take a break and Clothilde delivers lunch. She's a wiry woman of about fifty, with gray hair and a lined face. We all call her "Smoke-thilde," because she chain-smokes cigarettes. You'll never catch her without a butt in her yellowed fingers, and she's very good at talking with a cigarette between her lips.

Since she's one of the few women in the barracks, the soldiers treat her with respect. Smoke-thilde knows exactly what she's called, but she doesn't take it the wrong way. She assists the canteen boss, and now, she's giving us thick liverwurst and cheese sandwiches. We devour them like young wolves. Between the drags on her cigarette, I can make out a thin smile on her lips.

"Can I have a puff?" asks one of the boys, jokingly. Without a word, Smoke-thilde holds the cigarette in front of his nose. Heinz takes a long drag and tries to suppress a cough, choking in the process. Now he has to endure the laughter of all the others.

I grab one of the good seats on the back of the truck for Gerhard and me to eat our lunch. We let our legs dangle, drink the lukewarm, grain coffee substitute, and enjoy the break. I look over the ditch in the snow that we and the other groups have dug in the last few days. From here, it seems neither wide nor deep enough to stop the Russian tanks.

What's the point? I ask myself, not for the first time.

It's still quiet on the eastern front. The Red Army seems to be lurking, maybe waiting for reinforcements, or for the right moment to surprise us. But they will come—that much is certain. The Allies have made clear that they won't let up until Germany surrenders unconditionally.

After the brief lunch break comes the hardest part of the day. I long for an end to the drudgery, but now the hours start to crawl, and the sun sinks toward the horizon at a snail's pace. My exhaustion regularly reaches the point where my body works on autopilot, like a machine. I don't feel it anymore, don't think about what I'm doing, don't think at all.

Everyone is silent and dogged as they work. Even Wilhelm looks less than enthusiastic about serving the Fatherland this way. Gritting his teeth and glowering, he puts his muscles to work. He shovels like a crazy man, heaving an avalanche of snow and dirt over the wall.

August leans on his shovel and coughs again. His face has gone gray, though I'm not sure if that's just the late afternoon light. An officer passes by and tells him to keep working, and he complies. But a few minutes later, he stops again.

"Hey, is everything okay?" I ask softly.

August looks up at me with tired, oddly glazed eyes. He nods. Then he collapses and lies sprawled in the deep trench, a little pile of a person in a mountain of ill-fitting clothes. I throw down my shovel and bend over him.

"August, don't give up now. We're almost done for today." I hear the panic in my own voice.

"Done," mumbles August.

"Yeah, we're almost done. The sun's almost down."

"Yes…" And then he says something very strange: "Please don't give the rat any of my cheese."

I put my hand on his forehead. "What?"

"It's so big and pink…why is it so pink?"

Gerhard is standing next to me, looking alarmed.

"Hello!" I call. "Man down. I need help! Orderly!"

I try to lift August up so he's not lying on the cold ground. I can hold him easily—he hardly weighs more than the shells and hangs limply in my arms.

Finally, Swarowski arrives wheezing. "What's wrong, Köhler?"

He shines his flashlight into August's face. I'm astonished that he knows my name.

"Sir, *Wehrmacht* helper Hubrich collapsed on duty. He's hallucinating. I think he's got a fever."

"Blimey, that so?" Swarowski slaps the unconscious August on both cheeks with his bear's paws, but August doesn't react. Now the other boys have stopped working and are staring at us. Swarowski just stands there, indecisive.

"Sir, he needs a medic. Right away," I urge.

"You're probably right." Swarowski nods and picks up August, who probably feels light as a feather to him. "Come along," he orders.

Swarowski carries August to the truck and hoists him effortlessly into the passenger seat. I'm supposed to sit beside him and look after him. He orders the driver to take us back to the barracks immediately, and then to turn around and pick up him and the rest of the boys.

I do my best to keep August sitting upright as the truck bounces over the frozen snow. With every bump, his head lolls side to side, back and forth, but he doesn't wake up. Only when he has another coughing fit do his eyes open. He gasps and wheezes; sometimes he doesn't seem to be getting any air at all. Even the driver, an older soldier, peers at us with concern out of the corner of his eye.

"Drive faster, please!" I say, but I can't tell if he hears me. It's getting darker and darker, and he has to make sure he doesn't slip off the road. Because of the blackout, he can't turn on his headlights, so only the snow lights our way.

When we arrive back at the barracks, the driver jumps out of his seat and helps me lift August out of the truck. Since he's conscious, though only barely, I sling his arm around my shoulder and hold onto him as we stagger across the dark courtyard to the infirmary. The driver gets into the truck to return to the trenches.

An iron fist clenches my stomach. Dammit, August, why did you have to work until you dropped? I should have seen the signs sooner. I should have gotten him an extra blanket for his bed. It's bitter cold at night because the stove is only fired up in the early evening. Once the heat dissipates, at around midnight, the blankets don't do much good. But August didn't want special treatment from his groupmates. Stupid, stupid August!

With the last of my strength, I hoist him over the threshold to the infirmary. The door to the examination room is open. I can see a man sitting behind the table—an orderly, recognizable by the red-cross band on his sleeve. He's folded his arms behind his head and put his legs up on the table. When he notices us, he nearly tips over backward.

"Well, well, look what the cat dragged in!"

What an idiotic thing to say. Can't he see that August needs help? He has nearly passed out again and hangs like a sack of rocks on my right side.

"Can you help us?" I call.

"Why, two little soldiers!" Finally, the orderly jumps up and takes August's other arm. He lifts August effortlessly and carries him into the sickroom, where the cots for in-patient treatment are lined up. They're all empty.

"What's the matter with him?" I ask, as soon as the orderly has set August down on one of the beds.

"Just you wait, young man. Let me examine him first. What happened?" He places a hand on August's forehead and feels the pulse on his wrist.

"We were digging tank trenches when he collapsed. He has coughing fits—bad ones. I think...I think it's pneumonia."

"Slow down, boy. Leave the diagnosis to me. And pull off his boots, they're getting the bed dirty."

He retrieves a stethoscope and places it on August's chest. Squinting slightly, he listens to breathing noises. I can hear the rattling even without the instrument.

"Mhmm, very wet, but it doesn't seem to be affecting his lungs. Just his upper airways."

"And the fever?" I ask, pulling August's other shoe off his foot. August has wrapped cloths around both feet to keep them warm and make his boots fit better.

"That can happen with acute bronchitis."

"So what do we do?"

The orderly looks at me, astonished. "Are you gunning for a position as a nurse, *Herr*...?"

"Köhler. Anton."

"So, Köhler, Anton, what's your recommendation for treatment?"

I'm annoyed to feel myself redden. "I...would take him to the doctor."

The orderly scratches his cheek thoughtfully. "If he's not better tomorrow, I'll call the doctor or transfer him to the hospital. But unfortunately, we can't do anything but wait. Of course, he'll spend the night here. He needs rest and warmth."

"Maybe a vapor bath?" I say, remembering Mother's home remedies.

"A good suggestion, Nurse Köhler. But for that, our little patient has to regain some of his strength."

He holds out his hand. "Willi."

"Anton."

"So you said."

I can't help but grin. Willi is an *Obergefreiter* by rank, but that doesn't seem to matter to him.

"Is he your friend, Anton?"

"Yes, we're from the same town."

Willi places August's head on a soft pillow and changes his clothes so that he can sleep more comfortably. "I'm going to take good care of your little friend, Anton. You can go eat now. It's time, isn't it?"

I hesitate. "Can I visit him?"

"Of course. As long as you don't bring the whole horde with you. Peace and quiet, as I said."

Before I head to the canteen, I go up to our room. My roommates are not back yet; maybe they went straight to dinner. I pull a thick wool sweater from August's locker, one that his mother knit for him and made sure he took along, even though he can't wear it under his uniform. I pack all his things in his little suitcase—including his trading cards, in case he gets bored—and take them over to the infirmary.

When I enter the canteen, Gerhard immediately spots me and waves me over. After I've reported to Swarowski and received my tray of food, the boys slide together on the bench so that I can squeeze in between Gerhard and Herbert.

"What's wrong with August?"

"Is he doing better now?"

They whisper because we're not allowed to talk at meals.

"He probably has bronchitis. He's in the infirmary now," I whisper back.

"Malingerer," scoffs Wilhelm, who's sitting across from us. "Trying to slack off. You too, right, Köhler?"

I want to retort, but at that very moment, the loudspeaker comes on, broadcasting the *Wehrmacht* report like every evening. We stop talking so we can listen.

It says that, in the west, our troops are fighting for the Ruhr Valley. They're trying in vain to defend the left bank of the Rhine against the advance of the American forces. I prick up my ears when the bulletin starts talking about the eastern front. The monotonous voice of the announcer reports that, as of today, the Soviets have begun their offensive on the Vistula River.

An electric current runs through my body, making my fingertips tingle. I lean over to Gerhard and whisper, "Here we go."

Chapter 10

Since there's been movement on the eastern front in the last two days, the officers drive us even harder. But nobody is grumbling, not even under their breath: now we know why we're slaving away. All at once, the Russians' arrival has become tangible.

It started yesterday. We stood crowded in the back of the truck on the way to the trenches when, all of a sudden, we had to stop. A whole column of horse-drawn carts passed by us, most of them overloaded and rocking like ships in distress on the snowy road. People were huddled in the wagons or walked alongside—women, children, and the elderly. All were refugees, ethnic Germans from the borders of the Reich fleeing the Russians.

The wagons were piled precariously with chairs, lamps, bedding, and other furniture. Those not fortunate enough to own a horse-drawn cart or to know someone who did had to carry all of their possessions. Some pushed bicycles or strollers, to which they'd tied large bundles. Old and young alike hauled knapsacks and bags.

They trudged through the dusk, a ghostly pageant. The snow swallowed the sounds of footsteps and hoofbeats, a silence broken only by the clattering of furniture and the squeaking of wheels, and, every now and then, the crying of a small child. Bundled up against the icy wind, the refugees were probably searching for a place to stay and something to eat before the cold night ahead.

The whole time, I was thinking about my family. If we can't stop the Russian advance, Mother will have to flee, too.

Every evening, Gerhard and I visit the infirmary. August's condition has improved some: his fever is down and he isn't delirious anymore. But he's still weak and spends most of his time sleeping. Tonight, we stop to see Willi after visiting August. Willi sits at his desk, legs propped up and arms folded behind his head like they were during our first encounter.

"What's up, boys?" he asks, as we peek into his office.

"Any news?" I ask.

He exhales through his nose, then shakes his head. "Nothing. The mayor has forbidden anyone from leaving Breslau because the *Führer* has declared the city a fortress. And a fortress must be defended at all costs, you know. If the fortress goes down, its inhabitants go down with it."

"But the women and children..."

"Our *Führer* doesn't give a damn about them, does he!" Willi spits on the floor. Then he beckons us over and places a finger on his lips. "But that's just between you and me, understood?"

One morning, as we cross the courtyard to the canteen, I glimpse Willi smoking in front of the infirmary. He sees me and frantically waves me over. Gerhard and I come running.

"The little guy isn't doing so hot," says Willi as soon as we're within earshot, stubbing his cigarette out. Deep lines have appeared on his forehead. "He took a turn for the worse last night. I don't understand—yesterday things were looking up. Now the fever's back and his lungs are whistling like a teakettle."

We rush to the infirmary. August lies in bed, his eyes closed, face as pale as the pillowcase. My stomach clenches.

"Why doesn't the doctor come already?" I ask, hardly managing to keep my voice low.

Willi shakes his head. "They're totally swamped," he says gravely. "The reserve hospital is overflowing with the wounded. And then there are the refugees. They've all fled to the city. The doctors don't have time to make house calls."

"Then we have to take August there," I urge.

"Hang on. Right now he's too weak to move. We just have to wait and see how he's doing tomorrow."

"Wait," I repeat tonelessly. I know what waiting did to my brother Frank. "He has to go to the hospital," I insist.

Willi shrugs helplessly. "I'm doing everything I can."

We stand by the bed for a little while, then Willi whispers, "You've got to go do your duty, now."

"We'll be back later," says Gerhard, and drags me away.

But as soon as we're done with our work that evening, we turn up in front of Willi again. "The doctor was here. He gave August something to bring the fever down. Now we have to wait and see if it works. We'll know more tonight."

Tonight. I sink into the chair that Willi pushes toward me.

That's what the doctor said about Frank. That's the turning point. If the fever's down by then, he's in the clear. If not...

"I want to stay here tonight," I say.

"I'll tell Swarowski," offers Gerhard. "He won't mind. And I can cover your room leader duties."

I shoot him a grateful glance.

After Gerhard has gone, Smoke-thilde arrives, carrying a dinner tray with noodles and goulash. But Willi and I aren't hungry, and August isn't well enough to eat. I sit quietly by the bed and place a fresh compress on August's forehead every now and again. Willi smokes cigarettes almost end to end but leaves the sickroom to do so.

At one point August has a coughing fit that sounds like a dog barking and ends with a rattle. The sound makes my chest tighten. I tilt his head up slightly so that he doesn't choke on the phlegm. The fit lasts minutes, and beads of sweat appear on his forehead. *Hold on, August*, I think.

The night passes slowly. August has fallen into a restless sleep. I start to hum softly: Schumann's *Träumerei*. As I hum, I see Luise in front of me. She's sitting at the piano with her eyes closed, swaying to the melody. Only when Willi returns do I stop. He pulls up a chair and sits on August's other side, reeking of tobacco.

"Do you want something to eat?"

I shake my head, but my stomach growls traitorously.

Willi hands me the apple from August's tray. "You're not helping him by starving yourself."

I turn the apple around in my hand. Its smooth surface glows in the wan light of the bedside lamp. "I'll save this for August. Vitamins are good when you're sick."

"He can have as many apples as he wants when he wakes up."

I put the apple back on the tray. Willi shrugs. Then he leans down to take August's temperature.

"Still hot as hell," he mumbles, his face ashen. He sits back again and peers at me. "It's awful having to wait, isn't it? Not being able to do anything?"

"His mother asked me to look after him," I croak.

"That's what you're doing."

"If I'd looked after him properly, he wouldn't be here."

Willi waves dismissively. "This isn't on you, Anton. I've lost a lot of people in the field. You can't save them all."

I look up. "Were you at the front?"

He nods. "In the Great War. Don't give me that look—it wasn't *that* long ago. I'm older than you think." He winks at me with one tired eye. "I enlisted in 1917, back when I was young and stupid. I'd always wanted to be a doctor, so I trained as an orderly and went to France."

"What was it like?" I ask, straightening up.

Willi frowns. "Different than it is now, I can tell you that much. Now the units charge ahead or pull back most of the time. Back then, they didn't move an inch for years and years. The trenches were hell. Nothing but holes in the ground, full of rats and cockroaches… And the smell! Have you heard of gangrene? It's what took the unlucky ones, the ones who didn't die immediately from a bullet to the head. Especially the amputees. Everything was filthy. Wounds got infected, and then you couldn't do anything but sit and watch the rot eating away at you, until your body failed…" He stops, shaking his head, and waves off the memory.

I slide my hands under my thighs and sit on them to keep from fidgeting. "Why didn't you become a doctor? After the war, I mean."

"After the war, I couldn't even think about studying. I hadn't finished school—I was an idiot. Then came the famine and the crisis. You were lucky if you had a job at all."

I nod, remembering the stories that Father told me.

"But it was worst for the boys my age," continues Willi thoughtfully. "When we came home, we didn't have enough strength left to behave like normal people, to re-enter normal life. It was years before I felt human again. The war destroyed all of us, an entire generation... And now the same thing is happening again." He scratches his cheek and looks at me. "And you're caught up in it, too..."

"Do you really think they're going to get us involved in the fighting?"

"You can bet on it."

I shiver. Didn't Uncle Emil say the same thing?

Chapter 11

"Anton? You awake?"

I startle; I must have fallen asleep on the chair. My head snaps up as if it's been lying on my chest. It takes me a moment to realize where I am: cots in a half-darkened room, lit only by a dim lamp on the nightstand. The smell of disinfectant, medicine, and cold food hovers in the air. August's eyes are open, gleaming in the semi-darkness.

"How are you feeling?" I ask.

"I've been better," he wheezes, but the very fact that he's talking gives me hope. "Why...are you still here? Isn't it late?"

"It's the middle of the night," I admit, shrugging. "I wanted to keep you company. In case you woke up."

He looks at me strangely. "Because of what Mama said?"

"No," I reply. "Because you're my friend."

August's pale cheeks gradually darken as he blushes. "Really?"

"Of course. Why so surprised?"

He coughs into his fist. "I just thought...you have Gerhard."

"I can have more than one friend, can't I?"

He falls silent, pondering this, his expression suddenly dreamy. I consider how I might cheer him up.

"Anton," August whispers, before I can think of anything.

"Yeah?"

"The Russians are coming, aren't they?"

I shift in my chair. "Yes…"

"I want to get better before they arrive. So I can fight for the Fatherland too."

"I don't know-" I begin.

He interrupts me. "They all think I'm weak."

I want to contradict him, but he shakes his head slightly, preventing me.

"It's true," he says softly. "I'm not as athletic as you or Gerhard. Or as brave."

"Don't be silly," I object. "You're all that, and a lot smarter than I am. Remember how you always had to help me with dictations? I'm even too dumb to write properly."

"You're not dumb. Really."

"And you're not weak!"

He doesn't look convinced. Then I think of something else. "Hey, that soccer game in the summer, remember? When we played Wilhelm's team?"

August's eyes light up briefly, and he nods.

"You were our hero that day!" I continue. "The way you defended against Braun's penalty kick…"

The corners of his mouth lift in a slight smile. "But that was because of you. If you hadn't cheered me on, and told me which corner of the goal Braun likes to shoot at…"

I shake my head. "You were the one who blocked the ball."

August falls silent, and I hope I've persuaded him. "You should rest." The talking seems to have worn him out.

He lies still for a long time. I'm beginning to think he's asleep when he says in a weak voice, "I'd like some music…"

"What kind of music?" I ask, surprised.

"Something beautiful." He closes his eyes. "Something to help me sleep."

I hug myself, feeling a sudden chill. At this moment, he reminds me so much of my little brother: the way his curls fall over his ears, his eyelids thin as paper. August coughs again, his chest rattling. There are bright red spots over his cheekbones.

I start to hum softly as I pull the comforter up to his chin and he seems to nod off for real. His cheeks look hollow in the lamplight, but there's a trace of a smile on his lips.

At some point, I must have fallen asleep again, and Willi must have moved me into one of the sickbeds. Still, it feels like I haven't gotten more than a couple hours of sleep. The shades are tightly drawn, so the daylight can't filter in. August is lying peacefully, his eyelids covered with tiny spidery veins that lend them a blue shimmer.

I jump out of bed and tell Willi that August was up during the night. He says that's a good sign. Then I have to get ready for duty. The day's work blurs by as if in a dream, I'm so exhausted from the short night and from worrying about August.

As soon as we're back in the barracks, Gerhard and I go see Willi again.

"How's he doing?" I ask hopefully. "Is his fever down?"

Willi sits slumped behind his table, staring at the desktop. A half-smoked cigarette hangs forgotten between his fingers.

"Willi?" I ask again. My stomach clenches with fear.

He doesn't answer. The embers eat along the cigarette paper as if in slow motion; the blackened corners shrivel, leaving behind gray ash, which sits on the tip of the cigarette, frozen in the air for an instant. Then Willi's hand trembles slightly, and the ashes float down in little wispy clouds, light as snowflakes.

Willi's eyes are red-rimmed.

"It's over, boys," he rasps.

Gerhard and I trade glances, uncomprehending.

"He didn't make it." Willi sighs and rubs the bridge of his nose. "His body was just too weak. He couldn't hold back the fever."

What's he talking about? He can't mean what I think he means. "But...he was doing fine last night," I stutter.

Willi shakes his head, still not meeting our eyes.

"Are you saying...?" asks Gerhard tonelessly.

Willi spits on the floor. Then he nods slowly. "There was nothing else I could do for him."

That's impossible. I spoke to him; he was getting better. Should I have called Willi over during the night? This must be a mistake! My gaze travels through the open door and into the sickroom. August's bed is empty, sheets and blankets piled in a disorderly heap next to it. Slowly, the realization sinks in.

"Maybe it's better this way," says Willi, snapping me from my stunned paralysis.

"What?"

"With everything that's coming... Believe me, it's better that he doesn't have to go through all that..."

I'm barely aware of what happens afterward. Gerhard stands next to me and speaks to Willi. My eyes are burning. After a while, Gerhard drags me through the freezing, dim courtyard into the canteen. I tell him I'm not hungry, but he doesn't listen. Smoke-thilde puts a plate in front of me. I push my food around without really tasting it.

Our table is silent; even Wilhelm can't find anything to say. Only when Swarowski enters the room and announces the arrival of *Hauptmann* von Leisner, the commander of our barracks, do I wake from my trance. None of us have seen the *Hauptmann* face-to-face before now, so we all straighten up when he comes in.

Hauptmann von Leisner has just one arm. His other sleeve hangs baggy and empty on his right side, and he's stuffed the bottom end into the belt of his uniform. But he stands straight and proud as he stretches his good arm out in a brief Hitler salute. Then he clears his throat.

"Today, we mourn the death of a comrade," he begins.

Tears spring to my eyes. The room is so quiet you could hear a pin drop.

"This morning August Hubrich succumbed to his illness. He was, I'm told, a bright young man with a good head on his shoulders and a thirst for action. His roommates will feel his loss, and we will miss his devoted assistance." He is silent for a few seconds.

A loud sniffing sounds from Swarowski's direction. I keep my eyes fixed on my plate so I don't have to look at the others.

"There's something else," continues the *Hauptmann*. His voice isn't loud, but it carries effortlessly across the room.

"Today the District Leader of Lower Silesia, Karl Hanke, has given the command to evacuate the civilian population from Breslau and its surrounding areas."

The news explodes like a grenade, tearing me out of my dull despair. My heart begins to pound.

Mother...and my siblings...

"All men fit for service and all boys sixteen and older in the *Volkssturm* will remain behind to defend against the enemy's advance."

An excited murmuring bubbles up. "We're going to stay here," I hear some of my groupmates say. Wilhelm has a sparkle in his eyes.

"I can't say what will happen to you," continues the Hauptmann, raising his voice to make himself heard over the whispers, his gaze sweeping the room.

"I know you're all prepared to give your lives to protect our Fatherland and your families. But I hope it won't be necessary. That's all, boys. *Heil* Hitler."

Chapter 12

As we're driving to our deployment site the next morning, we can already see the effects of the evacuation command. The roads leading out of Breslau are filled with throngs of people wheeling carts and laden with bags. The trains trundling by are hopelessly overcrowded; some people even cling to the cars' outer railings.

Did Mother manage to get on a train? If only I'd get a message from her.

We arrive at the antitank ditches and begin our daily work. The hard labor and the shock I still feel in my limbs keep my thoughts in check. As we're digging, I suddenly have a vision of August standing just a few feet from me, lifting his shovel. I rub my eyes until the image vanishes and keep on working silently for a while. Then I see August lying on his sickbed, so quiet and peaceful. His face melds together with my brother Frank's. And once again, I'm back to worrying about my family.

Furiously, I drive my shovel into the hard earth, tearing clump after clump from its unyielding body. Today the cold is so harsh, there's no chance of getting warm. With each breath, the cold claws at my nose, and the glistening snow stings my eyes until they fill with tears.

In the evening, Willi tells us that trains have stopped running altogether, and anyone still left in Breslau and surroundings has to flee on foot. The temperature is below zero. "Most of them won't survive the march," he says grimly. "Especially children and the elderly."

"What's going to happen to…you know…?" asks Gerhard with a nod at the now empty bed in the sickroom.

"I telegraphed August's parents," says Willi. "I don't know if they got the message or if they've already left. We're going to bury him tomorrow, in the North Cemetery. You can all come, of course, the *Hauptmann* has announced." Willi lets out a heavy sigh. "Maybe you could write his mother a note. That's the thing to do. Better than a telegram."

That night, a fire eats at the wood in the stove, bringing little warmth to the frosty room. It feels like an eternity since I sat by August's bedside. Except for the soft crackling of flames, the place is quiet. Our groupmates sit or lie on their bunks, staring glumly into space, some flipping through a book.

Herbert is scribbling something on a sheet of letter paper, his brow furrowed. When he finishes and releases his pencil, I ask him for a piece of paper and take a seat at the table. At first, I can only stare at the blank sheet. What should I write? What can I possibly say to comfort his mother?

I poise my pencil to start, then drop it again, several times. Finally, I realize I can't do anything but tell her about August, as I knew him.

> *Dear Frau Hubrich,*
> *I'd like to tell you about your son. Last night, when he took a turn for the worse, I sat with him. He was asleep most of the time, but I think he*

*appreciated it all the same. We all liked him a lot,
even if he wasn't the fastest runner or the best boxer.
During one of our soccer games last summer, he was
a real hero. He blocked a penalty kick with his face.
It broke his glasses and gave him a bloody nose. But
when he came around, he just looked up proudly and
asked, "Did I get it?"*

*Did you know that back in school, he was al-
ways writing poems on scraps of paper under his
desk, secretly, when the teacher wasn't looking? He
would've been a great poet.*

No sooner have I written down one memory than another
occurs to me. By the time I'm finished, I'm surprised to
find that I've covered an entire page with my scrawl.

*I'm very sorry that I couldn't take better care of
him. He was my friend. You can be very proud of
your son.*

Sincerely yours…

I sign my name and wipe a hand across my eyes. It's not
exactly Theodor Storm, August's favorite author—but then
again, I'm only a watchmaker. The Hubrichs will understand. I just wish I could've done more.

Exhausted, I collapse into bed.

It feels like only a few minutes later that the sound of the
bell awakens me.

Blearily, I sit up, bumping my head on the low ceiling.
As I'm rubbing my head, somebody turns on the light. I
squint. There's movement in the hallway, boots pounding

on the wooden floor. Then Stoss bursts into our room and yells, "All of you—out of bed and listen! Report to the courtyard in fifteen minutes, dressed and with your marching packs on. This is not a drill! Stragglers will be left behind."

Suddenly I'm wide awake. I call to the others, who're still lying in their bunks or just sitting up groggily like me, "Let's go, you heard the man!"

I jump out of bed and slide into my uniform. There's a flurry of activity around me as my groupmates do the same. I grab my things from the locker and cram them in my duffel bag. The large backpack can hold a lot: change of clothes, toiletries, boot polish; even my old pair of shoes fits. I pack my civilian clothes, too. I don't know where we're headed, but I probably won't be going home any time soon. Adrenaline floods my body. Why couldn't this wait until morning? And why do we need our marching packs?

"Are they crazy? It's the middle of the night," moans Gerhard.

"It's 2:30 a.m., to be exact," I say, glancing at my watch before I quickly stow it in the inside pocket of my coat.

"They're going to send us to the front," Herbert says. "That means the Russians are almost here."

"You don't know that," Gerhard argues.

"Finally! It's starting," interjects Wilhelm. "Real men don't dig trenches."

"You're not a real man," Herbert scoffs.

I don't have time to speculate. "Let's go. Everybody ready? We have to get down there," I call, trying to urge on the stragglers.

I wait until everyone has left the room and turn off the lights behind me. I may not know where we're going, but I won't miss the barracks at all. In the courtyard, we hastily fall into formation with the other boys and wait for what's to come. Suddenly, I think of Willi.

"Save my place for me," I whisper to Gerhard, and sneak away in the darkness before he can protest.

Light's still on in the infirmary. Willi is sitting at his desk with his legs propped up as usual. He fixes me with a calm gaze.

"Willi!" I stare at him in disbelief. "Didn't you hear? We're supposed to get ready to march!"

Willi pushes his cigarette into the corner of his mouth. "That doesn't apply to me. Somebody has to hold down the fort."

"But..."

He takes the cigarette out of his mouth. "Don't worry about me—I'll be fine. You all should be worrying about yourselves."

"Do you know where we're going?"

Willi shrugs and scratches one stubbly cheek. "I know about as much as you do. I'm guessing you're supposed to leave the city before the Reds surround us completely. *Hauptmann* von Leisner is a sensible guy. He knows that a bunch of kids can't do anything against the Russian army. And before Hanke puts the city on total lockdown and forces you to join the *Volkssturm*, he's probably going to take you somewhere safe. Whatever *safe* means, nowadays." He nods slowly. "That's how it is."

I hear Stoss yelling and grab Willi's hand. "Please make sure you send my letter to August's mother. If she's still here..."

"I'll take care of it, kid, you can bet on that." He squeezes my hand firmly. "Now go. Watch out for yourself!"

He coughs slightly and turns away, his face melting into the shadows. I hurry out of the infirmary and slip into place next to Gerhard in the dim courtyard. The shadow of *Hauptmann* von Leisner is towering in front of us.

"There's no time for lengthy explanations. You will leave Breslau and march in the direction of Liegnitz, where cargo trains will be waiting to take you further west. Outside of Breslau, you'll meet up with some of the other youth units. Tonight you'll march until dawn, then you'll rest in a nearby town. If you see planes flying low overhead, lie flat on the ground or throw yourselves into the ditches by the side of the road, and cover your heads. Understood?"

Nobody moves. The wind whistles through the barracks.

"Division—halt!" Stoss cries. "Eyes left! Division—left! And—march!"

We march through the barracks gates, out into the icy, driving snow, in the middle of the dark night.

Chapter 13

The snowstorm makes the march torturous. Snowflakes form an impenetrable curtain, so thick that I can barely see the boys in front of me. The wind stings in my eyes and tears the breath from my mouth. This must be how the soldiers felt back in '41 when they had their first taste of the Russian winter. Only near dawn do we finally reach a small town.

Someone yells something, but I can't make it out over the howling of the wind. Light pours from an open door, piercing the snowdrifts. I'm pushed over the threshold. A loud howling sounds as the door closes and the storm batters against it. Then we're surrounded by the quiet and warmth of a heated room.

I tear my scarf from my face and take a deep breath. We seem to be in a small inn. Rustic wooden benches line the walls; a spruce-green tiled stove radiates heat, and a pair of antlers hangs on the opposite wall. A short, round man receives us in slippers and a bathrobe. "There are a few rooms available upstairs. And we can set up straw mattresses in the common room," he says in a tired voice.

I help push the tables aside. Others bring in thinly filled sacks of straw, distributing them across the floor and benches. Gerhard saves two spaces for us on the bench by the stove. Exhausted, I take off my marching pack and sink down onto the makeshift mattress where I pull off my boots and massage my numb toes until they start to tingle painfully. My stomach is rumbling, but my exhaustion is greater. I just want to lie down.

An officer pops his head into the room. "Get some sleep, boys. We'll leave around noon. When the storm has passed."

I fall asleep as soon as I lie down, wrapped in a scratchy military blanket and lulled by the heat of the stove.

A loud bang tears me from slumber. *Gunshots?* Instantly, I slide off my mattress and hit the deck. "Get down!" I yell to Gerhard. He just mumbles something incomprehensible and rolls onto his other side. Someone laughs. I lift my head and glance around, confused. Then I see the window: someone has thrown open the blinds to let the light in.

An officer is standing in the doorway, clapping. The sound echoes across the room. "Very good," he booms. "You're ready for the real thing!"

My ears burning, I sit up. At least, I'm one of the first awake.

"Get up, groundhogs! We're moving," the officer calls before leaving the room.

I shake Gerhard, who's still sleeping like a log. But once I whisper that there's food, he opens his eyes. We each get a couple of slices of bread with margarine and artificial liverwurst. I devour one right away; the other I put in my duffel bag. Gerhard eats both of his immediately and says, disappointed, "That's all we get?"

"Let's go, let's go," the officer commands.

Shivering, we dash to the little outhouse behind the inn. Then we form rows of four in the street, preparing to march onward. Now that the storm has passed, the rooftops and surrounding fields are covered by a beautiful white mantle, as yet unblemished by footsteps. The sun is climbing in the cloudless sky, surrounding us with a fairytale glittering.

As we trudge on, I stare at the snow until my eyes sting and tears well up in them. Suddenly, Luise appears before me. She's wearing a snow-white dress, so bright it's almost blinding, and her blue eyes shine like the winter sky. Her hair falls in thick braids over her shoulders. Does it feel as soft as it looks? I pretend I'm picking her up for a concert, wearing my Sunday best. *You look lovely,* I say to her. Luise blushes. *Really?* she asks. *You think I look lovely?* I nod. Luise gazes deeply into my eyes. Then she says…

"I have to pee. Again."

The daydream vanishes with a pop. Disgruntled, I turn to Gerhard, who's tramping through the snow next to me. "You shouldn't have had so much to drink, then."

"I had to fill my stomach with something," he protests. "I'm a growing man!"

I concentrate on stepping in the footprints of the boy in front of me. Is my family walking this way too? It must be awful for the kids, having to travel in the freezing cold and biting wind, completely unprotected, all day long. The vision of a girl lying in a roadside ditch just won't leave me, her tears frozen on her ice-cold cheeks. I shake my head to chase the image away.

"I have to get in touch with Mother. Let her know I'm okay, tell her where they're taking us," I whisper to Gerhard.

"We don't even know where that is," he replies.

"The *Hauptmann* said westward. To Liegnitz. But where do you think we'll go after?"

He shrugs. "I'm just happy to be out of Breslau," he says. "Things are getting pretty hairy there."

We're on an open country road, lined on both sides with old cherry trees. Thick, gnarled trunks stretch their bare branches skyward.

"I wonder if they made it to Leipzig," I murmur, mostly to myself.

"Of course they did," says Gerhard, but he can't dispel my worries.

"If I could just slip away," I ponder in a low voice. "Go and find them…"

Gerhard looks at me. "*Shhh*," he hisses.

"I…" I begin, but he interrupts me with a wave of his hand.

He tilts his head up, wrinkles spreading across his brow. "Did you hear that?"

That's when I hear it too: a fast-swelling buzz overhead. We look up. Over the tree line, in the direction of the forest we just crossed, a plane comes into view. Then another. And another.

"Russian fighters! Hit the deck," somebody yells. The cry echoes down the line.

They snuck up on us, flying against the wind so we couldn't hear them until they got close.

"Come on," I yell to Gerhard, plowing through the deep snow in the roadside ditch toward the cherry trees.

Around us, chaos has broken loose. My groupmates are falling all over each other, rushing to take cover behind the trees. Someone steps on my heels. I stumble, but Gerhard catches me and drags me onwards.

"Yaks," he wheezes.

I really don't care what kind of planes they are. We take shelter on the side of the trunks opposite the fighters, cowering, huddled close together. A moment later the machine guns begin their rapid-fire pounding.

I cover my head with my arms. Fountains of snow spray up around us...people scream...the old tree shudders, riddled with bullets, but the shots remain buried in its thick trunk. My heart hammers in my chest; my hands and feet are numb from the snow. I listen intently to the roaring of the engines, trying to guess their path.

They pass over, only to wheel around in a wide arc.

Fast as lightning, we switch to the other side of the trunks. Again, the shots whiz by us. My groupmates cry out. Some are running through the snow, panicked, scattering in all directions. They're making themselves better targets. I watch in silent horror, unable to look away.

The airplanes change direction again. As we scramble to our original positions, I falter in my step. In front of us, a boy lies face-down in the snow, a red stain spreading out from underneath him.

I should turn him over, check who it is, whether he's still alive, but we have to stay close to the tree. I feel Gerhard's body trembling next to mine as the shots whip past us. Another boy crawls toward us, groaning softly.

Finally, they retreat. The buzzing of the engines fades. We remain perfectly still, frozen in our hiding spots like frightened rabbits in their burrows, afraid they'll turn around and attack us again. I repeat the same prayer over and over: *Please make them go away. Please make them go away...*

"Hey, Anton," says Gerhard, his voice quavering. "I think I wet myself."

I can't hold it against him.

The moaning of the wounded and the officers' bellowed commands bring me back to myself. Hesitantly, I crawl through the snow to the boy who's lying on his stomach in the red spot. I don't want to turn him over, but I do it anyway. I don't recognize him: his face is expressionless, his eyes closed. Ice crystals have formed on his eyelashes, which are ridiculously long, and his upper body is riddled with bullets. I fight off my rising nausea.

On shaky legs, Gerhard and I lift the dead boy and carry him to where the troop is assembling. We're met with tear-streaked, horrified faces. Twelve dead, twenty wounded. With piercing whistles, the officers try to restore order.

The boys from our room are standing together in shocked silence. Herbert, Johannes, Heiner, Achim—even Wilhelm. "Gustav didn't make it," chokes Herbert as we join them. He's fighting back tears, others are crying openly.

"Pull yourself together, man," barks Wilhelm, but he, too, looks pale. "Gustav died for the Fatherland," he adds, more gently.

What a glorious death, I think bitterly.

I look over at Gerhard, relieved that he's not the one lying in the snow with his eyes closed; then I feel guilty for thinking that. Still, I make a solemn promise to myself: we're both going to make it home alive. I'm not going to lose Gerhard, too.

Chapter 14

Gerhard jabs me in the side and points straight ahead. We're near the front of the marching column. I'm constantly peering into the overcast sky, listening for the low thrumming of engines, searching our surroundings for places to hide. Cautiousness has become second nature. Currently, we're in an unprotected area, and I don't like it. Snow-covered fields stretch out on both sides of the street, and farther off a row of trees marks the beginning of a small forest.

When Gerhard tries to point something out, I immediately fear for the worst, but I can't see any low-flying planes. Then, at a curve in the road ahead, I can just make out some figures—little more than dark spots in the snow.

"Maybe they're refugees?" I suggest.

I stand taller, trying to see over the heads in front of me, but I only manage to discern that they're a fairly large group, like our own column.

"They look like they're barely moving," says Gerhard.

After another day and a half of marching through the snow and ice and a night spent in an unheated barn, always in constant fear of another air attack, we're all exhausted. Still, we're rapidly closing in on the group in front of us. Maybe they're moving slowly to accommodate children and the elderly.

Suddenly, my heart beats faster, and I hope, completely irrationally, that mother might be in the group.

A shot rings out. I startle, and our column falters. Everyone is looking around, confused. "Move along," calls an officer from the front of the line. "It's none of your business."

We march onward. I can see men in black coats with guns slung over their shoulders, bringing up the rear of the column. And then they come into view: dozens, hundreds of people in the blue-and-white striped uniforms that always remind me of pajamas. Prisoners.

I glance over at Gerhard, who returns the look with a furrowed brow. Our column begins to fidget. Suddenly, I spot something to the right of the road.

"Eyes forward!" yells a petty officer, but nobody's listening. On the edge of the road, there's a bundle of clothes. No, not just clothes—a person lies curled up there, the sleeves of the striped suit pushed up over thin arms. A bony, shaven skull is barely visible above the snow, and with a start, I see a black bullet hole in its back. There's hardly any blood, but at the sight of it, I feel as if my veins are flooded with ice.

"Company—halt!"

We stop. The officers must have noticed that we're distracted. An uncomprehending murmur starts up among us as another shot rings out ahead. Rough voices scream insults and curses. "Move it, pigs! Faster! Go on! March!"

Our column leader runs ahead and catches up with the column of prisoners. He speaks to one of the guards, gesturing heatedly.

Which concentration camp did they come from? And why are they being marched through the cold? Maybe they're being deployed to work? Or evacuated, like us? The overseers scream something. As we look on, the gray mass of prisoners divides and streams to either side of the road, where they sink down onto the snow, trembling.

"They're letting us through. Now go, on the double! March!" yells our column leader. The command is passed back down the line as we begin to move. "No dawdling."

Feeling very uncomfortable, we practically run past the prisoners, urged on by the officers who I suppose don't want us to be exposed to this scene any longer than necessary. A rotten smell lingers in the air—an odor I can't identify, unlike anything I've ever smelled before. What with their thin suits, it's a wonder half of the prisoners haven't frozen to death. I'd be glad to give them some of my bread, but I know that I'd be shot for it, and the prisoners too. Most of them stare right past us or at the ground, their eyes empty. Those skeletal faces…you can hardly tell if they're male or female. I'm appalled, and yet I can't tear my gaze away from these emaciated figures that look like walking corpses. The SS guards, meanwhile, are standing at the edge of the road, lighting cigarettes, talking and laughing.

Then something happens at the far edge of the crowd. Even as I watch, a few of the prisoners jump up and run, fast as rabbits. They seem so fragile that I didn't think it was possible. They bolt across the fields towards the forest, just a few hundred yards away. Within seconds, the SS men have recovered from their surprise and put their machine guns to their shoulders. A wave of heat courses through my body. My chest tightens.

"Get down!" someone yells, as the Mausers unleash an ear-splitting hail of bullets.

I pull Gerhard down with me and throw my arms over my head, but I peer out between them so I can see what's going on.

More and more of the thin figures jump up and try to flee in what seems to be a suicide attempt. The guards are aiming directly at them, even at the ones who remain on the ground. Screams ring out...I don't know whether it's the prisoners screaming, or us. One of the prisoners stumbles and falls into the snow with a cry. But a minute later, he stands back up again, wearily, and limps on. I follow him with my eyes...just a few more yards and he'll reach the forest. Then there's another round of gunfire. The man falls a second time, rolls over, and lies motionless in the snow.

The guards scream furiously, the prisoners cry and groan, and we're right in the middle of it.

No more than a few feet from me, there's a tangle of arms and legs and blue stripes: a heap of people. I can't make out how many there are. They fell over each other as the bullets flew toward them. They didn't move, they didn't try to flee, probably didn't have the strength left—and yet they were mown down. One face is turned toward me: a young man with sharp cheekbones, hollow cheeks, and a long, red scar across his bald scalp. His eyes stare sightlessly into the empty sky and his mouth is slightly open, revealing rotten teeth between bluish lips. He looks like he died in the middle of a scream.

Suddenly, something moves in the heap of clothing and bodies. I look closer, riveted with horror. From the bottom of the pile, out from under all the corpses, a hand emerges. The fingers look like a bundle of sticks, the skin between them as thin as paper. The hand clutches helplessly at the snow, then sinks back down. I turn away, but the image won't leave me.

The SS guards are still dashing about in a mad rage, bellowing hoarsely and shooting at everything that moves.

A few minutes—or hours—later, it's over. Dark heaps lie scattered across a white field.

"Fucking shit, was that really necessary?" screams our column leader, enraged.

The SS men don't answer. They have wounded among their own to tend to since they were shooting blindly in all directions.

"Everyone up! Get in your rows!" That's directed at us.

I get up automatically, though my legs feel like jello. Next to me, one of my groupmates is vomiting into a roadside ditch. I hold my breath as my stomach is threatening to turn, too. My face is wet, and there are frozen tracks of tears across Gerhard's pale cheeks. We can barely look each other in the eyes.

They drive us hurriedly past the fields of bodies. Stumbling, I try to stay in lockstep with my groupmates. Somehow, I succeed in putting one foot in front of the other. I don't know how many miles we've walked when we finally stop in a small town.

The word comes down: "We're taking a half-hour break, then we're back on the move. We'll be in Liegnitz by tonight."

It's too cold to rest outside, so we spread out among the houses that are willing to take us in. In the schoolhouse, which only has one room, I sink down on a bench next to Gerhard. He jams his fists into his eyes. Nobody says a word; there's no way to describe what just happened. We should unpack our bread and have something to eat, but no one's hungry. I'm shivering in the unheated room.

My eyes flit to Wilhelm, who's leaning against the wall with a grim expression on his face, arms folded in front of his chest. My jaw clenches as I consider that his father is also an SS officer, the commander of a labor camp near Breslau...a murderer.

An officer enters the room and stands at the lectern in front of us like a teacher. He calls us to attention, a serious expression on his face, and waits until everyone is focused on him.

"Boys, what you just witnessed...you shouldn't have had to see that," he begins carefully.

He glances to two soldiers who have entered the classroom behind him. The crescent-shaped metal badges dangling around their necks indicate that they're members of the *Feldgendarmerie*, the military police. We call them watchdogs because of the chains around their necks. What are they doing here?

"Most of you probably don't understand why that had to happen," continues the officer, an *Oberleutnant* by rank. He doesn't use the usual, jarring voice of the military; instead, he speaks softly, cautiously.

Now we all lift our heads and look at him, almost pleadingly. We're hoping he'll give us some sort of explanation, help us understand what we've just experienced.

He clears his throat. "The prisoners were trying to get away—you all saw that. If they hadn't run, they wouldn't have been shot."

"So it was *their* fault?" somebody asks. Everyone turns toward the speaker.

"Well, it's not *your* fault, in any case," replies the *Oberleutnant* evasively.

For a while, there's a deep silence. We sit motionless as the MPs shift from one leg to the other.

"Think of it this way," the officer continues, with another look at the MPs. "We're at war. In war, there are always victims…"

"Killing people in battle and slaughtering defenseless prisoners are two completely different things!" Herbert has stood up. "My father is a *Wehrmacht* officer. He would never tolerate such cowardly behavior from his soldiers."

One of the MPs steps forward. His face is unassuming, but there's a dangerous look in his eyes.

"Those people weren't like us, they're inferior races— *Untermenschen*, Jews, gays, Gypsies and the like. Understood? It's a public service to rid the world of vermin like that. Otherwise, Germany can never be victorious. They will eat us out of house and home."

"I'm going to be sick," I whisper to Gerhard, but he puts a finger to his lips in warning.

Herbert is still standing, his shoulders rigid, but doesn't say anything else.

A thin, pimply boy with glasses suddenly bursts into hysterical sobs. His name is Joachim Drechsler; he was in the room next to us in the barracks.

"Pull yourself together!" the watchdog orders harshly. But Joachim doesn't listen.

"My father…" he stutters, barely comprehensible through his sobs, "they came and took him, too…took him to a camp…he didn't come back…"

"He probably deserved it," the MP bellows, his face twisting.

"Please," says the *Oberleutnant*, but he appears helpless to stop them.

"You're murderers, all of you!" Joachim screeches. "If that's Germany's future, then I hope it goes to the dogs!"

"Quiet!" cries the MP, his face bright red now. "That's treason! Subversion of the war effort! Punishable by death!"

The *Oberleutnant* tries to intervene, pleading: "The boys are just worked up, and understandably so."

But the MP nods at his sidekick, who grabs the boy by the arm and shakes him. "You will stop *now*!"

My heart is in my throat. *Stop, Joachim, please!*

But Joachim pulls himself up and looks the MP in the eyes. "Pigs," he whispers, tears still streaming across his face. "I don't want anything to do with you!"

The second MP seizes the boy's other arm. Together, they pull him to the door. Joachim doesn't resist; head lowered, he allows himself to be dragged. Suddenly, the *Oberleutnant* is standing in front of them. "Let the boy go. He only—"

"Out of the way, or you'll be next!" yells the watchdog, pushing Joachim out the door and into the snow. He falls on his hands and knees. The other MP draws his pistol. I'm trembling all over.

"No!" somebody cries. A shot rings out. Joachim falls face-first into the snow, which reddens beneath him, like a white tablecloth soaking up grape juice.

"Let that be a lesson," shouts the MP, slamming the door shut again. This time, I have to throw up, too.

Chapter 15

When we finally reach Liegnitz, no cargo trains are waiting. We have to keep on marching through the cold, on foot, just like the countless refugees we encounter on the road. I haven't had clean clothes for days, and though I've wrapped my feet in rags, I have to hold my toes up to the fire and massage them for at least half an hour each night if I want to feel them again.

Every day is the same as the last; there's only before the prisoners, and after. I ask myself the same questions over and over: am I a coward? Should I have protested, like Joachim? Then I'd be dead too…just like Stauffenberg and the conspirators who tried to assassinate the *Führer*. By myself, I can't do a thing.

I pull Father's watch out of my coat pocket, which I wind every day. Undeterred, the little hands continue their movement around the face. With my thumb, I rub the inscription on the cover, feeling the thin lines beneath my fingertip. *In the end, a man answers only to his conscience, Anton,* I hear Father say, and in that moment I can see him clearly, though he's already fading from my memory.

I grip the watch tightly. There's only one thing I can do: resist. Refuse to go along with this madness. And if they press weapons into our hands—I will never use them against another human being. Germany has sinned enough;

I don't want to add to that sin. Maybe it doesn't matter what I do. Horrible things will still happen. But at least this way, I'll have a clear conscience.

The question is whether I'm brave enough to do it.

Our group reaches Bautzen by evening. We still have no clue what our final destination is, but as long as we're heading west, and I'm getting closer to Leipzig, I can live with it.

We spend the night in a refugee camp near Bautzen, a school they've outfitted to accommodate hundreds of people. We're sent to the gym, where straw mattresses cover the floor with thin army blankets spread across them. An oven in the corner barely manages to heat the big space. But at least they've set up several field kitchens, which are offering warm meals. We sink down onto our mattresses and eat in silence.

Our *Oberleutnant* Schwarz enters the gym and stands in the very center of the room so everyone can see him. In his quiet voice, which we have to strain to hear, he says, "Boys, our trains are finally ready. Tomorrow morning you'll get on board and head to your deployment site." Almost regretfully, he looks around at the assembled boys.

Silence greets the announcement as we allow his words to sink in. Nobody was expecting this. Deployment site? Are we going to the front after all?

"Our troops in the Protectorate of Bohemia and Moravia under *General* Schörner's command need reinforcements," continues Schwarz and takes a deep breath. "You're all on fatigue duty to help with defense. Tomorrow, you're going to the Protectorate. Right now I can't tell you exactly where you're headed; the front lines change every day."

Schörner. The name gives me goosebumps. From my groupmates' faces, I can see that they're thinking the same thing. Schörner is famous for sending his soldiers into hopeless situations. The word "defeat" isn't in his vocabulary—let alone "surrender."

After Schwarz has left the room, a loud murmuring arises in the gym. Some of the boys seem happy about the deployment, but most of them look as shocked as I am. Nobody admits he's afraid.

"Suicide mission," I mutter to Gerhard.

Wilhelm straightens up. "A German man faces the enemy fearlessly. Even if the situation is hopeless."

I shovel some soup into my mouth, ignoring him.

"I'm glad we're done running around like chickens with our heads cut off," he continues. "It's about time!"

When the gym has fallen quiet, when the last excited conversations have died away and we all lie down to sleep, I ask myself whether I'm the only one with this gnawing feeling in my gut, even though I've just eaten a big meal. I pull out my photos, which have curled and faded from the damp weather, and look at Mother and my siblings.

My brain is working feverishly. If they take us to the east, I may never see my family again. Who's going to take care of them? I can't let them down. I promised Mother that we'd meet up in Leipzig; I have to get there. And if we leave Germany, there's no way that will ever happen. So we have to escape before then…wait for some distraction and slip away.

"Gerhard," I whisper, rolling onto my other side so I can look at him. It's not completely dark in the gym: the oven emits a weak firelight, and a ceiling lamp glows in the front of the room, where two guards are standing by the door.

"I won't die a hero's death in a war we've already lost."

"What's that supposed to mean?" Gerhard whispers so softly I can barely hear him.

"We have to disappear. The next chance we get."

The decision, once made, stops the trembling inside of me.

For a moment, Gerhard looks like he's going to object. Maybe, like me, he's thinking about the watchdogs. Everyone knows what they do to deserters. But he simply asks, "Where do you want to go?"

"To Leipzig. Are you with me?" I won't go without Gerhard.

He doesn't hesitate, just nods decisively.

I sigh with relief. "The next chance we get," I repeat. "Get ready."

A whistle jolts me awake. I sit up and look around blearily. The other boys are getting up, but there's still no trace of daylight. A glance at my pocket watch tells me it's 5:00 a.m.

The officers herd us into the school courtyard once we've put on our boots and coats. I shiver. A cold moon is hanging in the grayish-black sky. Though we've practiced our formations hundreds of times, today there are careless mistakes. Some people turn their heads the wrong way, some fall out of step with the others. The officers shout, but nobody's really listening.

We march to the train station, where I steal glances in every direction. Behind us is a long brick building, dark and apparently abandoned. Train tracks, which gleam dully in the moonlight, stretch out to either side, crisscrossing in several places and disappearing in the distance. Across the tracks is a broad area covered only with low bushes and weeds. No good escape route—we'd be too visible. A long cargo train is waiting at the platform.

They herd us into the cars like we're cattle going to slaughter. There's no place to sit, just a suspicious-looking heap of straw in one corner, which I prefer to avoid. It reeks of sweat and urine. I have a horrible feeling that this train hasn't been used for cargo in quite some time.

"We're trapped in here," I whisper to Gerhard

Despite the cold, I'm starting to sweat. The darkness on the train is oppressive. The high windows, nothing more than rectangular slits, don't yet let in a glimmer of dawn.

Gerhard saves us a spot next to the door, and I feel a little better. I sink down onto the wooden floor and pull my legs to my chest. My duffel bag becomes a cushion for my back.

It takes a long time for the train to start up. Finally, the engine puffs, and with a squeaking and jerking we set out. How long is the ride to the Protectorate of Bohemia and Moravia? I don't care! I don't intend to be on the train when it arrives.

As we boarded, I noticed that the car doors were secured with hooks on the outside. Our platoon leaders fastened them so that no one could jump off the moving train. But our door isn't completely closed: there's a small gap, through which an icy wind is blowing. I could probably stick a finger through the gap, push up the hook, and open the door.

The problem is doing so without anyone noticing. If the others jump out of the car too, it's less likely we'll escape. I'd rather that Gerhard and I could steal away unnoticed. But in a train car with dozens of other people, that seems almost impossible.

I mull the problem over, rubbing my hands together from time to time to see if I can still feel my fingers. After a while, my eyelids get heavier and heavier and want to shut.

Just then, a loud crash startles me awake. I feel a blow to the back of my head and see yellow lights dancing before my eyes. I'm shoved roughly to the side and fall against Gerhard's shoulder. In the back of the car, our groupmates are also sliding about, tumbling all over each other. The wheels of the train screech—a hair-raising sound, like fingernails on a chalkboard.

A low roar fills the air. Plane engines?

The ground seems to quake and the vibrations spread through my whole body. Outside, there's a shrill whistling, followed by the sound of an impact...then another...and another...in ever-faster sequence.

They're bombing our train! If we stay here, we're done for.

"Grab your duffel bag," I yell to Gerhard, strapping on my own.

I crawl to the door and begin to work on the hook. My finger does actually fit through the gap. But then the train shakes from another impact and my finger is trapped between the door and the frame. I bite my lips from the pain, drawing blood.

"Are you crazy? We can't leave. Nobody's allowed off the train, that was the command." I don't recognize the voice, but I'm not overly concerned about it. Not anymore.

Finally, my finger comes free again. I resist the urge to immediately pull it out and stick it in my mouth; instead, I grit my teeth and keep groping around for the hook. There. I try to push it up, but it doesn't move.

An explosion resounds close by, followed by the crashing and groaning of wood. I yank desperately at the hook.

Gerhard, who's figured out what I'm doing, throws his whole body weight against the heavy steel door.

"Shit, shit, shit," I hear him mutter. Outside, the chorus of whistles is getting louder.

"If you hear a bomb whistling, it won't hit you. The ones that'll hit you are the ones you don't hear coming," I call to him. That's a pearl of wisdom I got from Willi.

"Very comforting," he grinds out.

At last, the hook gives way. By now the other boys are crowding around us, vying to get out. Regardless of our orders, no one wants to be trapped in a cage of steel and wood during an attack like this.

The door bursts open. Gerhard nearly tumbles over me and almost pushes me out in front of him. I just manage to catch hold of the frame.

Once again, there's an ear-splitting crash. Around us, more and more shells are dropping. Now there's no holding back. I'm shoved out of the train by the wave of bodies behind me, so I jump onto the tracks and look around.

Our surroundings are lit bright as day by parachute flares—a frozen shower of sparks in the sky. We've stopped at an open stretch of land, there's no train station, no town in sight. Just a small pine forest, about two hundred yards away. Between the tall, slim trunks, inviting shadows beckon. That's where we need to go, hopefully unnoticed!

A soldier dashes by, hunched over. "Everyone take cover! No one runs away!"

These last words are drowned out by more explosions. Gerhard and I throw ourselves to the ground simultaneously. I wrap my arms protectively around my head, opening my mouth so the pressure doesn't shatter my eardrums.

Pain courses through my little finger as if I've been stabbed. I ignore it and stand up again, still trying to reach the forest.

But…where's Gerhard? I don't see him. There are too many people.

I call out to him, but I can't even hear my own voice. The pressure wave from another detonation knocks me over again. I crawl into a bomb crater and look back at the train. The only thing that remains of our car is a ragged skeleton. Some of the other cars have been opened, too. Dark figures are rushing around, trying to find shelter.

Finally, I see Gerhard. He's stumbled a few yards away but is picking himself back up again. I wave, gesticulating wildly until he sees me.

"Let's go! To the forest!" I cry. He nods and hobbles toward me.

Then a large soldier grabs him by the scruff. I freeze.

"Where are you going, boy?" he demands.

"I have to…I have to…," stammers Gerhard.

The officer releases him as if he had the plague. "You've wet yourself, haven't you? Well, stay where I can see you!"

Gerhard nods and crawls toward me in the bomb crater. After a minute, the soldier has to take cover himself and loses sight of us. I'm afraid we've missed our chance to run; we should have done it before the flares, when it wasn't so bright. Still, I creep toward the far side of the crater, Gerhard following close behind, both of us on our knees and elbows. My hands are numb from the snow. The inferno seems to have passed, and the officers are whistling to call everyone to order. Not us.

We reach the bushes at the edge of the forest and, finally, the protective shadows of the trees. For a while, we keep crawling across the forest floor. Snow trickles into my sleeves and down the back of my neck. Luckily it isn't as deep here, thanks to the tree cover. Behind a thick trunk, I stop and wait for Gerhard. Did we make it?

Chapter 16

We stand leaning against the trunk. My knees are trembling. I'd like nothing more than to sink down into the snow and fall asleep on the spot, but I force myself to remain on my feet and peer around the trunk. From here, hidden in the trees, we can no longer see the track bed. Apparently, no one's on our heels. Yet.

"What now?" asks Gerhard, wheezing.

"Let's go," is all I say. "Can you walk?"

Gerhard takes a tentative step with his right foot and flinches. "It'll be okay, I just twisted it when I fell. What happened to you?"

I stare at him, uncomprehending.

"You're bleeding…" he points to my left hand.

I'm surprised to find that the hand is completely covered in frozen blood. But then I remember the pain in my little finger. I inspect the wound: a small, sharp-edged metal splinter has bored into my fingertip. It's lodged fairly deep, and when I pull it out, fresh, dark blood pours from the cut. Gerhard rummages for his bandages, but I wave him off.

"Let's get out of here first!"

"Where are we going?"

I try to orient myself. I can see the first pale-red light creeping up from the eastern horizon. The train can't have gone far from Bautzen during the short ride. I point in the opposite direction, to the west, and we start to move. Although Gerhard grimaces when he takes his first steps, he follows me at a crisp pace. There's no time to waste. Who knows when they'll let the watchdogs off their leashes.

Beneath the thick crowns of the evergreens, it doesn't get light for a long time. I listen carefully for any noises. The forest, wintry and still, is just waking up. A few birds chirp, but the only other sound is the crunching of our footsteps in the snow and the occasional cracking of a pine cone underfoot.

I startle at a quick movement in front of us. There's a rustling in the underbrush, then something white flashes before our eyes and hops away on two lanky hind legs. Just a deer.

We keep going and going, trying to put as much distance as possible between ourselves and the train tracks. I cool my injured finger with snow until the blood stops flowing and the pain is numbed by the cold. Behind me, Gerhard curses. I turn around. His right leg is stuck up to the ankle in a snowbank. When he tries to pull free, he falls forward onto his hands. I help him up and notice that he can no longer put weight on his foot, though he's trying hard not to show it.

"Let's take a little break," I say. "We've already gone a long way."

He leans on my shoulder, and together, we hobble toward the south side of an old pine, where the wind has swept away the snow. If someone is following us, they won't spot us there right away. Then I remember that our tracks in the snow would lead them to us anyway. Still, we need a break.

Carefully, I pull off Gerhard's boot and unwrap the rags so I can examine his ankle. It's swollen and he cringes when I gently move his foot.

"I'm sure I sprained it. Or twisted it at least," he says. "I did that once, playing soccer. When Herbert ran me over." The snow helps to cool the ankle. There's nothing else I can do, at the moment.

We each eat some chocolate from our rations. The cold bar cracks loudly as I bite off a piece, and the chocolate warms me from the inside, calming me. Only now do I notice my inner trembling—not from the cold, but from the tension. After eating a handful of snow to quench my thirst, I feel refreshed.

"So what's the plan?" asks Gerhard, winding the rags back around his foot.

I think for a moment. "We can't stay here until we freeze. Or starve," I say.

"I'm with you so far. Then what?"

"That's all I've got."

"*That's* your plan?"

"I haven't exactly had time to think about it…"

Gerhard pauses in his attempt to pull the boot over his swollen ankle and begins to laugh. It starts as a soft chortling, but it soon turns into a hysterical laughing fit. At first I'm annoyed; then I have to laugh too. I don't know why, but I can't seem to help myself. The laughter bubbles up out of me, shaking me so hard that I have to hold my stomach and gasp for air.

"Help," Gerhard wheezes, bent over and trying to catch his breath.

There's a cracking among the trees behind us. Abruptly, we fall silent; it sounded like the far-away echo of a branch snapping underfoot. Another deer? My heart resumes its drumbeat. What if they've found us?

Now we can hear crunching footsteps. They're much too regular to be coming from an animal. Somebody is fighting through the snow just like we are. He murmurs something out loud. I'm guessing he can't be more than fifty yards away. Did he see our tracks? I hardly dare breathe, or even turn my head to look at Gerhard.

Suddenly, the steps stop. "Damn it," I hear him say. I think I recognize the voice. But surely it can't be...? I feel torn between distrust and relief. Is he friend or foe?

As I lift myself up, Gerhard looks at me questioningly, then nods. I step around the trunk. In the morning light, between two slim trees, stands Wilhelm Braun, examining our tracks in the snow. His gaze follows the footprints and settles on me.

We stare at each other silently. A squirrel rustles in the treetops above. In Wilhelm's face, I read nothing but surprise.

Finally, Gerhard emerges from our hiding place, still limping. There are two of us, while Braun is alone. No reason to be afraid.

Wilhelm stands with his fists clenched at his sides. He has a bloody scratch beneath his eye. "Aha! You're deserting!" he challenges us, his loud voice echoing in the forest.

"Looks like we're not the only ones," Gerhard replies.

Wilhelm glares at us. "I've been looking for thugs and deserters like you," he sneers, but it doesn't sound very convincing.

"And what are you going to do, now that you've found us?" I cross my arms.

Hesitantly, Wilhelm moves a few steps closer. "I'll take you back. The train is waiting."

"Cut the crap," I say. "You can't take us both with you. Plus, if you really wanted to go back, you'd be heading in the other direction."

His mouth opens as if he wants to say something, then closes again.

"Admit it! You're deserting too. Do you really think the watchdogs will believe it if they catch you? That you're only looking for runaways…"

His face darkens. "I don't see the point in being beaten to a pulp by bombs. They should deploy me like a real soldier. I'm going to report voluntarily as soon as I reach the nearest city."

I'm still standing in front of him with my arms folded. "Good idea. You do that."

He hesitates. "Where are you guys going?" he barks in a commanding tone.

"What do you care?"

He glares at us, but after everything we've experienced, he doesn't seem so threatening anymore, even though he's a head taller than I am.

"Then stay in the forest and die," he says, setting off again decisively.

We stand there, listening until the crackling steps disappear amid the sounds of the awakening forest.

"He's such an asshole," murmurs Gerhard.

"Do you think he'll really do it? Report voluntarily? Or is he full of hot air?"

"No clue."

I think about *SS-Hauptsturmführer* Braun, Wilhelm's father. Unwittingly, I once witnessed how he thrashed his son when I was repairing the grandfather clock in the *Hauptsturmführer's* office. But I don't want to feel sorry for

Braun. Just because his father beats him doesn't excuse the fact that he's a jerk. It doesn't excuse him for not thinking for himself and bullying boys like August.

But then I remember my own father, who taught me so much, and to whom I owe so much. Maybe I'd be different if I had a father like Wilhelm's?

I haul my duffel bag out from behind the tree. "Will you be okay, with your foot?" I ask Gerhard.

He tests it carefully and nods. "I have to be. We can't sit here and freeze our asses off. I won't do Braun that favor."

"So let's go." I look westward, the rising sun at my back, and say determinedly, "To Leipzig."

Chapter 17

For Gerhard, every step is torture; still, he struggles dog-gedly on. I frequently declare that it's time to take a break, even though this means our progress is very slow. It's calm between the trees; they take the bite out of the cold. Every now and then, snow trickles from densely-laden branches onto our heads. As kids, we spent so much time in the forest that I have no problem orienting myself. Still, I don't want to spend the night here. We have to find shelter before nightfall.

Finally, the forest ends, and snow-covered fields stretch before our eyes, dotted with small clusters of trees.

"What does your internal compass say?" Gerhard asks.

"We're heading the right way." I sound more optimistic than I feel. The sun has long since passed its zenith and is sinking rapidly toward the western horizon. My stomach protests. We haven't eaten anything since the chocolate this morning.

"I think there's a town over there." I point to the hori-zon, where little plumes of smoke rise into the air behind the silhouettes of the trees.

"Do you think they'll give us something to eat?" asks Gerhard.

"If we're lucky, some nice farmer may even let us sleep in his barn."

Gerhard presses forward with new energy. The hope of a meal and a warm, dry place to sleep spurs us on. We slog across the field through knee-high snow. Its top layer has frozen, and with each step, we break through the ice with a crack. I walk in front so Gerhard can follow in my tracks.

After we cross another stretch of trees, a collection of farmsteads comes into view. By now, dusk has set in, and a red glow covers the sky. There's no one to be seen. Most people will be inside their houses since with darkness come low-flying planes.

Inviting smoke rises from the chimney of the nearest house. It's a small farm, with a main house connected to the barn at a right angle.

Gerhard wants to head over immediately, but I hold him back.

"Hang on. We can't just show up in our uniforms—they might report us. Or they won't let us in in the first place, because they're afraid."

Gerhard wrinkles his brow. Luckily we have civilian clothes in our duffel bags. It's painfully cold, but there's no way around it. As fast as humanly possible, we slip out of our uniforms and into our old clothes. Immediately, I feel different, in my brown woolen pants and the sweater that Mother knit for me. I quickly pull on my coat, feel in the breast pocket for the watch and the photos, and stuff the uniform into my bag.

"We should leave the duffel bags here too. Hide them somewhere," I suggest.

"And preferably never pick them up again."

Gerhard's got a point. Soldiers' equipment would give us away if they caught us.

We find a suitable tree and hang the duffel bags as high as possible in the bare branches. My equipment gone, I feel like a normal person again. Still, my heart is pounding as we approach the farm. The blackout blinds are pulled down, so we can't see inside. But a warm light is streaming through cracks in some of the windows.

"You know what you have to say…"

Gerhard nods. We've agreed on a story, which I'm hoping sounds plausible. I knock on the wooden door of the farmhouse. No response. A minute passes and I knock again. Then we hear noises inside. I imagine that the farmer and his wife are sitting at dinner in their cozy room, looking at each other with shock and distrust. Who could it possibly be, calling at this hour? Or maybe the farmer's been drafted and the farmer's wife is tending the farm all by herself.

A door inside the house opens, creaking, then floorboards squeal under heavy footsteps, and the bolt is drawn back. A haggard man opens the outer door a crack, poking his head out. I try to look as innocent as possible. When he sees that we're just kids, he opens the door all the way and stands before us with folded arms. A warm current of air caresses my face.

The farmer is wearing threadbare brown corduroy pants with suspenders over a coarse cotton shirt, and clogs with wooden soles. The hair on his head is thinning and his eyes, ringed with wrinkles, examine us suspiciously. "What do you want?"

Behind him, light streams into the hall from an adjacent room, out of which a plump woman in a blue-flowered apron is peering at us.

"Good evening, sir," Gerhard says, respectfully. "Sorry to bother you. I know it's late. We're refugees from Silesia.

We lost our parents when we fled. If there's maybe a hay bale we could sleep on tonight…and perhaps a piece of dry bread to eat? We're lost."

"So you're refugees?" growls the farmer, drawing his brows together.

His wife steps into the hall, pushing her husband aside with her broad hips.

"Manfred, they're just children… You lost your parents, you say? Let them sleep in the barn tonight!"

"Sure, sure," the farmer mutters and steps to the side.

"Come in, warm up a bit! Fleeing from the Russians, you say? How terrible! And you had to leave house and home behind…" The farmer's wife steers us into the living room with a hand on each of our backs. Her husband obviously has no say in the matter.

The living room is simply furnished. A green-tile stove in the corner radiates a homey warmth. On the bench, a black-and-white cat lies curled next to a sewing basket. A large, sturdy dining table occupies the middle of the room, and its white lace tablecloth is heaped with goodies, so many that for a moment I think I've died and gone to heaven. Gerhard's eyes are as big as mine. Bread, cheese, sausages, something that looks like real butter—even a plate of fried eggs. And there's a jar of applesauce. Where did they get all this food? I feel myself starting to drool and hardly take notice of the two girls sitting at the table.

At their mother's command, the girls bring two stools from the kitchen. Passively, I allow myself to be pushed down onto the chair by the farmer's wife. I can hardly believe our luck; the smell of food is fogging my brain.

"Help yourselves," she says. "You must be starving." The farmer furrows his brow again, but his wife waves him off. "Look how thin they are! They can't have had a proper meal for days! And God knows we have enough."

"Sure, sure."

Hesitantly, I look at the mountain of food in front of us, feeling suddenly overwhelmed. The farmer's wife snatches our plates and serves us some of everything. Gerhard begins stuffing food in his mouth right away. I try my best not to look like a ravenous animal, but it's difficult.

After the first bite of dense, aromatic rye bread, I can't hold back anymore. The egg yolk is soft and runny; it melts in my mouth and trickles down my chin. Impatiently, I wipe it away with my hand, and alternate taking bites of spicy salami and bread. Food has never tasted so good. The farmer's wife places two steaming mugs of cocoa next to our plates. I hear Gerhard moan with pleasure as he swallows the sweet, creamy liquid.

Only when my hunger is sated do I notice the two girls staring at us, wide-eyed. They must be about our age. One of them wrinkles her nose when Gerhard wipes his mouth with the back of his hand and crams more food in, even though he's still chewing. We must look like barbarians.

"You see, completely starved," says the farmer's wife to her husband. She babbles on, but I'm barely listening. "The Russians…when they make it this far…can't imagine…what will happen to our animals…our home…?"

The farmer remains silent, focused on his food. Carefully, he saws thin slices from the sausage and places them evenly on his piece of bread.

"So, my boys, are you quite full now?" asks the woman, as I set my knife down and wipe my mouth with a red-checkered napkin. "By the way, I'm Bertha Besecker, this is my husband Manfred, and our daughters Johanna and Lena."

I swallow the last bite and nod. "Good to meet you, *Frau* Besecker. I'm Anton Köhler." Since Gerhard's mouth is still full, I add, "and this is Gerhard Engler."

Gerhard nods at her with shining eyes.

"Good German names. See, Manfred?" The farmer doesn't react, but *Frau* Besecker doesn't seem to expect him to. "How old are you?"

"I'll be sixteen soon," replies Gerhard, with a look at Lena, who's peering at him from beneath her eyelashes. She has brown braids and big brown eyes.

"Ah, so you're Lena's age. She's fifteen as well."

Johanna, the one who wrinkled her nose, remains aloof. That's fine by me. Now that my stomach is full and a pleasant warmth has seeped into my limbs, I can only think about sleep. What a day! We've been on the road since five, survived a bomb attack, and then marched for hours through the forest…

But now that he's done eating, Gerhard seems flustered by Lena's looks. He keeps glancing over at her, and she replies with more shy smiles. Luckily, her mother and father don't seem to notice.

"You must have come a long way," *Frau* Besecker says. "And how are you going to find your families now?"

"We're making our way to Leipzig," I say. "I have relatives in the city. Hopefully, my family will be there." At least that much is true.

"So you lost them along the way?" That's the grumpy voice of Manfred Besecker.

Suddenly I feel hot. "Yes, in a bomb attack," I murmur.

The farmer looks as though he'd like to add something, but *Frau* Besecker interrupts him again. "My goodness, and then with all the snow! These poor people,

Manfred. Carrying everything they own on their backs… And even families with children just have to slog on. Those horrible Russians."

"Did you see the Russians?" asks Johanna, leaning forward. For the first time, she seems interested.

"Johanna, don't interrogate our guests!" *Frau* Besecker reproves.

Johanna makes a sour face and sits back again.

"So, is it true what they say?" asks her mother in the same breath. "The Russians cut out children's tongues? And with the women and girls, they…" she falls silent, looking at her daughters.

"I know as much as you do," I respond curtly.

"Oh, well then." She sounds a little disappointed. "I hope you can find a train. *Frau* Heinemann told me yesterday that they're all hopelessly crowded. People are actually standing on the running boards, hanging onto the outsides of the cars. Can you believe it? They don't even have tickets."

"Our guests must be tired from their travels," interjects *Herr* Besecker.

I nod with relief.

"Oh, of course. Excuse me, boys. Where are my manners?" *Frau* Besecker says.

"Come, I'll show you your quarters," the farmer grunts.

Gerhard and I stand up. "Thank you so much for the meal!"

"Oh, you're good boys," *Frau* Besecker says. "Why don't you stay a few days? Instead of trudging on in this horrible snow…"

Gerhard exchanges a glance with Lena, then with me. I can tell from his expression that he wouldn't mind staying here for a few days and resting his foot. But I can't bring myself to sit around uselessly, while I still don't know what happened to my family.

"I don't think we can, *Frau* Besecker. But thanks anyway."

Gerhard looks disappointed but doesn't protest.

Chapter 18

Our bed is an empty stall in the barn that Besecker fills with some fresh straw. I don't mind sleeping in the straw. Gerhard and I must have slept in farmer Moltke's hayloft hundreds of times in the summer. But now it's winter and the animals' body-heat the only source of warmth—barely enough to stop our breath from freezing in our nostrils. Still, it's better than sleeping in the forest, and the sweet smell brings back memories of my childhood and of home. I settle down on the prickly padding with an old horse blanket. Gerhard lies close beside me. This way, we can keep each other warm.

"If your foot still hurts tomorrow, we'll stay," I murmur sleepily. "The farmer's wife was so nice. And she did offer."

He rolls to face me. "Lena isn't half bad, is she?"

"Mhmmm…"

"What with that she's only fifteen…not bad at all!"

"You're fifteen yourself!"

"Only for another month," retorts Gerhard.

"Whatever…better get her out of your head."

My eyes are already falling shut when I'm woken by the creaking of the barn door. I bolt upright. Next to me, I can feel Gerhard doing the same. It's pitch black. The only sound is the soft tapping of footsteps on the stone floor.

I'm already searching around for something I can use as a weapon when a soft voice says, "Hello? It's me, Lena."

"Lena?" asks Gerhard, flabbergasted.

"Shhh!"

A moment later, the door to our stall slides open. The glow of a flashlight momentarily blinds me. I squint, and when she turns it away from me, I see her standing before us, wrapped in a thick wool coat.

"I just wanted to see if you're comfortable. If you have everything you need."

"Yes, everything's fine," Gerhard says.

"That's good."

"It's nice of you to come and ask," he adds.

Her face brightens. "I also brought cookies, if you want. Mother forgot them before, but I'm sure she wouldn't mind if I offered you some."

The whole time she's talking, she's staring directly at Gerhard. It's as if I don't exist.

"Man, you're *fan*-tastic," says Gerhard, and Lena beams.

I would actually prefer to sleep, but I remain silent as Lena slips through the door and, after a moment's hesitation, lowers herself into the straw where Gerhard has made space for her. She sets the flashlight down at her side, so it casts its dim beam of light onto the ceiling. Lena pulls a linen cloth out of her coat and unfolds it. A pile of crumbly cookies appears.

"Dig in."

Gerhard pops one into his mouth immediately. I'm still stuffed from dinner, but I take one just to be polite. I could have saved myself the trouble; Lena hardly notices me.

"Do you like it?" she asks Gerhard, after watching him eat in silence for a few moments.

He nods, his cheeks full.

"Do you think…" she licks her lips, "Do you think the Russians will come here?"

Gerhard swallows and hastily reassures her: "Our troops will do everything they can to hold them back. If we were sixteen, we'd be helping," he says grandiosely.

"I'm so afraid that they'll be at our doorstep all too soon. And then we'll have to leave our beautiful farm and our animals, or worse… Everyone says the Russians are savages. Some refugees came through not too long ago. We took them in, too. There was a girl, a few months younger than I am. She confided in me, told me what those…beasts did to her. She said it like it was completely normal. Four or five men, one after the other…she bled." Lena pulls her coat closer around her.

"I would defend you to my dying breath," Gerhard says.

I can hardly keep from rolling my eyes, but Lena seems impressed.

"That's very courageous," she breathes.

Gerhard grins and wipes the cookie crumbs from his hands.

"So you'd fight to defend me?" She leans toward him with an expectant expression, no more than a few inches, but Gerhard holds his breath. I feel even more like a third wheel.

"Of course." Gerhard clears his throat. "It's our duty."

"You know," whispers Lena, "before a soldier goes to war…" She pauses.

I would love nothing more than to stuff the blanket into my ears.

"What then?" Gerhard's voice quavers slightly.

"I just mean…he shouldn't go to war before he…"

I jump up as if I've been bitten by fleas. Lena and Gerhard look up with surprise as though they've just realized I'm still here.

I clear my throat. "I'm going to have a look at the horses. The, um…mare reminds me of Liese, farmer Moltke's horse back home…" My voice trails off, but they're not listening, anyway. They've locked eyes again.

"Have you ever kissed a girl?" I hear Lena whisper, as I wrap the blanket around my shoulders and slide out of the stall.

Gerhard coughs. "Of course I have! I mean, not very often… Actually just once, to be honest…"

Finally, I'm out of earshot. I stand at the barn entrance, next to the stall with the small brown mare. Her long white blaze seems to glow in the semi-darkness, and as I lean on the stall door, she stretches her head out curiously. I stroke her soft coat and warm nostrils until I almost fall asleep on my feet. Still, I can't hold it against Gerhard. I kind of wish Luise could be sitting there, instead of Lena.

At some point—I'm not sure if I dozed off—I hear soft footsteps. A cold blast of air sweeps in through the barn door, and I see the tails of Lena's blue coat disappearing in the glow of her flashlight. Then it's dark again. Too exhausted to ask questions, I crawl onto the straw beside Gerhard and instantly fall asleep.

The next morning, we're woken before dawn when the farmer enters the barn to feed the animals.

"So, are you staying or not?" he grumbles as we jump up from our straw beds.

I look at Gerhard; he nods. The swelling in his ankle has gone down.

"We have to go," I say.

Frau Besecker hands us a huge pile of sandwiches and pats me encouragingly on the shoulder with one strong hand. Standing on the top step, still in her nightdress and slippers, is Lena. She fumbles bashfully with one of her braids. Gerhard waves at her when *Frau* Besecker isn't looking, a wistful smile on his face.

Outside, gray clouds blanket the sky, half concealing the dim orb of the sun hanging over us. Good weather for low-flying planes. We avoid big roads and walk on paths through the forests and fields, heading west.

"It was decent of you to leave last night," Gerhard starts suddenly.

"No worries." I wave him off. "I was happy to cuddle with the horse while you were…busy."

Gerhard actually reddens a little. Or maybe it's the cold. "We just kissed."

"Okay," I say quickly. I don't want to know the details.

He shrugs. "If you ever need a favor…you can count on me."

I nod without looking at him. Gerhard is my best friend, but I haven't told him about Luise. Maybe I'll see her again—if we ever make it to Leipzig.

Chapter 19

That evening, we knock at another house on the outskirts of a small town. Thick icicles hang from the low eaves. I break one off while we wait to suck on it.

"Who is it?" demands a grumpy female voice. Through the small peephole in the wooden door, an eye regards us, bordered by deep wrinkles.

"We're refugees from Breslau. We're looking for a place to stay the night," Gerhard says. "A straw mattress would be more than enough."

The woman slides back the bolt and opens the door. She's wearing a green wool headscarf over her gray hair and peers at us over the rim of small, oval glasses. "So you're from Breslau, ey?"

"Yes. We fled with our families but lost them in a bomb attack," Gerhard recites our story again.

"Hmmm." The old woman wrinkles her brow, pulling her headscarf tighter.

Steps sound on a wooden stair at the end of the hall. A man emerges from the shadows. "Who are these boys, Mother?"

As the woman repeats Gerhard's words, the man draws closer, his right hand resting casually in his pants pocket. A cigarette dangles from the corner of his mouth as he inspects us from top to bottom. I'm uncomfortable, though I can't say exactly why.

"How old are you?"

"Fifteen."

He grins. There's a gap in his teeth next to his canines. "Do you have your papers with you?"

This can't mean anything good. My Hitler Youth ID—a little paper booklet with my personal information and a photo—is in my coat pocket, but I don't want to show it to him. Gerhard hesitates, too.

"We lost them," I say. I'm afraid it doesn't sound very convincing.

"And what are your names?" he asks, not letting on whether he believes my lie.

"Anton Braun and Gerhard Hubrich," I say quickly; they're the first names that come to mind. Gerhard looks at me sidelong, quizzically, but doesn't say anything.

"Alright. Come in, then."

He steps out of the way and makes an inviting gesture, one that seems excessively theatrical. He's grinning the whole time. With a slight limp, his mother moves into an adjacent room, and we follow hesitantly.

"My name is Strober," the man says.

Strober's about thirty and seems to be in good shape. I immediately wonder why he hasn't been drafted. Maybe he's on home leave, or he has a different kind of wartime duty.

"There's an extra room upstairs if you don't mind sharing a bed." He grins wolfishly.

We shake our heads and take a seat on the kitchen bench. I still have a funny feeling in my stomach. Strober's mother busies herself at the hearth, while Strober himself pulls a bottle out of a top cabinet and sets it on the table in front of us.

"A little something to warm us up."

Without asking first, he fills three shot glasses with schnapps. His mother sets buttered potatoes on the table.

"Thank you very much," I say to her.

She mumbles something incomprehensible and wipes her bony hands on her apron before she leaves the kitchen.

Strober puts his glass to his lips and peers at us over the rim, waiting.

"No, thanks," I say.

But Gerhard shoots me a look, eyebrows raised, warning me not to be rude. He lifts his own glass and downs it at the same time as Strober while I just sip at the drink. The liquid burns my lips. Gerhard coughs and Strober claps him on the back.

"Good, isn't it?" He laughs.

We dig in as Strober pours Gerhard and himself another drink. He's sitting across from us, backward on a chair, his elbows leaning on the backrest.

"So. You're from Breslau," he states.

Gerhard nods, chewing.

"I've heard it's all blocked off now; nobody goes in or out. Things must be getting really crazy there, huh? Lucky you got out."

Strober toasts Gerhard and drains his glass. Gerhard does the same.

"It's a mess," Strober continues.

"You can say that again," responds Gerhard. I'm seized with the urge to stamp his foot.

"And what're the people there supposed to do? Old men and young boys who can hardly hold a weapon? It's an unpleasant business."

"If we were older, we'd have been drafted too," says Gerhard, still chewing.

Worried, I watch Strober fill his glass a third time.

"I'm about fed up with it all," Strober starts again. "Sometimes I ask myself…" He stops and lowers his voice. "I ask myself whether it wouldn't be better if…"

Gerhard pushes his empty plate away. I swear, that boy can eat like a horse. "If what?" he asks.

Strober traces a circle on the table with the bottom of his glass. He appears to be thinking. "Everybody in this town wants the war to end. Surely your parents do, too."

Gerhard shrugs. Almost unconsciously, he downs a third shot. As long as he doesn't give away our real names…

"Our parents want Germany to win," I interject.

Strober sits upright. "Don't we all want that! But is it even still possible? They're already on our turf."

I don't trust him; something's off here. "You know the motto, land in exchange for time," I say, as casually as possible.

"Land in exchange for time—*hah*! How much more land do we have to give up? How much time do we have left?" Strober puts the schnapps bottle to his lips.

My glass sits untouched in front of me.

"'Do you want total war?' That's what Goebbels asked us. And we all screamed back, 'Yes'! And do you know where it got us?" He sets the bottle back on the table with a bang. "*Up to our eyeballs in shit.*"

Gerhard starts to laugh until his whole body shakes uncontrollably. We both stare at him as he wipes tears from his eyes.

"I just had to…hee hee…think…ha ha ha! Anton, the way you…used to imitate Goebbels… He can do that so well," he gasps.

"Oh?" Strober looks amused. "Let's see, Anton."

I grow cold with fear and lick my lips. "I…he's kidding. I can't do it."

"Can too! You're so good at it" Gerhard is still giggling, laughter bursting from him in waves. "Even the limp… And Hitler, too!"

I kick him in the shin. Hard.

"Oho! Hitler?" asks Strober.

Gerhard rubs his leg. Way too obvious. "Yes, yes! The way he screams and rolls his eyes… Like some kind of clown."

"So. Hitler's a joke to you?" asks Strober. Now he seems completely sober.

I swallow. "We…I'd like to go to bed now."

Strober gets up. "Come on, stay awhile! Entertain me with your…talents."

I stand up too. "I'm really tired, *Herr* Strober."

We stare at each other. I try to hold his gaze. Gerhard stops laughing, sensing the tension between us.

"Second room. Upstairs, to the left," Strober says finally, indicating where we should go with a tilt of his head. He moves out of the way but doesn't let us out of his sight.

I shove Gerhard past him and up the narrow stairs to the second floor.

"That was really stupid," I start after I've closed the door.

In the tiny bedroom, a single kerosene lamp burns on the wardrobe under a sloping ceiling. The wooden poster-bed is narrow, but the down-filled comforter with its clean, red-checked coverlet, looks inviting, as if you could just sink into it.

"What? I just—"

"You shouldn't have had so much to drink. We have to get out of here."

"Get out?" he asks sleepily, sinking down on the bed.

I hurry to the window and peer out beneath the black shade into the night, which is just as black. A mountain of snow has accumulated under the window, against the wall of the house. We could jump out...

Behind me, I hear a soft snore. Gerhard is lying across the bed, his legs dangling over the edge. I shake him, but he only stops snoring for a moment. Sighing, I decide to leave him alone. Maybe it's better to let him sleep. We can only leave once everything's quiet in the house, anyway. I go to the door and listen carefully. Do I hear a voice downstairs? What if he calls someone? A door squeaks, and heavy steps trudge up the stairs and down the hall. The steps halt outside our room. I hold my breath. Then they retreat, and another door closes.

I sit down on a hard wooden chair next to the bed and stare into space. The lamplight flickers in the faint breeze blowing through a crack under the window frame. It's cold in the unheated room. I hug myself, regarding Gerhard's form stretched out on the bed. One arm is curled next to his head as if he were a young child—a very lanky, tall child. Suddenly, I think of August. Tears well in my eyes. I remember how his curls fell over his ears; and his eyes, so big behind the thick glasses. Then images of skeletal figures with shorn heads rise before my mind's eye, and I blink rapidly to fight off the vision.

Chapter 20

By the time I wake up again, the lamp has gone out, and I can hear Gerhard's steady breathing on the bed. My aching neck and stiff legs tell me that I've once again fallen asleep in a chair.

This time, Gerhard stirs when I shake him.

"What time is it?" he mumbles.

"It's a little before five. We've got to go. Now!"

I pull up the shade and try to open the window as quietly as possible. A blast of cold air hits my face as I lean out. "Let's get out of here."

"Are you crazy?" asks Gerhard, sitting up.

"It'll be a soft landing. Come on!"

Since my voice leaves no doubt that I'm completely serious, he finally gets up, stretches and looks out the window.

"You first," I command.

Gerhard raises his eyebrows, but then he forces his long body through the open window, his knees on the windowsill. Carefully, he turns himself around and feels down the wall of the house with his feet, still hanging onto the sill.

"Let go," I whisper.

He obeys; I hear a dull thud, and snow flies up below. A moment later, Gerhard appears out of the white heap, giving me a thumbs up. It's my turn. I climb onto the windowsill and let myself fall without hesitation. The snow gives way underneath me, and for a second, cold wetness engulfs me. Then a hand grabs my collar and pulls me out. I surface, coughing and spitting snow.

As I'm shaking the snow from my clothes, I hear Gerhard mutter "Uh-oh!" He points upward.

A dark figure has appeared at the window next to ours. It's Strober. He looks down at us and tries to open his window.

"Run!" I cry.

We sprint off. The snow is so deep that we sink with each step. It feels like an eternity before we reach the dark edge of the forest, but I don't hear anyone in pursuit. Only then do I take a deep breath.

"What was that all about?" grumbles Gerhard after catching up to me. "Couldn't we have used the door like normal people?"

"That guy was sounding us out. Probably a fink. You didn't notice because you were drunk."

Now that the danger has passed, anger wells up in me. I barely slept, while Gerhard was out cold like Sleeping Beauty. "Luckily he didn't know our real names. If he'd found my family…"

Gerhard bites his lip. "We didn't do anything wrong."

I turn around to face him. The moonlight reflecting off the snow illuminates his features as clearly as daylight. "Oh yeah? Last night you made a big show of how I can do Hitler and Goebbels impressions, remember?"

Gerhard digs the toe of his boot into the snow. "Okay, I guess that was stupid."

"You have to control yourself," I hiss. "First the thing with Lena and now this…" I place a hand on his chest and shove him backward.

Gerhard pushes me back. "Leave Lena out of this. We just... Chill out, man." He lifts his hands appeasingly. "I thought you'd be happy for me, as my best friend and all. And yesterday—how was I supposed to know the guy had ulterior motives? Okay, so I had a bit too much to drink..."

"A bit!?"

"Not everyone has to be as uptight as you."

That does it! I shove Gerhard with both hands, harder this time; he falls backward into the snow, landing on his rear. Steaming clouds of breath billow in front of us as we stare each other down. For a minute, I think he's going to jump up and tackle me. But then a grin spreads across his face.

"Feel better now?"

After a second's hesitation, I nod. I'm just relieved that we made it out in one piece.

Gerhard stands up to his full height and rubs his backside. "Man, and here I thought snow was soft..."

We regard each other uncertainly. "Shall we go on?" he asks.

"Yep. We better."

I tramp off. After a while, I hear Gerhard mutter behind me, "I didn't mean it, Anton."

"It's okay. I didn't either." But I'm not sure I can forget it so easily.

The next night, we slip secretly into a barn to sleep because I don't want to risk another encounter like last night. In the morning, the farmer drives us out, threatening us with a snow shovel, but not before we steal two eggs from the chicken coop. I feel like a common thief, but what else can we do? Hunger gnaws at us constantly. Since we don't have a way to cook the eggs, we swallow them raw.

Toward the end of the day, I'm exhausted. The hours of strenuous marching through the cold, constant hunger and sleepless nights have worn me down; I don't know how much longer I can go on. Just then, we stumble on something that gives me hope: train tracks.

We follow them to a train station at the edge of a small settlement. From a distance, I can see the black, metallic body of an engine, its smokestack puffing clouds of steam into the blue sky.

As we approach, we discover that the cars are jam-packed with men, women, and children; still more people crowd the platform. Everyone is trying to force their way onto the train. Those who don't succeed hang onto the outside, clinging to the railings or standing on the running boards and the connectors between the cars. Just like *Frau* Besecker said.

"I think it's going west," I say. "We have to get on."

We hurry toward the train. Gerhard calls out to one of the people on the platform: "Excuse me, where's this train headed?"

The man turns to us. "To Magdeburg," he says absent-mindedly, craning his neck as he searches for a path through the crowd.

I grip Gerhard's shoulder. "So it's got to be going through Leipzig." What a lucky break.

If we fight our way onto the train, we could be in Leipzig tonight—or at least a good bit closer. But a lot of people are thinking the same thing.

I pull Gerhard off to the side. "We won't be able to get through this crowd. Let's wait farther down the line until the train goes by. Then we'll try to jump onto the back.

Gerhard's eyes light up. "Like bandits!"

The train starts off, puffing and clattering. People are hanging off every available surface, clutching their backpacks and bundles tightly against them. Maybe some of them came to the countryside to swap food, and now they're headed back to the cities. It doesn't look like there's room on board, but we have to try anyway.

"Aaaand—go!"

We start to run. The train picks up speed, but we're right on its heels. The people standing on the running board look at us suspiciously. As I'm sprinting, I try to grab onto the railing, but a man blocks me with his body. "There's no room," he grumbles.

"Please, we have to get to Leipzig! To our mothers," calls Gerhard, who always has an answer ready. "We lost them...on the run...they don't know whether we're alive or dead."

"There's room for two skinny boys," scolds an older man.

He stretches out his hand and pulls me onto the back of the train. Gerhard jumps up behind me. Since we don't fit on the platform, we have to hang onto the back railing, clutching it as tightly as we can. Uncomfortably, yet happily, we jostle toward Dresden, and on toward Leipzig.

Chapter 21

Everything looks so different in my aunt's neighborhood! There's bomb damage everywhere: burnt attics, broken windows, some of them patched over with cardboard. The streets are filled with rubble and fallen roof tiles. Gerhard and I skirt around a deep crater in the middle of the street. The attacks must have become more serious in recent months.

The closer we come to the street where Aunt Martha and Uncle Emil live—and Luise—the faster my heart beats.

Please, let Mother be there. Please. And all of my siblings, too, I plead in silence.

What are we going to do if their house looks like the one we just passed? Through the torn-away front, we could see the burnt-out interior as if it was an oversized dollhouse. The rooms were eerily empty except for some leftover debris: charred rugs, shreds of curtains, and broken glass… Everything that was still usable seems to have been carted off, maybe by the former residents, or else looters. There's not even any broken furniture left; I guess they used that as firewood.

Gerhard seems to understand my nervousness. He doesn't say much, just nods at me encouragingly every now and then. Since the moon is already climbing in the sky and the first stars are twinkling, I walk faster. There won't be anyone left on the streets when darkness falls.

Finally, we get to a park just a few blocks from Aunt Martha's. I remember there's a shortcut through it that Luise showed me once. The shortcut is really just a dirt path, which weaves through the old oaks and chestnuts, past a deserted playground with a rusty jungle gym and a squeaky swing. A cold wind whistles through the bare branches, and I pull the collar of my coat tighter and jam my hands into my pockets.

Someone is walking in front of us. Judging from the skirt peeking out under the long, thick coat, it's a girl. She's carrying a large basket under her arm. Something about her seems familiar. I walk a bit faster, trying to catch up with her so I can see who she is.

The girl glances back over her shoulder. She spots us, chasing after her in a deserted park in the semi-darkness, and picks up speed. But she has to fight against the wind just like we do. I'm about to call out to her when she trips, loses her balance and falls to her hands and knees. Her basket rolls a few feet up the path.

It takes the girl a moment to pull herself together. In the meantime, I've caught up to her. I stand in front of her, holding out a hand to help her to her feet.

"Everything okay?" I shout over the whistling wind.

She stares at my hand; then her gaze travels slowly up my arm to my face. My heart skips a beat. I was right. Blonde braids peek out from under her cap, shimmering almost silver in the twilight. Her mouth opens slightly and her eyes widen.

I hold out my other hand, and she reaches for it, her eyes never leaving mine. She lets me pull her to her feet, all the while staring at me like I'm a ghost. Strands of hair that the wind has pulled from her braids whip around her face.

"Anton?" she whispers. And then louder: "Oh my gosh! I don't believe it!"

I can't say a word, my throat feels constricted. Luise looks for a moment as if she'd like to fling her arms around my neck, but then she blinks and only grips my hands tighter.

"Everybody was so worried about you," she cries.

Everybody? Even her?

"I can't believe you're standing here. In front of me. Like you just appeared out of nowhere! Your mother…"

"Mother is here?"

She nods.

My knees almost give way.

Gerhard clears his throat. "Um, Anton? Who is this?"

Only now do I remember Gerhard. His gaze wanders back and forth between us. While I've been helping her up, he's collected the basket and holds it out to her now. Luise looks at him warily.

"Oh, um, Luise, this is my best friend, Gerhard. Gerhard, this is Luise Hofmann. My aunt's neighbor," I explain after a brief pause.

"I see!" is all he says. I know what he's thinking: why have I never told him about Luise? I can feel my ears reddening, but luckily the darkness covers it up.

I turn back to Luise, who has let go of my hands to take her basket.

"Is everybody okay—?" "How did you get—?" Luise and I both start talking at the same time, then stop.

Luise smiles and starts over. "Everybody's fine. Come on! They're going to be so happy to see you."

We start out across the park. By now, darkness has fallen completely.

"You're out late," I note.

"I've just run some errands," she says casually, then changes the subject. "How'd you get here? We all thought you were trapped in Breslau."

I tell her briefly about how we'd marched from the barracks, got caught in an air raid and made our way to Leipzig by ourselves.

She looks at me, wide-eyed. "Sounds like an odyssey."

I shrug. "It wasn't exactly a walk in the park. I'm glad to finally be here."

"I am too. I mean, I'm glad that you made it alright... both of you," she says with a glance over her shoulder at Gerhard, who's trailing behind us.

We come to the end of the park and step out into the street. Here, too, the bombs have left their marks. On the opposite side of the road sits another burnt building, with charred beams and dark, sightless windows. I remember that there used to be a shop on the ground floor. The owner always gave us candy. But Aunt Martha's and Luise's houses are still standing, even if a few window-panes have cracked, and the old apple tree in the garden looks as unshakeable as ever.

When I ring the doorbell at Uncle Emil's house, there's a tingling in my stomach. I shift from one foot to the other. Finally, Aunt Martha opens the door and peers cautiously out. She's wearing her flowered apron and looks the same as ever. When she recognizes me, she lets out a little scream and covers her mouth with her hands. The next moment, she pulls me against her and squeezes me hard. "Hanna! Come quick!" she calls over her shoulder.

My mother looks smaller than I remember. Silver threads shimmer in her hair, more of them than there used to be. Her eyes tear up when I pull her into a hug. I breathe in the familiar smell of her hair with its lingering kitchen-scent. It makes me think of home, and how we may never see it again. I have to rub my eyes.

"Oh, there's another one," I hear Aunt Martha say behind me. She beckons Gerhard into the hall from where he stood awkwardly on the step.

Luise watches our reunion with a smile, appearing both happy and sad at the same time.

Aunt Martha babbles with excitement. "Emil, look! Anton's home. And he brought a friend…Gerhard? It's nice to meet you, Gerhard. Are you hungry? You must be hungry!"

Now I'm surrounded by children, my brothers and sisters and cousins. They tug at my arms and grab onto my legs. Mother pulls Gerhard in for a hug like he's another lost son. Then Uncle Emil emerges, feeling his way along the wall until he stands in front of me. He reaches out a hand and I shake it. His eyes are hidden behind dark sunglasses.

"It's good to have you back, son."

Luise takes her leave, almost unnoticed in the hubbub. I would've liked to ask her to stay, but it's too late for that now.

"Can Gerhard stay here?" I ask Aunt Martha.

"Of course! There's enough room for everyone," Aunt Martha assures me, leading us into the kitchen.

Enough room for everyone? I cast a skeptical glance into the living room as I pass: the floor is covered in mats and blankets. It looks like summer camp. Except for the sofa and the armchair, all of the furniture has been pushed against the walls to clear space for the makeshift beds. Aunt Martha and Uncle Emil's apartment only has a small kitchen, a living room, and two bedrooms. Not enough space to house ten children—and now two more.

My youngest siblings were probably already in bed, but now they all gather around us as Gerhard and I sink onto the corner bench by the kitchen table. The small room is fuller than I've ever seen it. It's nice to have the little critters close again, even if the attention soon becomes too much. Gerhard is great at talking to the kids and answering all their questions. Max wants to know whether we met the Russians. "Only their planes," says Gerhard, changing the subject because the details aren't appropriate for young ears.

"Let the boys eat now. Hush! Go back to bed. You can ask questions later." Aunt Martha finally shoos them all out.

She serves us cold cooked potatoes, a slice of dry bread, and a handful of walnuts, which, Aunt Martha tells us, the children picked in the fall. It's not as rich as our meal with the farmer's family, as people in the cities have a much harder time finding food. Aunt Martha keeps apologizing that she doesn't have any butter or oil to fry the potatoes in. But after days with almost nothing to eat, everything tastes good to me.

Uncle Emil, Mother, and Aunt Martha sit down with us after the brouhaha has subsided. They don't ask us anything. While we're eating, Mother tells us how they escaped from Breslau.

"The day before the evacuation notice, I heard *Frau* Weber gossiping that we were going to be evacuated. I knew the trains would be full as soon as the news got out, so that evening, I packed everything we could carry and took the children to the train station. I was hoping I'd hear something from you, or at least be able to send you a message, but there was no time." She looks at me apologetically.

"We rode to Breslau in farmer Moltke's hay wagon to catch a train to Leipzig. But when we arrived at the main station, there was only one more train going out of the city—and naturally, everyone wanted to get on. I've never seen a crowd like that in my life. It was terrible. Later, I heard that some children who'd lost their parents were trampled to death…"

I almost choke on my food.

"Max and Fritz squeezed in through a gap in the door, but I couldn't follow them with the little ones… We ran along the train looking for where there was room. Then a man called out the window, 'Pass the children, ma'am!' I was so desperate, worried that we would get stuck in Breslau, that I did it. I lifted the girls and Erich one by one through the window, and the friendly man pulled them in. Then I ran to one of the doors where there was a crowd of people, and just before the train started moving, I managed to squeeze in. The whole time I was worried that we wouldn't find each other ever again."

"But everything worked out in the end," Aunt Martha says, patting her hand.

Gerhard sets his fork aside and leans back. I'm done eating, too, though I'm still hungry.

"And how'd you two manage?" asks Uncle Emil.

Gerhard and I glance at each other. There's so much to tell, but neither of us wants to relive all of the details. Besides, it would only get Mother all worked up.

I start hesitantly, running through the most important points as concisely as possible: how we had to dig ditches at the barracks, how they snuck us out of Breslau at night, in the fog, only to announce after days of marching that we were supposed to board a train going east again. I don't mention August's death and also leave out the encounter with the concentration-camp prisoners and the air raids. I try to describe our flight as undramatically as possible, telling the story as if we slept in friendly farmers' houses every night until we found a train. I don't feel guilty about lying—Mother has enough worries. And Gerhard seconds everything I say.

"You fought bravely, boys," says Uncle Emil.

Mother shakes her head. "It's just as well I didn't know any of this. Though it was just as bad not to know whether you were still in Breslau."

"I hope you've had enough to eat," says Aunt Martha, practical as ever. "I wish I had more to offer you."

I assure her that we're full, but Mother looks at our empty plates with a frown. "I'm afraid we can't feed another two mouths for long... You'd better go register at City Hall tomorrow. They'll give you ration cards."

"But if they register officially," says Uncle Emil, "then they'll be leaving again before too long."

He seems to sense our questioning looks because he adds, "You'll be sixteen soon, won't you, Anton?"

"Yes."

His head turns in my direction. "And I'm assuming Gerhard is about the same age?"

"Yes," Gerhard says.

"You mean...they'll be drafted?" asks Aunt Martha softly. "At sixteen?"

"They're the right age," he says. "That's how Hitler likes his soldiers...young, fresh, and full of vigor."

"Emil!" protests Aunt Martha, her brow furrowed.

"If they don't register, they're living here illegally," says Mother. "If someone finds out..."

"And there definitely won't be enough food," Aunt Martha adds.

"I won't take food out of anyone's mouth," I say. "Or put you in danger. So we'll register." Still, the thought gives me a queasy feeling.

"I don't want to dance to their tune again," Gerhard whispers later that night as we're lying on the corner bench in the dark kitchen, covered in a thin blanket. It was the only place to sleep that wasn't already occupied. We're lying head to head. Gerhard is too long for the bench and has to pull his legs in, so his knees are jutting out from the narrow seat. But we've slept in worse beds. At least here it feels like home.

"I don't think we have a choice," I reply. "If we don't register, they'll arrest us. And I don't want to be a burden on my family."

Gerhard sighs. "I know."

"But maybe Uncle Emil's wrong. Maybe the war will be over in a month."

It takes a while for Gerhard to respond. "That sure would be nice. And Anton… now I know why you never spared a second glance at any of the girls at home." I can hear the grin in his voice.

I pretend to be asleep, but my thoughts stray to Luise and the look on her face when she recognized me. The image produces another fluttering in my stomach.

Chapter 22

When we leave the house the next morning, there's a blood-red veil over the eastern horizon. Today is Ash Wednesday, February 14. Last night they bombed Dresden, and the city is still ablaze. It's where the eerie red glow emanates from. It's alarming that we can see it from as far away as Leipzig.

Slush sprays out from under our feet as Gerhard and I tramp down the street, toward the streetcar stop.

"Hello, you two!" I immediately recognize the bright, melodious voice that calls out to us from behind. I stop short.

Gerhard elbows me in the ribs, grinning, as we wait for Luise to catch up, but I ignore him.

"Are you on your way to the streetcar?" she asks. Her cheeks are red from the cold, and she's pulled a blue woolen cap down over her ears and forehead. It brings out the blue of her eyes.

"Yep," says Gerhard, and I realize that I was staring at her.

"I'll come too," she says.

We set off down the street together, turning into the park where we ran into each other yesterday. I'm walking in the middle, between Gerhard and Luise. For a while, no one speaks, as if absorbed in our own thoughts. I find the silence increasingly uncomfortable. Finally, Gerhard nudges me subtly and looks at me, eyebrows raised expectantly—an expression that says, *Do something already! Talk to her!* I'd like to, I really would. But once again, I seem to have turned into a blubbing cod and can't think of anything to say.

"Where are you going, anyway?" Luise asks, startling me.

"Oh, um…to City Hall. To register. The streetcar will take us to the main station, right?" I know the answer, but I ask anyway, just to keep the conversation going.

"Yes. City Hall's not far from there. You can walk via Augustusplatz."

"I still have a bad feeling about this," mutters Gerhard. "If your uncle's right…"

"We talked about this already," I interrupt impatiently. "We don't have a choice."

Luise looks curiously from Gerhard to me. "What is it?"

"Nothing," I respond a bit too curtly.

She turns away, and immediately I'm sorry.

"Don't you get it? If—" Gerhard starts again. I shoot him a dark look, but he won't be deterred. "If we register, we're back on their radar."

"What does *that* mean?" Luise asks and looks past me to Gerhard.

"We're going to be sixteen soon," says Gerhard, before I can stop him. "His uncle thinks we're going to be drafted…"

I remember my conversation with Luise last summer. I haven't forgotten a single word of it. What if she still thinks that way?

"Then we'll fight for the Fatherland," I add quickly.

Gerhard looks at me askance.

Luise appears thoughtful. "They've already drafted all the boys from the upper classes in my school for anti-aircraft service."

"Yes, my brother Helmut too," I say.

"Oskar's complaining because he's not old enough to be drafted." She snorts. Oskar is her younger brother; he must be thirteen by now. I get where he's coming from. When I was his age, or maybe a little younger, I thought war was an adventure. I wanted to grow up as fast as possible so I could join in.

Silently, we walk onwards.

"What if you don't register?" Luise asks abruptly, twirling her braid in one hand absentmindedly.

I'm so surprised by her question that I forget to answer.

Gerhard jumps in again. "We'd be in trouble if they found out…"

"But we need ration cards," I add. "We can't eat all my aunt's food. There's little enough as it is."

"That's true," admits Luise, still twirling her braid. "You do need ration cards…"

I prick up my ears. Her voice has taken on a strange undertone like her words have hidden meaning. Suddenly, she stops and looks around. We're alone in the park; there's nothing but bare trees on either side and behind us the deserted playground with the rotten swing.

She fixes us with her gaze and lowers her voice. "You know, there are other ways to get ration cards…"

"You mean…?" I ask, though I have an idea where this is going.

Luise seems to be wrestling with something. "I know…ways."

"Are you thinking what I'm thinking?" Gerhard asks, suppressed excitement in his voice.

"I might be able to help you…" She looks directly into my eyes and my stomach does another flip. "If you have something to barter with."

I must have been gawping at her, because she adds impatiently, "I know people."

My head is swimming. *Luise* has contacts in the black market? The same patriotic German girl who lectured me last summer? Lectured me about the *Führer* and his pride in the German youth? About courage, and the civilians who have to stand with Hitler so we can win the war?

"This girl is *fan*-tastic," says Gerhard.

Luise grins at him.

"Mother would never allow it," I object.

Gerhard and Luise look at me like I'm crazy. Suddenly I find myself outnumbered.

"She doesn't have to know," Gerhard suggests.

I want to protest, but Luise's cornflower-blue eyes have put me under a spell.

"I don't want you to go away again," she says softly.

Her concern sends warmth trickling through my body. "But it's dangerous. And we don't have anything to trade, anyway."

"Nothing at all?" she asks. "Cigarettes, alcohol, watches, jewelry…"

Gerhard makes a face. "I'm poor as a church mouse. I've got nothing but the clothes on my back." He turns out his empty pockets to illustrate. "Hang on a sec—Anton! You've got that watch."

I cringe, my hand flying to my coat pocket.

"What watch?" asks Luise, glancing at me curiously.

"I inherited it from my father!"

"Well you can't give that away," she responds immediately. I shoot her a grateful glance.

Gerhard shrugs. "Then we really have nothing."

There's unmistakable disappointment in his voice.

"I got it for Christmas," I say. It sounds like an excuse, though Gerhard isn't accusing me of anything.

"Do you have it with you?" asks Luise quietly.

I open the top button of my coat and reach into the inner pocket. My fingertips touch the cool, smooth metal casing of the watch, and I twist the chain around my index finger to pull it out. In the process, something flutters onto the ground, landing in the slush at our feet. I bend down swiftly, but Luise is faster. She snatches up the photo and turns it over. The dirty, heavily worn black-and-white picture still portrays its subject clearly. I feel my ears reddening and watch the expression on her face as Luise examines the photo of herself. It changes from one of surprise to confusion to something like embarrassment. Without a word, she passes the picture back to me.

"It's from a couple years ago. I took all the photographs with me that I had…as souvenirs," I mumble.

Her cheeks suddenly seem even redder than they were before. Quickly, I put the picture back and catch Gerhard rolling his eyes. Then I turn the watch over in my hand. The tiny inscription interrupts the smooth gold of the cover: *When heart and conscience are aligned, the right path you'll always find*…would Father want me to give it up?

"It's nice," says Luise.

I nod and open the cover. The watch has stopped at eleven thirty because I haven't wound it in a few days. When I turn the wheel on the side, it begins to tick again. The mere thought of giving it away makes my throat tighten.

I squint at Gerhard, who, like Luise and me, is staring at the watch as if it were magic. Maybe the war will end soon; all the signs point that way. So we just have to get through a few more months. A few more months…what if Gerhard were drafted because I refused to give up the watch, and I could have prevented it? I know I'd never forgive myself. What's a watch compared to my best friend's life? Didn't I swear to do everything I could to protect him?

I draw in a deep breath of the cold-humid February air. "That's the only thing of value we have," I say. "So I have to give it up."

Both of them look at me with surprise.

"Are you sure?" asks Luise. "You don't have to!"

I nod determinedly. "If it'll help my family, then I have to." Father would have wanted that, right?

Gerhard places a hand on my shoulder. Luise holds my gaze for a moment, and I think I glimpse admiration in her eyes. But that's probably just wishful thinking.

"So then…let's go," she says. "I wanted to meet my contact at the main station anyway. He gets me the ration cards."

"Why do you need so many?" I ask.

She doesn't answer right away but stares down at her feet, which are spraying through the slush. "For a friend," she mutters and changes the subject.

We get off the streetcar at the main station and head toward its large, pillared entrance. The city center is riddled with bomb craters and burnt houses, but the station itself is still standing. Its size always impresses me. It's one of the largest terminus train stations in Germany. The façade is damaged but not unrecognizable and still looms across our entire field of vision. From our arrival in Leipzig I know that part of the platform inside was destroyed, so the passengers have to walk across wooden planks to reach their trains.

As we enter the station, my stomach clenches. I remind myself that I'm not just helping my family, but Gerhard and myself as well. Still, the whole thing makes me uneasy.

We climb the stairs to the platform. It's busy up here. People with suitcases and backpacks are hurrying about, soldiers are saying goodbye to their families, others are returning home with bandages or amputated limbs. Refugees disembark from incoming trains, recognizable by their worn clothing and the household goods they're carrying with them. Two little boys with dirty faces and holes in their pants and shoes are zig-zagging through the crowd as if playing tag. It's an ideal place to meet discreetly with a contact. You could just be waiting for someone to arrive on one of the trains. Still, I scan the platform nervously; the *Gestapo* has its eyes and ears everywhere.

When a male voice addresses us from behind, I startle. "Luise?"

I'm even more surprised when Luise turns around and throws her arms around the neck of a young man whose right jacket sleeve hangs emptily down from his shoulder. "Martin! I'm so glad you're back," she cries loudly. It's almost as if she wants somebody to hear us.

"Come," she hooks her arm under his healthy one and pulls him toward Gerhard and me. We stare at each other distrustfully. I'm guessing he's nineteen or twenty. He has a stubbly chin, which makes him look rather roguish, and holds a cigarette between his fingers.

"These are my friends Anton and Gerhard," says Luise. "And this is Martin."

"Didn't we agree to meet alone?" he murmurs, though he maintains his friendly smile.

Luise walks on, her arm still linked in Martin's. We can't do anything except follow.

"I know," she responds quietly. "But the boys are in urgent need of your…stamps. They want to complete their own collection. You've always got some extras on you, haven't you? Think of it as a business opportunity."

Martin looks at her. His wrinkled brow smooths, and suddenly he bursts out laughing. "You've sure got guts, girl. I've always thought so," he says. "But the *stamps* are for someone else."

Luise smiles at him, batting her long eyelashes. Where did they meet? He must have been a soldier. Hopefully, this routine is just for show.

"Wait until you see what Anton's brought you," she whispers. "Anton, what time is it?"

I turn to look at the big station clock, but Gerhard elbows me in the ribs. Luise smiles.

"Oh—right. Hang on…" I pull the watch out of my pocket, open it up, and thrust it toward Martin. "See for yourself," I say, more gruffly than necessary.

"Hmm, it's getting late already," says Martin after a brief glance. I put the watch away and we keep walking.

"Real gold?" Martin mutters.

I nod.

"And the boy's a watchmaker," Luise affirms. "He knows what he's talking about."

The boy? I grit my teeth.

"How many do you need?"

We're still in the middle of the platform. I keep an eye on the crowd, but nobody's paying us any mind. I wish Luise would let go of Martin's arm.

"Two people, half a year," she says softly. Her voice is nearly drowned out in the hubbub.

"I can give you two months."

Luise purses her lips. "Three?"

Martin shrugs. "Two's all I've got."

Luise looks at me. Two months' rations for Gerhard and me. That's not much for a precious watch. But what choice do we have? With a knot in my gut, I agree. The deal is done. The watch changes hands inconspicuously, then Luise takes the ration books and tucks them into her wallet.

Chapter 23

Luise steps out of the huge, age-old school building. Her calves are visible under her knee-length uniform skirt. Despite the bulky wool stockings, she has the slimmest legs of anyone I know. Her cap has slipped slightly, and her silky blond hair gleams under the navy blue. She links arms with another girl, with whom I'd gladly trade places. As they move across the courtyard, I step away from the chestnut tree I've been leaning against. I don't want to look like I've been lying in wait to spy on them.

Luise spots me and dimples form in her cheeks. The other girl peers curiously at me as they approach.

"Is he waiting for you?" She whispers, loud enough for me to hear.

"Yes, that's…my cousin, from Silesia."

The girl's eyes grow wide. "Oh, your cousin! Don't you want to introduce him to me?"

Luise releases the girl's arm and gives her a playful shove. "Maybe later. Right now I have to go. See you tomorrow! Say 'hi' to Irmi for me." She leaves her friend standing there and comes toward me.

"Your cousin?" I ask, raising my eyebrows.

Luise blushes. "I just didn't want her to think…the girls here are all such gossips, see."

"Right."

There's a second of uncomfortable silence.

"Ready?" she asks, then, clapping her hands a bit too enthusiastically.

"Yes," I reply.

"Where's Gerhard?"

"He's not feeling well." As if! He left me in the lurch. Some friend he is! *Go by yourself,* he said. *You don't need me for this, do you?* I'm still not entirely sure what he meant.

"I see," she says. I can't tell whether she sounds disappointed or happy about it.

"How was service?" I ask, remembering Gerhard's suggestion that I should open my mouth. *Just ask questions*, he said. *Girls like it when they think you're interested in them.—But I am interested in her!* I replied.—*Sure.*

"Same as always," says Luise as we turn into the Heidestrasse. "I made friends with one of the patients. His name is Joachim. He used to be an opera singer, but now he's never going to be able to speak again—never mind sing. His larynx got burned. It's like if I lost both my hands…"

During our first trip into the city, Luise told us that her school has been turned into a field hospital and all the older girls have been assigned to help out there.

"And how do you communicate?"

"We write notes. It makes him so happy to hear me play. They pushed the piano from the music room out into the hall, and I'm allowed to play it for half an hour a day at the request of all the patients."

Suddenly, I wish I were a patient and Luise were taking care of me.

"So that's how you know Martin?"

She nods. "But we only see each other to do business."

We board the streetcar that just arrived.

"Uncle Philip promised me a dozen eggs today—you can have those," she says. We've already called on her uncle several times. He owns a grocery store on the west side of Leipzig. We can get food for our ration cards there without worrying that we'll be caught.

As we sit in the streetcar, side by side, I steal a sidelong glance at her. I'm still amazed at the way she talks about these illegal dealings without so much as batting an eye.

She turns to look at me as though she can feel my gaze. I notice something new in her eyes—an earnestness, and perhaps also a trace of sadness. It makes her look older than her years.

Ask questions. I remember Gerhard's advice. Show that you're interested in her.

I wrack my brain. "So… How have things been for you, these past few months?"

She shrugs and looks past me out the window into the bombed-out streets of Leipzig, her face expressionless. Apparently, I asked the worst possible question. Great!

We ride on silently as the streetcar jerks over the tracks and people get on and off at the stops. I think feverishly about what else I could ask, something harmless. But she surprises me by answering my question after all. It seems to take a lot of effort for her to talk.

"My father has been reported missing in action." Her whisper is nearly lost in the squeaking of the wheels.

It takes a while for me to find my voice again. "Since when?"

"Right after the start of the year. That's when the telegram arrived, anyway."

"I didn't know that," I begin, licking my lips. "You haven't heard anything else since then?"

She shakes her head and looks down at her hands, folded in her lap. "Apparently, he was transferred to a penal battalion. They had to stay and fight while everyone else retreated—a suicide mission. That's all we know. He's either dead or in prison camp. I don't know which I should wish for...."

I'm trying to digest what she said. A penal battalion? I thought you get transferred to those if you've done something wrong. Insubordination, or something. But surely, her father...?

"Not knowing...that's the worst part," she continues.

I gulp. "And how are you all dealing with that?"

Luise snorts scornfully. "Mother isn't dealing at all. That's why I'm taking care of everything. We sent Gerda to Grandma, and Oskar is even wilder than he was before."

"Does your mother know that you...you know..."

"That I am dealing on the black market?" she whispers. "No. And she doesn't know that I go visit my uncle, either. She and Uncle Philip had a falling out years ago." She sighs. "My siblings and I haven't been allowed to visit him for a long time."

When the streetcar stops at the main train station, Luise jumps up from her seat. I get off behind her and glance around. It looks like another refugee train has just arrived. Hundreds of people with sacks, suitcases, and strollers—the pitiful remains of their former existence—are being served tea in front of the station. They'll be assigned quarters here as well. Nobody even looks at them anymore; they've become part of the landscape. The refugees themselves are quiet, almost apathetic, as they stand in line.

Lost in our own thoughts, we wait for another streetcar that will take us to the Napoleonic memorial, close to where her uncle has his store. I ponder how, a few months ago, Luise was raving about sacrifices for the Fatherland. She's has changed so much, and now I think I understand why. I wish I could help her.

Suddenly, from loudspeakers up and down the length of the street, we hear the shrill ascending and descending howl of sirens. We stare at each other, shocked. No pre-warning this time? The bombers must already be over the city.

I look up into the sky that is blanketed in clouds. No wonder we didn't see them before. Luise gasps as the first silhouettes of planes emerge from the clouds above us. Suddenly there are more and more, too many to count, bearing down on us like a menacing black swarm of insects.

"Flying Fortresses," I mutter—Gerhard has explained to me one too many times how to recognize the different types of planes.

Around us, people are shaking off their stupor and run, searching for a place to hide. My ears are filled with the nerve-wracking wail of the sirens. Then the flak starts, thundering quietly in the distance like a drumroll. Spotlights pierce the sky.

"Come on! We have to get out of here," I cry to Luise, who's still staring upward, transfixed.

"Where should we go?" she shouts over the sirens and the ever-louder roar of engines.

The teeming crowd makes it difficult for me to orient myself. Most people are pushing up the steps into the train station to take shelter under the pillared roof. But it's clear to me that we won't survive a direct hit in there.

"Are there emergency bunkers?" I yell. Now the roar is deafening.

Luise points toward the left side of the train station. "Deep bunkers…on the east and west sides…"

Her words are drowned out by a shrill whistling, followed by the first impacts. I pause for the briefest instant to think, then grab her hand and break into a run.

Chapter 24

The world seems to explode around us as bombs start to drop on all sides. In front of us, a woman is running with two small children in tow. One of them trips and falls. The mother tries to pull him up, but other people are stampeding by, threatening to trample him. I let go of Luise's hand and scoop up the little boy, who's screaming his head off. Pressing him into his mother's arms, I look around for Luise, but she's disappeared into the crush of people.

I'm swept up by the crowd as still more detonations send rubble flying around me. Flames crackle and dust and smoke shroud the air in a thick fog. People are screaming, and I watch in horror as some go hurtling through the air, while others are torn to shreds before my very eyes

"Luise?" It's hopeless; my voice won't carry over the noise. Still, I keep running.

Somewhere in front, there's a bottleneck—people seem to be slowing down. This must be the line leading to the bunker. Damn it! We'll never get in.

Suddenly, I crash face-first into someone. I recoil, but then I recognize Luise's face.

"Anton." I have to read her lips because I can't hear her.

Thank God! I try to take her hand and pull her along, but then something explodes right next to us. A shell has fallen on the train station; stones and bits of rubble rain down on us. Luise presses close to me, holding her arms over her head.

We have to get inside the bunker, line or no. I grab Luise by the arm and pull her out of the throng of people, all of whom seem to be heading to the same place. They're so absorbed by their own fear that no one notices us as we edge alongside the line until we reach the narrow stairs leading down to the bunker. Dozens of people are fighting to get through a tiny door at the bottom of the steps. The air-raid warden guarding the entrance is hopelessly overmatched.

A shot rings out. Then another. The people at the very front of the line pull back.

"Order!" screeches the warden, a strong man with a steel helmet. He's holding his pistol high in the air. "Two at a time!"

One of the men raises his fists angrily and begins to argue with the warden. I take advantage of the confusion, which has caused a space to open on the stairs. I slip down the steps, towing Luise behind me. We squeeze by the waiting people until we're directly in front of the door. A moment later, the air raid warden waves us through.

We made it. People are shoving us from behind, jostling and pushing us further into the anteroom, which already seems full to bursting. I keep a tight grip on Luise's hand.

The walls quake in time with the falling bombs. Dust sifts down from the ceiling. Suddenly, the light goes out and the earth shakes under our feet. The air raid warden hastily closes the bunker doors. Now it's completely dark, and all I can hear is a muted banging and roaring from outside. With each hit, I'm terrified the ceiling is going to come crashing down around us. Luise's hand is cold and damp in mine, even though it's hot in the bunker. It smells like sweat and urine—the smell of fear.

I try to calm my breathing, concentrating on my own body. I've been through this before, but last time I was out in the open. Here in the bunker, I feel like a trapped animal. And then there's the darkness.

"We're safe," I whisper to Luise, though I barely believe it myself. "We just have to wait it out."

"I know," she says. It's strange to hear her disembodied voice. "I just don't like the dark."

It occurs to me that, under different circumstances, I would never have had the courage to hold her hand. Yet here we are, standing side by side, her hand in mine. With each hit, Luise presses closer to me. I'm just living from one detonation to the next. How many have there been? Hundreds? I haven't been keeping track. A child whimpers behind me, voices whisper, and I feel Luise trembling close beside me. With each brief lull, I fervently hope the attack is over. But then it continues. It feels like it will never end.

Finally, the crashing stops, and when the sirens sound the all-clear the air raid warden opens the bunker doors. A white ray pierces the room, blinding us after the long time in the dark. We allow ourselves to be jostled along by the crowd of people streaming out of the bunker. At last, we're outside, in the dim daylight.

The air is still heavy with dust and smoke, making my eyes water. Luise coughs. We pull our scarves over our mouths and noses and stand there, stunned.

There are heaps of debris where just a few—minutes?—hours?—ago buildings stood. Flames are licking at the remains of houses and shops, and sparks of burning rubble fly through the air like quickly extinguished shooting stars. People run through the streets, frantically searching for friends and family members. Some wear gas masks that make them look like huge insects; others have tied damp cloths around their mouths and donned diving goggles.

Luise gasps at the sight of bodies scattered on the ground, the corpses of those who didn't make it. I swallow the lump that has built up in my throat, a lump of equal parts disgust and dust, and pull Luise onwards. We have to get out of here. There's nothing we can do for them anymore.

I try to forge a path through the ruins without glancing at the bodies. With every step I think, *don't look*. But then I do anyway. Some appear quiet and peaceful as if they've just fallen asleep on the street. Their lungs were probably torn apart by the pressure of the explosions. They were the lucky ones. Others were horribly maimed by the bomb fragments, and still others became so shrunken in the fire that they look like children's bodies. Maybe they *were* children, but now they're burned beyond recognition.

Luise stumbles next to me through the rubble, one hand pressed over her mouth. At last she stops and, to my disappointment, lets go of my hand. "What now?" she asks hoarsely through her scarf.

"Home?" I rasp, struggling to suppress a coughing fit.

"The streetcars won't be running," she says.

"How long to get there on foot?"

"At least two hours," she replies. "I'll bet my mother is beside herself. If she even noticed I'm not there…" She looks at me fearfully. "Do you think they were hit?"

"The bombers dropped most of their loads over the city center," I say reassuringly, though I'm afraid too.

I follow her as she starts in the direction of home. What else can we do? Silently, we pass smoldering ruins, and buildings with collapsed walls and burned-out attics. At last we reach an area that wasn't hit so hard. Here we can breathe more easily.

"That was the worst attack so far," says Luise, after she's pulled her scarf away from her mouth. "But you were so calm. Like you weren't afraid at all."

Calm? If only she'd heard my heart beating. "I was scared shitless," I say.

Luise looks at me strangely.

"I'm just being honest," I murmur, shrugging. "Anyone who says anything else is a show-off or a liar."

She smiles. "Have you been in an air raid before?"

"Only once, on a train. But that time the bombs helped us flee."

"You haven't told me how you escaped…"

"No," I say.

"You don't have to talk about it if you don't want to. I get it."

"It's a long story," I give in, staring at the ground.

"We have a long road ahead of us."

"I haven't even told my mother everything. I mean, not in detail because…"

"Because you didn't want to upset her?"

"Yeah."

"I understand."

I shoot her a sidelong glance. She probably does understand. She really has changed.

Hesitantly, I begin to talk. I tell her about the drudgery in the barracks and about August, for whom it was all too much. How news of the evacuation broke and we were marched out of Breslau. After a while, I notice that I'm speaking more freely. I thought it would be hard to talk about, but instead, it feels like a great weight is being lifted off my shoulders. Luise listens silently and I almost forget she's there.

When I get to the part about the prisoners from the concentration camp, I stop. It's difficult to put the horror into words, but I try anyway. "They looked like skeletons, half-dead... But those bastards were still driving them on. They had steel whips and guns... And then they made the prisoners stop so we could pass. Some of them took the opportunity to flee...and the SS just mowed everyone down. All of them. Down to the very last one."

Luise stops abruptly, and I already regret that I told her.

She looks at me, wide-eyed. "Oh God, you really saw all that?" The intensity of her voice startles me.

"I'm sorry, I shouldn't have..."

"So it's true," she says tonelessly.

I look at her, uncomprehending.

"My father..." She stops to take a deep breath. Her brow is furrowed. "My father wrote us a letter before he... He wrote that he was riding through a forest near Lemberg in the Ukraine. This was during his recovery—it was the first time he was allowed to ride out again... Anyway, he came across a group of prisoners. The guards were tormenting them. Father was so horrified that he confronted the SS men, demanding to see a superior...but even though he was an officer, they just told him to look away. Said it was none of his business."

She looks past me, her eyes glassy. "He said in his letter, 'This is a stain on our Fatherland. A stain we'll never be able to wash away.'"

As the full meaning of her words sinks in, I get goosebumps on my arms. "Is that why he was transferred? To the penal battalion?"

"We assume so."

Of course! They would have wanted to get rid of him if he'd lodged a formal complaint about what he'd seen.

Silent tears run down Luise's cheeks. I search feverishly for words to comfort her.

"At first I didn't want to believe it," she says. "That Germany could do something so horrible…"

I look sheepishly at the ground.

"Father loved Germany," she continues, as if she has to get something off her chest. "He thought he was fighting for a country he could be proud of. It must have been a heavy blow, seeing that."

"But he did what he thought was right. That was really brave," I say.

She looks at me through her tears. "You think so?"

I nod. "My father always said, 'In the end, a man answers only to his conscience.'"

Suddenly, I don't know how, her head is on my shoulder and she's crying into my coat. We stand there for what seems like an eternity. I hold her close, feeling the shaking of her shoulders as she's wracked with sobs. Luise smells of smoke and burnt things, but I still like the way her hair tickles my cheek.

Slowly, her breathing returns to normal. She gently withdraws from my embrace, wiping the tears from her eyes, and blows her nose.

"Strange," she says, sniffling. Her face is streaked with white where the tears have washed away a layer of dust.

"What's strange?" I ask.

"I haven't cried once since we got the telegram. This was the first time."

"Then I guess it was high time," I say softly.

Chapter 25

"You're not going out there anymore, Anton!"

I've never seen Mother this upset. But when I catch a glimpse of myself in the hall mirror, I find that I'm covered head to toe in dust. My pants are torn from when I tripped and fell in the rubble. It looks worse than it is.

"I'm fine," I try to assuage her. "It's just a little dirt."

"No! I mean it. I was so worried. You and Luise all alone… I had no idea where you were, if you'd been hurt. Why were you going into the city center, anyway?"

Gerhard must have told her where I was. He's leaning against the kitchen doorframe, hands buried in his pants pockets, looking guilty.

"We…we were trying to get some food."

"At least let the boy clean himself up," interjects Aunt Martha. But she too looks pale, as if she spent the past few hours worrying.

"I don't understand why you had to go into the city for that. We can get everything we need right here," says Mother.

I can't tell her about the illegal grocery runs—Mother has made clear what she thinks of this kind of activity. Plus if I told her, I'd be involving Luise, and I'd sooner bite off my own tongue than do that. So I just stare at the floor.

The living room door opens by a crack. Max and Fritz's big brown eyes appear in the narrow space between door and frame. I wink at them to indicate that everything is okay.

"The stores here don't always have everything," I say evasively.

Mother scrutinizes me with narrowed eyes, hands on her hips. It's difficult to hold her gaze without blushing. Finally, she sighs and takes my coat off its hook. "I'll wash this."

She reaches into the pockets to empty them. Only then do I realize that I haven't taken my ration cards out. I stretch out an arm, trying to snatch the coat away from her, but I'm too late.

Her hand is in my right inner pocket and she pulls out the ration book. My breath catches as the cards appear. Gerhard and I exchange a frantic glance.

I'm so stupid! Why did I leave them in my pocket? Why didn't I put them someplace safe?

Mother wrinkles her brow, counting the sheets in her hand.

"Where on earth did you get so many ration cards?" Her voice is expressionless.

I feel nauseous. It's over; we've been discovered. Because of my stupidity.

"We got those…as an advance," says Gerhard, but he doesn't sound like he buys his own story.

"An advance? I'm supposed to believe that?" She fixes me with her gaze again. "Anton?"

Shit! I stare at the floor. It's difficult enough to hide something from Mother, but to lie to her outright? "We got them…"

"Don't tell me you—"

"…from the black market," I finish lamely, trying to look remorseful. "We traded for them."

Her eyes widen. "Why? Didn't you get any ration cards from the office?"

I draw a deep breath and croak: "We didn't go to the office."

"Oh, dear," I hear Aunt Martha murmur.

Mother looks at me aghast. I have no choice. The cat's out of the bag, so I might as well tell her everything.

Mother's gaze hardens. "You didn't register? Are you out of your mind?" Her voice is strained.

"Why are you so angry, Mother?" whispers my sister Wiebke.

Mother tucks a loose, silver-gray strand back into her bun. "Why am I angry? Because Anton is putting all of us in danger if he's here illegally." She looks directly at me. "And he knows that."

"I just wanted to help. You already had too many mouths to feed…and then Gerhard and I came along, and we eat a lot…" I explain weakly.

"You let *me* worry about that," she says. "I can find a way to feed all of my children. Legally."

She sighs deeply. "First thing tomorrow we're going to the office and registering both of you." Her tone allows for no argument. "And these ration cards are going straight into the oven."

I want to object, but the words get stuck in my throat. I think about Father's watch. It was all for nothing.

When Gerhard and I enter the kitchen a few weeks later, I notice Mother's eyes are red, though she quickly turns away.

Aunt Martha is looking at us oddly, too. Her hands are still wet from washing up. As she wipes them on her apron, she exchanges a meaningful glance with Mother.

I stand frozen in the doorframe, a sack of coal over my shoulder, while Gerhard shakes the contents of his sack into the stove box. We've only received half the coal ration to which we're entitled—a pitiful heap. It's already the beginning of March, but this year spring just won't come. It's still very cold.

Mother is peeling potatoes at the table while Lieschen and Erich are playing with blocks at her feet. With a happy crow, Erich knocks over the tower they've built, causing wooden blocks to clatter across the floor.

"Oh, *Erich*!" says Lieschen, shaking her head like an old woman. "Now I have to start all over again."

"What's going on?" I ask, finally setting down the sack of coal. Thoughts of my brother Helmut enter my head. What if something's happened to him…?

Mother points her peeling knife at two postcards sitting on the table in front of her. "Those came today. For you and Gerhard."

Gerhard wipes his sooty hands on his pants and approaches the table to pick up the cards. I watch his face as he takes a quick glance at them, paling noticeably. Hesitantly, he hands me one of the cards. It bears the stamp of the *Wehrmacht* office in Leipzig and the national crest: the eagle over the swastika. Below are my name and Uncle Emil's address, which we used to register a few weeks ago. I skim the short, typewritten text that contains no greeting at the top.

> *On Saturday, March 10, 1945, at 9:00 a.m., you*
> *are to report to the barracks in Leipzig-Gohlis for a*

physical in preparation for your deployment. A sign
will indicate the precise meeting point. If applicable,
you will be issued a Wehrmacht ID there and be in-
formed of your training site. Training will begin on
Sunday, March 11. You must bring sufficient cloth-
ing and toiletries with you, as well as this card and
your identification papers. From this point onward,
the German Wehrmacht will provide your food and
accommodation.

I look at Gerhard. My own emotions are mirrored in his face. This is exactly what Uncle Emil predicted, but it's happened even sooner than we expected. My sixteenth birthday isn't until March 17. Still, we're being drafted at the end of this week. In four days.

Mother shakes her head sadly. I suppress the urge to say, *This wouldn't have happened if we hadn't registered.* Accusations will do us no good now.

I put the postcard on the table and squat down next to Lieschen and Erich. Erich crawls over and proudly shows me the tower they're rebuilding. I pull him close, burying my face in his soft brown hair. I'm going to have to abandon my family. Again.

Chapter 26

In the next few days, I spend as much time as possible with my family. We don't discuss the upcoming physical and what will happen after because it's all too clear. Gerhard and I are healthy and athletic—there's no chance we'll be rejected.

Only on the evening before we leave can I bring myself to go over to the Hofmann's. I haven't seen Luise since the bomb attack. With our secret revealed, we didn't have any more reason to take these trips together, and her service has been keeping her busy. I spend the entire day thinking about what to say to her.

When I tell Gerhard that I'm going to see Luise, he grins and advises me, "Tell her that this might be the last time you'll see each other. She might just give you a parting kiss."

"Ha-ha!" I say, jabbing him in the ribs.

"No, really, girls like that stuff. The emotional stuff. Why do you think Lena flew at me?"

"You shouldn't joke about that."

Gerhard doesn't know what Luise told me about her father. I'd be a jerk if I took advantage of her vulnerability.

Gerhard sighs resignedly. "Whatever you say. But don't come crying to me if you never land a girl."

I ignore him and put my coat on. Once outside, I stand in front of Luise's door for a long time, trying to think of the right words to say, but it's like my mind has been swept clean.

When I knock, Luise's mother opens. She has dark rings under her eyes, and she's no longer well-coiffed or neatly dressed. Though she's smiling, I notice deep furrows around the corners of her mouth.

"Hello, Anton. What's up?" she asks in a tired voice.

"Good evening, *Frau* Hofmann. I wanted to see Luise," I croak and clear my throat.

"Of course. Come in. She's practicing right now."

I can hear the piano from the living room and follow the sound. When I reach the open door, I stop and listen silently until she finishes the piece. Only then does Luise notice me. Her eyes widen.

"Oh, a secret listener!" She smiles at me.

"I didn't want to disturb you…"

"No worries. I was just playing around, doing some improv. Would you like to hear something real?"

I nod, happy that I can put off my news for a while.

She leans over the keys again and taps out the first notes. "Tell me if you recognize it."

And of course I do. It's *our* song, Schumann's *Träumerei*. I imagine that she's playing it just for me. As her fingers dance across the piano, as the familiar, melancholy notes sound, I can't help but think that this could be the last time that… No! I'm coming back. I have to. But…then what?

So you're going to be a watchmaker. Again, I hear her asking the question from last summer, hear the disappointment in her voice.

Luise has closed her eyes. A single tear trickles down her cheek. I would so like to reach out and wipe it away.

When the last notes fade, she turns and looks at me. I feel a prickling from head to toe and have to force myself to hold her gaze.

"Well…?" she asks. "Recognize it?"

I can only nod. Then I remember why I'm here. Shit! "Do you have a minute to talk?"

"Of course!" She closes the piano lid. "What's up?"

"I just wanted to talk to you."

Her eyes narrow. Does she suspect? Is my face really so easy to read?

"Would you like to go for a walk?" I ask.

She looks surprised, but nods and stands up. I'm pleased with my idea. If we're walking, I don't have to look directly at her, and the lulls in the conversation are less uncomfortable. Plus this way nobody can listen in.

She pulls on her coat, and without thinking about it, we head down the path into the park, the path we've walked so often before. Luise strolls close beside me. Our hands could touch, but they don't. What was so easy during the air attack now seems like an insurmountable obstacle.

"How come you haven't stopped by before now?" she asks offhandedly.

"Mother found out about the ration books after the attack. I had to explain everything. But don't worry—I left you and your uncle out of it."

"Oh! Well, thank you. If my mother found out…" her voice trails off.

I wait for her to continue, but she remains silent. "What have you been up to?" I finally ask.

"This and that, you know…hospital duty and all the other stuff. Do you have enough to eat now?"

"I guess." I hesitate. It's now or never. "But it won't be a problem pretty soon anyway."

She turns to face me. "Why?"

I stare down at the gravel path riddled with puddles.

"Gerhard and I have to report for a physical tomorrow, and if we pass, it's off to the barracks on Sunday," I say, as quickly as possible. "We got the draft notice a few days ago."

We're silent for a long time. Only the splash of her feet through the puddles reminds me that she's still there. I glance at her sidelong and she returns my gaze with a slight frown. I wish she would say something. She opens her mouth but closes it again immediately.

We pass the playground. As always, it just sits there, abandoned, the lonely old swing squeaking in the wind. Suddenly, Luise turns off onto a narrow dirt track. I follow her curiously. I've never been here before, but Luise seems to know where she's going. The path winds through overgrown hedges; we have to bend branches aside or duck under them. The bare trees surround us like shadowy guards.

She stops before a weeping willow. The thin, naked branches sway slightly in the wind, sweeping over the bare ground. She lifts a handful of branches up and to the side like she's opening a curtain, and lets me slip through; then she follows. The branches fall back behind her, enclosing us. I imagine what it would feel like to be here in the summer, like in a green, light-filled cave.

She sits down on one of the knobbly roots that's sticking out of the ground and leans back against the trunk. With her eyes, she signals that I can sit down next to her. When I do, our shoulders and knees are touching. She smells like violet soap and cookie dough.

"This is my favorite place," she says, hardly louder than the whisper of the wind. "Father's and my secret place. When he showed it to me the first time and held the branches aside, I felt like he was opening a veil and a magical world would appear behind it. We'd sit here, and he'd tell me stories about that fairy tale place. And sometimes I had my flute with me, and I thought up melodies to go along with the stories."

She starts to hum softly. I listen, spellbound. It's a simple but enchanting sequence of notes.

"When you're sitting here, you can forget everything else... The real world doesn't exist anymore."

"Is that why we're here?" I ask.

"Maybe."

My throat is tight. I feel like I should thank her for telling me her secret, but I don't know how. Gerhard's voice echoes in my head, nudging me. *Do something! What do you have to lose? You're leaving tomorrow!*

Hesitantly, I lift my arm to put it around her shoulders, but at that moment she starts rifling through her pockets, and I let my arm drop, feeling awkward. Another missed opportunity.

"I wanted to give you something." Luise pulls her closed fist out of her coat pocket and thrusts it toward me. Slowly she opens her fingers. Something in them catches the light and flashes at me. I recognize a matte gold casing, a golden chain, and on the cover, the etched lettering...I can't believe my eyes. Is it really Father's watch?

I'm much too surprised to react, so she presses it into my hand. In the process, our fingers touch briefly. I have to swallow a few times before I regain my voice.

"Where did you get that? I thought..."

"I traded back for it," she says.

I stare at her wordlessly.

"I couldn't just let you give it away," she explains. "I know what it's like to have only one thing left of your father."

"Thank you," I say.

She smiles sadly. "You have to promise to bring it home in one piece. Okay?"

I nod. Now my throat feels like there's a tennis ball stuck in it. I slide the watch into my pocket and decide to defend it at all costs.

"What did you trade to get it back? It must have been expensive."

She shrugs her shoulders. "Nothing you need to worry about."

"The food wasn't all for your family, was it?" I ask as something else crosses my mind.

She looks down at her hands, encased in woolen gloves. Finally, she shakes her head. It seemed odd to me from the beginning that Luise would be involved in illegal dealings if there wasn't a very good reason for it. Suddenly, I'm worried about her.

"I can't tell you about it. I'd like to, but…it's just too dangerous." She speaks so softly that I have to read half of the words from her lips. "The more people who know…do you understand?"

"Dangerous?" I ask, hearing the tension in my own voice.

She waves me off, as if she's already said too much, and stands up. "Come on, we should get going. It'll be dark soon."

Right before she parts the willow curtain, I stop her. I don't mean to—my hand just reaches for her arm. She turns around, looking at me curiously.

Her face is so close to mine that I can feel her warm breath on my skin. A delicate trail of freckles runs across the bridge of her nose, and her blue eyes are as inviting as a cool summer lake. Briefly, I see something soft, almost tender there that gives me hope. Then she frees herself gently from my grasp, moistens her lips, and turns around again. Her cheeks are red.

I follow her, disappointed and frustrated with myself. Once again, I feel how Gerhard is kicking me where it counts.

She doesn't look at me again until we're standing in front of her garden fence. "Take care of yourself, Anton." Her eyes glisten in the twilight. "And Gerhard, too!"

"I will."

Hesitantly, she opens the gate and walks through. I stand in front of it, watching her. *If she turns around again, then she likes you*, I think to myself, even though I know it's a silly notion.

She walks the length of the path through the garden, stops in front of the house and fumbles for her key. I turn away, suddenly feeling stupid, standing here and staring at her back. But when I hear the door creak on its hinge, I glance back. Her right hand is on the latch. She takes one step into the hall; then she turns to look over her shoulder. Our eyes meet, and we both grin like we've been caught.

With a spring in my step, I walk the few yards over to our house.

Chapter 27

"What kind of tired heap is this?" bellows *Feldwebel* Müller, our drill sergeant, in a voice that's surprisingly sonorous for a person of his size.

"Dishrags! Blindworms! All of you…"

The insults roll off my shoulders like the icy rain that has plagued us for days. The sun hasn't come up yet, and I'm still exhausted after a two-hour night watch. I got back at 4 a.m., only to be woken up again at 5:30 for morning roll call. It's no wonder we look like a tired heap.

"Well, nothing a little exercise can't cure!" yells the sergeant after firing off another round of curses. The thought of whipping us into shape seems to cheer him up. "Drop and give me fifty squats. Let's go!"

His eyes bore into mine, and I quickly bend my knees. He reminds me of a snappish little terrier: a head shorter than I am, wiry, with a loud bark and a pointed face. Stubbly gray hair is visible beneath his cap.

While I'm squatting, Müller passes me over and over, shouting in my ear, "Lower, Köhler!" Once, he grabs my shoulders and pushes me to the ground, so I almost lose my balance. "You call those squats? That half-baked shit? You'll do ten more!"

I grit my teeth. My only consolation is that, even squatting, I'm almost as tall as this guy.

Afterward, he chases us on a ten mile run around the barracks and through the woods. We're carrying all of our equipment—duffel bags on our backs, gas masks and shovels clattering on our belts. My hair's been cropped short, but I'm still sweating under the heavy steel helmet.

As I'm belting out marching songs, my boots spraying through the mud, I begin to calculate how long we've been here and how many days of torture lie ahead. I wonder whether what comes after will be better or worse.

We arrived at the barracks near Rossleben in Thuringia just three days ago, but it feels like an eternity. As soon as we got here, *Feldwebel* Müller made it clear that the next fourteen days wouldn't exactly be a picnic.

"There's no room for weaklings here! Think the war'll go easy on you? It's keep up or die! You're going to learn how to handle weapons, how to comport yourselves on the battlefield, and how to tell enemy tanks from ours. But most importantly, you're going to learn how to follow orders. That's what really counts. Later on, it'll mean the difference between life and death. When your superior gives an order, you carry it out immediately—no hesitating, no asking why. If you don't…best case scenario, you'll be dead. Worst case scenario, your whole unit will be." He tapped his temple with one finger. "So you'd better learn to turn off that thing in there. I don't care if you were valedictorian. Anyone caught thinking will spend an extra week scrubbing latrines."

At 9:00 a.m., after breakfast, it's time for the theory lesson. Most of us use it to catch up on sleep—except when *Major* Schirmer is speaking, like he is today. Schirmer is our barracks commander and a forceful presence. Medals glint on his chest: the iron cross, the silver badge that indicates he was wounded in battle, the golden hand-to-hand combat medal, the infantry badge, and many others I don't recognize. His most striking feature, though, is his snow-white hair. It's completely white, not just white-blond, and it makes him look like an old man, even though his face is hardly lined. Schirmer's eyes are keen but kind, and his voice casts a spell over all of us.

"Good morning, recruits!" he calls, lifting his hand briefly in the Hitler salute. We respond in kind. "Weapons expertise is on the agenda today."

I'm sitting next to Gerhard in the cafeteria, where the tables and hard wooden chairs have been rearranged for our lesson. We all have a clear view of the white wall where they sometimes project slides.

"As you know, you're being trained as *Panzergrenadiers*, which means you will accompany our panzer divisions as infantry troops. So it's especially important that you can distinguish between ours and enemy tanks. I'm going to be honest with you: your training is short, and I'd really like to have more time. But as things stand now, that's simply not possible."

He allows his gaze to travel over the assembled boys, who are hanging onto his every word. "All of you, though you're still very young—some of you have yet to turn sixteen—all of you have been called to take up arms for the Fatherland. The *Führer* believes that young people like you are skilled and brave enough to stand by him and our country in this time of need. You will defend it, no matter the cost. Our enemies are advancing on all sides. According to the *Wehrmacht* report I just saw, the Americans crossed the Rhine at Remagen a few days ago."

A groan ripples through the crowd.

"And in the east," the major continues, "the Russians are looting and pillaging, attacking our women and children. It's every man's duty to defend his country, every day. So we'll do our best to prepare you as well as we can. I expect each of you to listen carefully. You will do yourself no favors if you don't pay attention. This isn't a high school—it's a survival school. Copying other people's work, sleeping in class…do it at your own risk." He looks at us insistently.

Then he begins the lesson. He makes it easy to listen. Instead of dry theory, he describes his own battle experience and keeps emphasizing the bravery of the soldiers he fought with, in 1944 on the French coast.

He also allows us to ask questions and answers all of them with patience. Somehow, he reminds me of my father, with his calm presence and prudent speech, and a little bit of Uncle Emil, though he's not nearly as cynical. I wonder if I could dare to ask him for his opinion. Normally, I wouldn't raise my hand in front of everyone, but the major makes it feel safe to do so. Tentatively, I lift my arm. When he calls on me, I jump up from my chair, almost surprised at my own boldness. I stand straight and tall. All eyes are on me; there's no going back now.

I clear my throat. "*Major* Schirmer, sir, how do you think the rest of the war will go?" I ask, holding my breath.

The major is silent for a moment. The atmosphere in the room has changed noticeably; suddenly, it's very quiet. Everyone wants to know the answer, but no one else dared ask. I'm almost afraid to meet *Major* Schirmer's eyes that are fixed on me.

"What's your name?"

I swallow. "Köhler. Anton Köhler, *Herr Major*."

"Please sit down, Köhler."

I drop back down into my chair, trying to make myself as small as possible. Gerhard raises his eyebrows. But the major continues, his eyes trained far away.

"You're asking if I believe in the ultimate victory?"

I sit up straight again, my heart in my throat. This was not what I meant to ask at all!

Softly, *Major* Schirmer goes on. "Now, I can't tell the future. But there's one thing I know for sure: as long as German soldiers keep fighting for the Fatherland with all they've got, we can't lose—no matter how the war ends."

The room is silent; then, a soft murmuring starts. The major's cryptic answer has caused confusion. I'm afraid that someone will read his words as doubting the ultimate victory and our military capabilities. I bite my tongue. Why did I even ask?

Gerhard elbows me.

"That was a brave question," he says.

I shake my head. "No, it was a brave answer," I whisper back.

After the lesson, my head swims with all of the new terms and technical details that we're supposed to memorize. *Two weeks*, I think again. *Two weeks' reprieve.*

Chapter 28

Behind the barracks is the training ground, a large, open area with trampled grass and muddy earth. They've arranged a variety of obstacles there: wooden walls, towers, ropes, barbed wire, and a firing range where we've gathered for our afternoon lesson.

I weigh my carbine in my hand. This morning, we learned how to take it apart and put it back together. We must have done it a hundred times. Now we're supposed to shoot. As I lie down on the hilltop, I remind myself how to put the clip in and lift the hammer. Resting my elbows on the soft ground, I squint at the target about sixty feet away. It's not the first time I've handled a weapon; we already had some target practice with air rifles in the Hitler Youth.

As the first shots crack next to me, no one is spared *Feldwebel* Müller's tongue-lashings. "Anyone who shoots that badly is a danger to his fellow soldiers, moron!" he bellows at Gerhard. I struggle not to let it distract me.

"My blind grandma shoots better than you do!" he yells at another boy. "We'd send you packing if we didn't need each and every soldier right now."

I concentrate on the center of the target, that little black circle. Everything else fades into the background as, slowly and with controlled force, I pull the trigger. The shot rings in my ears, and with the kickback, the butt of the rifle slams into my shoulder. But I think I've hit it. I've always had a steady hand—inherited it from my father. I fire the remaining shots. To my astonishment, Müller leaves me alone. Once we've all finished, he inspects the targets and calls out the number of the rings each of us hit.

"Köhler!" I cringe when I hear my name. "Neubauer! Böhm! You three will report tomorrow for sharpshooter training with *Oberfähnrich* Konradi. The rest of you are stuck with me until you can load and fire the damned thing in your sleep."

Gerhard nudges my shoulder. "Sharpshooter," he whispers as we move to the next station. I'm not sure if it's good or bad, so I don't reply. We stop in front of a long obstacle course. Just looking at it gives me an uneasy feeling, which only increases when I see the glint in Müller's eyes.

He claps once. "Now we're getting to the real thing. This morning was a walk in the park, but here, there's nowhere to hide. I will find and eradicate every weakness. Weakness is death—you should tattoo that on your foreheads. Now go! Line up! Rows of two!"

Unfortunately, Gerhard and I are at the head of the line.

"You know the drill. Scale the tower, slide down the rope, crawl under the barbed wire, and jump over the wall. You've got two minutes. And don't lose your guns! Starting now, they're your most important possession; they'll save your ass. Got it? Ready—and—go!" The sergeant starts his stopwatch.

I sprint off, my duffel bag on my back, carbine slung over my shoulder. Gerhard is running next to me. With his gangly legs, he's the first to reach the tower. It's about thirty feet tall, made of rough-hewn timber. Despite the wide spaces between the boards, we both reach the top quickly. We've practiced climbing trees often enough when we were younger.

I grab one of the ropes hanging from the platform at almost the same time Gerhard does. We slide down together. To save time and avoid chafing my hands, I let go a few feet above the ground. I land square on my feet, knees bending a little, and sprint off toward the long, barbed wire tunnel we're supposed to crawl through. Without a second thought, I throw myself down on the muddy ground and haul myself forward on my elbows and knees, gun in hands. Gerhard follows hard on my heels.

Müller's voice pursues us. "Go, go, go! Faster! Do you have tomatoes in your ears? You're crawling along like snails!"

"How are we supposed to get over the wall?" I puff, eying the ten-foot structure that now looms before us. There are no hand-holds or uneven spots—not that I can see, anyway.

"Gain some momentum and push through," replies Gerhard, gasping.

Somehow I don't think the hard wooden boards will give way... Müller is still bellowing insults as we crawl through the last of the barbed wire. His constant yelling makes me nervous, even though I'm trying hard to ignore it. He's like an angry wasp, buzzing around our heads, refusing to leave us alone. Mud sprays up into my face; I taste wet earth and blink to clear the dirt from my eyes. Finally, the end of the barbed wire! I need to keep going, get away from that voice...

I raise myself up on one knee and try to run onwards, only to find myself held fast from behind. For a moment, I think Müller has grabbed me and is going to rattle me like a dog his prey. But then I notice that my collar has caught in the barbed wire. I got up too soon. Gerhard overtakes me and runs off. When I don't follow, he slows and looks around. I struggle to free myself from the wire. Behind me, the next two boys are already closing in.

"Köhler! You wimp! Weakling! Lame duck! What the fuck are you doing? Hanging yourself? Bravo! We could really use soldiers like you—doing the enemies' work for them. Why don't you just take your gun and put yourself out of your misery?" screams Müller in my ear.

My fingers are trembling. I can't seem to find where my clothing is caught. The barbed wire slices the skin on my hand.

"And what are you gawking at?" That's aimed at Gerhard. "Move it! Now!"

I have no idea how Gerhard manages to get over the wall. I feel like a rabbit, shaking in his burrow while the hunting dogs howl for blood. Then suddenly, a strong hand grabs me by the collar and pulls me down. My face nearly hits the mud, but I catch myself at the last moment. I hear a tearing sound and discover that I'm free. Before I can lift myself up, I glimpse a wink from Fred Neubauer, our room leader and a great guy. He runs past me, toward the wall.

"Move it, Köhler! No napping, you're next!"

I struggle to my feet and race after Fred. He doesn't slow down and, elegant as a panther, actually runs vertically up the wall a few steps, stretching out his long body and holding fast to the top edge. He uses his momentum to swing his legs over and drops down on the other side. I want to imitate him, but Müller's bellowing confuses me so much that I come to a screeching halt just before the wall. I freeze, unable to do anything but stare.

"What's the matter now, Köhler? Are you scared of the wall? You're supposed to jump over it, not stop! And where the hell is your gun, you moron? What did I tell you about your gun?"

My gun! It's still lying in the mud by the barbed wire. I trot back, blood rushing in my ears. My face must be fire-engine red, though they probably can't see under the layer of grime.

"I asked you a question, Köhler!" Müller screams.

"You said our gun is our most important possession, *Herr Feldwebel*," I gasp.

"Exactly, shit-for-brains, and what did you do with your most important possession? You left it lying in the dirt. You're impossible, Köhler!"

Tears of anger prick at my eyes, but I blink them away as I bend down to retrieve my rifle. *Don't show any signs of weakness, or he'll taste blood.* Another boy has just crawled out from under the barbed wire and is running toward the wall.

"Step to the side, Köhler. You're going to do pushups until all of the others are finished. Then you'll get a special turn."

When all of my groupmates are through, Müller allows me to get up again. Out of breath, I stand up straight while he comes at me like a mad hornet.

"Now it's your turn! I'll time you, and you will keep going until you can do it in less than a minute. And—go!"

One minute? That's impossible! As I jog by Gerhard, I see sympathy in his eyes and am even more ashamed of my failure. I'm the only one in the group who couldn't complete the course the first time around.

I scurry up the climbing tower again, slide down the ropes, and throw myself on the ground in front of the barbed wire. This time, I crawl until I'm absolutely sure I'm clear of the tunnel. Then I jump up, sling my carbine over my shoulder, and race towards the wall.

"Faster, faster!" Müller hollers.

The ten-foot wall rears before me, filling my field of vision. Don't stop now. Just close your eyes and push through, like Gerhard said.

"Faster, Köhler!"

The wall is directly in front of me. I keep running. My feet lift off the ground and my legs move up the wall as if of their own accord. I grasp the uppermost board, swing myself over the edge, and drop down on the other side. Wheezing, I try to catch my breath, satisfied with the effort.

But then Müller appears beside me. "That was a minute sixteen, Köhler!" he yells, glancing at his watch. "Do it again!"

I gape at him for a moment, stunned, but his grim expression leaves no doubt that he's serious. This rotten, sadistic bastard! Worse than Wilhelm or *Unteroffizier* Stoss.

His whistle drives me on relentlessly. I run back to the start of the course and grasp the boards of the climbing tower again. My arms and legs are getting heavier, and though I try with all my might, I can't pull myself up as fast as I did the first time. When I've made it over the wall once more, I squint at Müller, resting my hands on my knees. He consults his watch.

"You're getting slower, Köhler! That was a minute thirty. Not good enough. Again!"

My legs feel like jelly now. I'll never beat my first time. Even the distance to the starting line feels endless. My lungs are burning. *He'll slave-drive me to death*—the thought shoots through my head as I scale the tower for the third time. If I fall down dead from the top of the tower, he'll get what's coming to him. But no—I won't do him that favor! I clench my teeth and keep going.

"Squeeze your glutes! You think this is hard, do you, mama's boy? This is nothing compared to what's waiting for you on the front. If you think you're going to sleep through the night or get breakfast in bed, you're sorely mistaken."

I hear Müller's voice as if from afar as I grasp the rope and try to slide down. There are red welts on my hands. I lose my grip and fall the last few feet. Landing badly on the ground, I think I've twisted my ankle. But I get up again and keep running. Again I drag myself through the barbed wire. The wall swims before my eyes as I sprint toward it. I can't even tell if I'm running straight. Still, I manage to land on the other side, somehow.

"A minute ten. Getting better. Now one more time, and—"

"That'll do for today, *Feldwebel* Müller." A deep, quiet voice cuts through Müller's rant.

I blink a few times until my vision clears. When it does, I can hardly believe my eyes: *Major* Schirmer himself is standing at the edge of the obstacle course, his eyes on Müller.

Müller opens his mouth and closes it a few times. Finally, he waves me off, a sour look on his face. "Go on then, Köhler. Stand with the others."

I drag myself away, gasping, and get in line with my groupmates.

"And now," the Major says evenly, "show the boys how to handle a grenade. That will be useful to them on the front."

Müller salutes succinctly. "*Jawohl, Herr Major*. Heil Hitler."

"Sure." The major turns around without giving Müller a second glance. Does he always come to watch the exercises?

Müller clears his throat. "Let's go, recruits. I want to see who was paying attention in theory class this morning."

Chapter 29

We've been at the barracks for a week now. Each day *Feld-webel* Müller forces me to play his sadistic little games. The major's rebuke seems only to have provoked him further. Before, I was on his radar only from time to time; now, nothing I do escapes his notice. And he keeps coming up with creative new ways to bully me.

It starts early each morning. Müller drags me out of the bathroom before I'm even done brushing my teeth and sends me into the courtyard to run a few laps because my bed wasn't neat enough. During our afternoon exercises, I'm guaranteed to have to climb the ropes more than anyone else or do squats just because I looked at him funny.

The time that Fred, Harald and I spend in sharpshooter training—the only time I'm away from Müller—becomes the highlight of my day.

Today, because I supposedly dawdled during barracks duty, Müller ordered me to sweep the whole courtyard while the others are sitting at breakfast: "So that you learn the meaning of cleanliness."

My comrades throw me pitying glances, but I know they're relieved not to be on Müller's list themselves. I hope Gerhard thinks to save me some breakfast. If I weren't so hungry, the punishment wouldn't be all that bad. It's a sunny day, the air is mild, and it already smells like spring. And it's my sixteenth birthday. Is my family thinking about me now? Is Luise?

I survey the large yard. How am I supposed to sweep the whole thing in an hour? Would Müller really make me miss my morning lesson if I didn't finish in time? The broom brushes over the asphalt, pebbles jumping away from the bristles. I'm pushing little bits of plants and dried mud, all the debris of a long winter, in front of me, making piles that keep getting larger. Suddenly, a gust of wind scatters everything across the courtyard. I sigh and lean on my broom. So much for breakfast...

Then I notice a window opening on the second floor of the main building. *Major* Schirmer looks out, glancing first at the sky—perhaps to check the weather or look for enemy planes—then down at the courtyard. His white hair shines brightly in the sunlight. I hurriedly resume sweeping.

After a few minutes, during which I don't dare look at the window, a sonorous voice calls down to me. "*Hallo*! Köhler! That is your name, isn't it?"

I stand up straight and salute the window. "*Jawohl, Herr Major*, sir. Anton Köhler, reporting for duty."

"And what is your duty?"

"I am sweeping the courtyard on *Feldwebel* Müller's order, *Herr Major*."

"I see." He falls silent, and I'm not sure whether to continue with my activity. But first he has to tell me to stand down, doesn't he?

"Come up to my office, Köhler!"

I'm flabbergasted. "But—"

"I will let *Feldwebel* Müller know that I have kidnapped his recruit for a while." He steps back and closes the window.

I hesitate, then lean the broom against the wall and tramp into the main building. On the ground floor, the inviting smell of fresh rolls, eggs, and bacon wafts toward me from the cafeteria. My stomach growls. I climb the stairs three at a time up to the second floor and knock on the door to *Major* Schirmer's anteroom. The adjutant opens the door and waves me straight through to the major's office.

Did I do something wrong? Why does *Major* Schirmer want to see *me*? Perhaps he's noticed how many *special tasks* I have to do, and now he thinks I'm a difficult case who needs extra discipline. I wipe my clammy and slightly dusty palms on my pants before entering the commander's office.

The major is sitting at his desk. Rays of sunlight slant through the window behind him, almost blinding me. I salute. "Recruit Köhler reporting as ordered, *Herr Major*."

He points to a chair in front of his desk. Hesitantly, I take a seat. On the right side of the desk, a telephone is sitting atop a stack of files. Fanning out in front of him are papers, pens, and other writing materials, with a tray of food in the center. Clearly, he's in the middle of breakfast.

I wait for him to speak, but before he can do so, there's another knock at the door. The adjutant comes back in, carrying another tray, which he sets down in front of me. The major pushes some of his files to the side to make room. I'm so surprised I can't decide how to react.

"Coffee?" the major asks in a friendly voice.

I nod, still speechless. I can smell the aroma of real coffee—not that surrogate brew made from grains. I haven't had that in ages.

"Dig in, my boy," he tells me.

Did he just call me *my boy*? But—a command's a command. And you don't look a gift horse in the mouth. So I start on my food, feeling suddenly ravenous. I can't believe I'm sitting here and having breakfast with the major. As I butter my bread, I keep glancing up at him. Schirmer holds a coffee cup in his left hand and a newspaper in his right, which he's scanning.

He looks at me over the paper and smiles. "So, Anton Köhler, I hope you're not too upset that I took you away from your important task of sweeping the courtyard."

Since I've just taken an enormous bite of toast with jam and my cheeks are full, I hurriedly shake my head.

"I see you in the courtyard during breakfast quite often," he notes.

I chew and swallow, unsure what to say.

"*Feldwebel* Müller is a hard master," he continues, "hard, but good. No one has ever regretted being trained by him. And he seems to like you."

I nearly spray my mouthful of hot coffee across the desk.

"What is it?" asks Schirmer, his eyes twinkling.

I debate whether or not I should answer, but the major's openness encourages me.

"Permission to speak freely, sir?"

"Of course. Honesty is a German virtue, and one that every soldier should master."

"*Feldwebel* Müller hates my guts. Since day one, when I didn't complete the obstacle course to his satisfaction, he has taken every opportunity to humiliate me in front of my compatriots."

The major grins. That's definitely not what I was expecting. Is he laughing at me?

"I think you've got it backward, Köhler. The sergeant only treats recruits that way if he particularly likes them."

I shake my head in disbelief. "He screams at me, insults me, and tells me that I'm doing everything wrong."

The major lays his newspaper aside. "He's only trying to get you to do your best."

He must see from my expression that I'm not convinced. "If you survive this week, you will be better prepared than most of the others."

"Yes, sir," I respond, though I'm still skeptical. How is sweeping the yard supposed to help me at the front?

"You know, Köhler, you remind me of my son Hans."

Suddenly, I understand why he invited me here.

"He's seventeen, and he's been a cannoneer with the *Luftwaffe* for a few months. At the moment, he's stationed in the west, in Remagen. Where are you from?"

"Breslau, *Herr* Major."

"Oh, a fellow Silesian. My family is originally from Liegnitz."

I would never have thought that someday I'd be sitting with the barracks commander, eating breakfast and chatting like we were old friends. We talk about our homeland. Then Major Schirmer looks at his pocket watch and says, "You'd better go now. The lesson will begin presently."

I stand up immediately, shoving the last bit of bacon into my mouth. "Thank you very much, sir."

Just wait till I tell the others about this! They aren't going to believe it!

Chapter 30

Surprisingly, Müller leaves me alone for the rest of the day. I don't know whether he heard about my meeting with the major, but I don't care, as long as I don't have to scrub the floors with a toothbrush again. Since tomorrow's Sunday, we get the evening off.

When I return to our room after cleaning the latrines, I almost jump out of my skin. Nineteen boys yell, "Happy birthday!"

Gerhard approaches me. "Congratulations on turning sixteen, old buddy!" He slaps me on the back. "Finally you're as old as me."

I snort. "Like you didn't just turn sixteen yourself." But I'm grinning.

The other boys wave me over. They're sitting on the swept floor in a circle or squatting on the lower bunks. Gerhard pulls a brown paper bag out from under his pillow and hands it to me. "For you."

The bag is heavy, and my suspicions are confirmed when I reach into it and pull out a bottle of schnapps. I stare at Gerhard. "Where did you get *that?*"

"I did a little *arranging* for you. Actually, for all of us, so we can drink to you. You've got to celebrate a birthday like this properly."

"Just don't drink too much this time," I whisper to him.

He looks at me with a guilty grin.

"I have dice," says Siggi.

I sit down with my groupmates.

"You start," Gerhard commands, pointing to the schnapps.

"To us," I say, setting the bottle to my lips. I take a tiny sip. The alcohol runs down my throat like a streak of fire. My eyes tear up, but I suppress the urge to cough and pass the bottle around.

"No, to you!" says Gerhard, taking a proper sip.

"To the upcoming deployment," toasts Fred. The bottle makes its way around the circle, finally returning to me. The second sip is easier as I'm prepared for the burning in my throat. Pleasant warmth spreads from my stomach through my whole body as the bottle makes its second go-round. The boys are laughing and chattering. We play cards and dice games and polish off the schnapps in no time.

"What did you wish for?" asks Gerhard softly, when no one is watching.

I shrug.

"Come on. If you could have anything you want?"

Anything I want? First, I think of Luise. I want to see her again. But for that, I'd have to make it home in one piece. Surrounded by the other boys, I almost forget we're not at summer camp, that we'll be sent to the front in just a week. The schnapps gurgles in my stomach.

"So?" Gerhard prods me again.

"That the war will be over soon?" I say softly.

Gerhard shakes the dice cup and sets it on the floor with a bang before he lifts it up to look at the dice. "Ha! Boxcars!" He collects the cigarettes we've been using to bet. As he stacks the cartons, he leans toward me again.

"Boring! I thought you'd wish for something else…"

"Fine—what should I wish for?"

He presses the dice cup into my hand. I shake it distractedly.

"Oh, I was thinking about a creature with big blue eyes, blond hair, and ruby-red lips." Gerhard bats his eyes exaggeratedly, puckering his mouth.

I suppress a grin and shake the dice cup. "Stop!" I say and lift the cup. One and six. It's not good.

"Anton, you've hit lucky sixteen," calls Knöppi, whose real name is Mirko Knöppke. "It's time for you to become a real man."

We all roll our eyes. Knöppi only talks about one thing: girls. More specifically, his girl back home. "Do you have a girlfriend?" he asks eagerly.

I can feel the blood rising in my cheeks, unable to prevent it, and I look down at the floor in hopes that nobody is watching me too closely.

Gerhard answers for me. "Yes, he does," he says. "She just doesn't know it yet."

The boys laugh. Gerhard slaps me on the back good-naturedly. I shoot him a dirty look, but I have to laugh all the same.

"Don't worry, Anton," calls Fred. "When you return home a hero, you'll win her in no time."

I awaken with my stomach churning. Today is the day of our swearing-in, our last day in the barracks.

At breakfast, I have to choke down my bread. I keep thinking about the last evening at Aunt Martha's, when Uncle Emil took Gerhard and me aside. He wanted to talk to us alone, man-to-man.

Uncle Emil sat across from us at the kitchen table, his sightless eyes uncovered. By now they'd scarred over, and his lids looked a bit like they'd caved in. Still, it seemed he could see right through us.

"Listen, boys," he said gravely. "Don't try to be heroes, okay?"

"I didn't intend to," I replied.

"I mean it," he stressed. "Run, take cover. And if you can, get yourselves captured. By the Yanks, not the Russians. Understood?"

"You want us to *try* to be taken prisoner?" Gerhard asked, confusion written across his face.

"Would you rather be alive in a POW camp or lying dead in the field?"

Gerhard and I glanced at each other. When he put it that way… "And what happens if we're captured by the Russians?"

"If the Russians get you, then you're better off shooting yourselves."

"You okay?" asks Gerhard, tearing me out of my memory. Worry lingers in his voice.

I clear my throat and nod. We grab our half-empty trays and put them away.

"Just nervous."

"I know what you mean. It's finally time…"

When we go outside, the recruits are gathering for the swearing-in ceremony, all wearing their uniforms and steel helmets. Müller directs us to our places. We're lined up in four divisions on all four sides of the courtyard, faces turned toward the center, where the Reich's military standard—red, with a black cross and the swastika in the middle—flaps in the breeze.

I shift my weight from one leg to the other. The sky is overcast, and my spring mood has vanished for the time being. We wait silently for the ceremony to begin.

Major Schirmer strides to the center of the courtyard, flanked by several officers carrying the regimental flag. He allows his gaze to travel over the crowd. I have a feeling that it lingers on me a little longer than the rest, but I probably imagined it.

"You have completed your training, and now you're ready to defend your country with your blood," he begins his speech. "I'm proud of each and every one of you. I'm sure you will honor us with your courage and bravery and do your duty as soldiers. From here on out, you aren't recruits anymore. I hereby proclaim you *Panzergrenadiers* of the German army. After you have taken your oath, you will be full members of the *Wehrmacht* with all the rights and responsibilities that entails."

I feel the hairs on my arms stand up. The officers lower the flag a little, and the major puts his hand on the staff. The courtyard is so quiet you could hear a pin drop. Even the wind dies down as the major recites the oath. Then the chorus of recruits' voices sounds, and I follow automatically. We all repeat after him.

"I swear to God this sacred oath that to the Leader of the German Reich and people, Adolf Hitler, supreme commander of the armed forces, I shall render unconditional obedience and that as a brave soldier I shall at all times be prepared to give my life for this oath."

As I repeat the words, I feel only emptiness inside. They mean nothing to me. I can't bring myself to feel an obligation to the *Führer*. I don't know what the others are thinking as they take their oaths. Many of my comrades still believe in the ultimate victory, in the *Wunderwaffe*, in Hitler. They are keen to prove themselves in battle, to give their lives for all this. But I'm not.

I feel like a traitor. Involuntarily, I glance around, as if somebody could hear my thoughts. In the process, I meet Gerhard's gaze, where I read the same insecurity that I feel—and fear of what lies ahead. I nod encouragingly to him. And then I take my own oath.

I want to survive. I want to return from this war with Gerhard so I can help my family. I want to see Luise again and make something of my life. I feel for the watch in my pants pocket.

I won't let you down, Father. I will try to stay alive and make it back home. I promise.

My heart pounding, I wait to see what happens next. The officers, including *Feldwebel* Müller, are now walking along the rows of newly minted soldiers and handing each of us our dog tags, inscribed with the name of our unit, and our pay books.

I incline my head slightly so that *Feldwebel* Müller can hang the tag around my neck. My heart feels a bit lighter at the thought that I no longer have to deal with him. Müller's sharp little eyes are fixed on me once more, but today I meet them directly, without fear.

"Köhler," he says, dropping his voice to a tolerable level for once, "don't forget what I've taught you. You'll need it."

I stare at him in confusion as he moves on to the next boy.

This is our last day in relative safety. I can't imagine what will come next. I lean over to Gerhard. "Whatever happens, we're going to stay together, okay?" I stretch out my hand, and Gerhard shakes it solemnly.

Then he grins: "'Til death do us part."

Chapter 31

I've lost all sense of time. I'm lying on the cold, hard ground between thorny shrubs, keeping watch over the road. When will the tanks come, the ones we're supposed to be defending against? Why are they taking so long? Gerhard squats next to me, his *Panzerfaust*, a single-shot anti-tank weapon, at the ready. My exhaustion is replaced for a moment by a rush of adrenaline as I think I hear a distant rumbling, but then it dies away. Must have imagined it.

I look around. My unit's gray field uniforms blend into the gray-and-brown tones of the bare landscape. Almost no one in the platoon is older than seventeen. Our commander is a young lieutenant, only twenty-one himself, with barely any battle experience. That's the way it is in our whole division and throughout the Twelfth Army. And *we're* supposed to be the Reich's last hope? The saviors of Berlin?

How long has it been since we were sworn in? Has Easter come already? The days and nights blur together, an endless series of the same events over and over…enemy attack, retreat, realignment, another attack. No one, not even our commander, knows exactly where the front line is. We're pawns on a blind man's chess board.

I've become disoriented, lost all sense of where I am. Somewhere in the middle of Germany, between Dessau and Berlin. Heaths alternate with barren fields, small settlements, and scattered farms, most of them deserted.

A weak buzzing sounds from a distance, then quickly swells. And then they come rumbling down the road from the east: Russian tanks. Dozens of them. My breathing accelerates at the sight of the steel monsters, with their long, rotating guns. The image seems to blur before my eyes. My palms are slick with sweat, forcing me to grip my weapon more tightly.

Gerhard licks his lips and lies down low beside me, at the ready.

"This is crazy; we can't stop them," I say. "We're just a handful."

Gerhard keeps his eye trained on his target. With a determined expression, he aims at the first tank in the approaching column.

I have to shoot as well—that's the command. This time it's just steel monsters, but I know there are people inside of them.

"Fire!" calls the platoon leader.

As Gerhard fires his *Panzerfaust*, a bang resounds in my ears. The projectile zips directly into the turret of the first tank. A moment later there's a powerful pressure wave and a brilliant flash. I recoil, deafened, but with my gaze locked on the drama in front of me.

The tank's turret flies several yards into the air, seems to hover there for a moment, then falls, trailing smoke, plummeting ever faster toward the ground, a fiery comet. Pieces of metal rain down on us. The rest of the tank lies smoking and torn apart in a crater on the side of the road.

"Come on! Who's next?" the lieutenant bellows at me. I still haven't fired my weapon.

But by now the enemy has spotted us. Their turrets swivel toward our platoon. I know the sparse roadside bushes can't shield us. Grenades and machine gun volleys hit all around, throwing clods of earth into the air, tearing the lieutenant's legs off. I pull Gerhard away, and then we run, like always. That's all I'm good at.

We race across the muddy field, the tanks following with unbelievable speed. Dirt flies up around us. We take cover behind a hill, then run onwards, into a small forest where we can catch our breath, filthy and sweat-soaked. Moving on…farther, faster…a piece of *Panzerschokolade* to boost us along…tapping our last reserves of strength.

Finally, we run into another division and report to their commander. Some of the soldiers overhear our news.

"Shit, what are the Russians doing in the hinterlands? I thought they were over by the River Neisse."

"Well, obviously not, or their tanks wouldn't be flattening us."

"We clearly underestimated the Russian advance," the commander says loudly. "Starting now, we're going to think of this as enemy territory. That means taking extra precautions. We'll remain here until we receive new orders. Now clean your weapons."

The weight of my equipment seems to pull me down, and I sink onto the soft ground beneath a pine tree, which provides a little shade. I take off my helmet, enjoying the cool breeze that dries my sticky hair.

"That was close. Again," says Gerhard softly, obviously still shaken. He sits down across from me, leaning against a boulder, and stretches out his long legs in front of him. On the other side of the boulder sits another soldier with his back to us.

"Damn it!" I say because I can't think of anything else. Shock has seeped deep into my bones. I take out my cleaning leather and begin to disassemble my carbine.

"You can say that again. I'm done playing cat-and-mouse with the Russians." Gerhard looks around uneasily.

The soldier on the other side of the rock turns toward us, twisting his neck. "I don't believe it," he mutters.

Gerhard jumps at the sound of his voice

"What are *you* doing here?" the soldier snarls.

I stare. I must be imagining things—it can't be...

Gerhard shifts to the side so I can have a better look at the soldier. Cropped blond hair, icy gray eyes, thick neck, broad shoulders...it's Wilhelm Braun. He scrunches his face up like a dog raring to bite.

"Oh, hello Wilhelm. Nice to see you, too," Gerhard scoffs.

I still can't believe it. We haven't seen each other in months and *now* we cross paths again?

"What are you doing here?" I ask stupidly.

"Isn't it obvious? The same thing as you, probably."

"Damn it," I say again.

"I thought I'd gotten rid of you two for good...that you kicked it back in the woods somewhere."

"Seems you were too quick to celebrate," says Gerhard.

Anyone else from back home, I'd be glad to see. But not Braun!

"And I thought you'd have joined the *Waffen*-SS by now. Isn't that what you always wanted?" I challenge him.

Braun shrugs, but his expression darkens. "I can fight for the Fatherland just as well here. So, you guys just escaped from the Russians, did you?"

I don't want to argue with Braun. To be honest, I don't want to talk to him at all.

"It was a…disorderly retreat," says Gerhard.

"Oh yeah? So you ran like frightened rabbits."

"I'd like to see how you handle yourself in front of a Russian tank," I growl back.

"Well, maybe one of these days you'll get the chance."

"If it means I have to deal with you a second longer, I think I'll pass, thanks." But even as I say it, our old squabbles seem suddenly laughable. We're all in the same boat. Wilhelm can't touch us now; he's just one soldier among many.

"Köhler has gotten bitchy," replies Wilhelm.

"Stop it, you two," Gerhard says in a tired voice. "I want to enjoy the peace and quiet. Who knows how long it'll last."

Wilhelm frowns and turns around so I can't see anything but the back of his blond head. I glare at him as if he could feel it, then turn away and try to forget him.

When we set out marching again, Wilhelm falls in right behind us, whether accidentally or intentionally, I don't know.

At daybreak, we arrive at the edge of a small town, where we're allowed to rest. My limbs are leaden, and I could drop right down onto the damp earth at the side of the road. But the houses beckon to us, offering a dry place to sleep, maybe even in a real bed. An early-morning quiet lies over the landscape, which is still submerged in gray, pre-dawn light. A blackbird flies over to perch in the bushes. Everything is peaceful—too peaceful.

I grab Gerhard's arm, holding him back while the first men in our unit approach a farmhouse at the edge of the town.

"Wait," I whisper.

"What? I want to sleep," mumbles Gerhard.

I'm not even sure myself what has set me on edge. In front of us, a stall door creaks open, shattering the morning peace. A bearded man steps out, yawning and stretching. He's wearing nothing but dirty long johns. Our unit stops and stares at the messy figure.

Farther up the street, more doors are opening, and sleep-drunk men are staggering out into the cool morning air. A man with a razor blade stands at a water trough shaving his chin.

Then the man who came out of the stall notices our expressions: befuddled and gaping. He utters a cry of surprise. But not in German—in Russian.

His cry startles the remaining men into action. Most of them aren't even in uniform yet. They scurry back into the houses, their hands raised, weaponless.

Suddenly I'm wide awake.

"Come," I whisper to Gerhard, pulling him backward by the sleeve.

We turn on our heels. So what if they accuse us of cowardice? Our comrades follow close behind. No one wants a confrontation this early in the morning, even if we have the advantage. A little later, we stop by the side of the road to catch our breath. The experience still seems unreal. A snorting laugh bursts from my throat. I can no longer suppress it.

Gerhard stares at me, flabbergasted. Then he starts to laugh, too. "The enemy…in long johns."

I wipe tears from my eyes, wheezing. "Oh man! Up close, they're not so scary. Not with shaving cream all around their mouths and messy hair."

"And the way they peered at us, standing there in their underwear."

Again, we're overcome by fits of laughter. I double over, my sides aching.

"They were just as surprised as we were," says Gerhard.

"I know!"

My laughter fades as I realize how it resembles gallows humor. Just a few hours ago, we were fleeing from the sleepy soldiers' countrymen, running for our lives. Their planes mowed us down, their tanks crushed us, their infantrymen charged at us with blood-curdling screams.

But in the end, we're just like the Russians. We too are filthy, tired, afraid. I don't know how I'm supposed to point my weapon at one of them and pull the trigger—and silently, I pray that I'll never have to.

Chapter 32

*I'm running, running, but I can hardly lift my feet off the ground—
it's like there's an iron ball chained to them. The quagmire I'm slog-
ging through clutches at me with sticky fingers. Gray twilight and
shadowy figures surround me. I turn to Gerhard, who's sprinting
behind me. Face twisted in a grimace, he stretches out a hand. I'm
waiting for him, trying to pull him along, yet the distance between us
is growing. Gerhard opens his mouth in a scream, but no sound comes
out. Then a shot shatters the eerie silence.*

I sit up with a gasp. Voices swirl around me. Through
the window, moonlight falls across the room's wooden
floorboards. Gerhard is squatting next to me, also startled.
So I didn't dream the gunshot.

My heart is still beating wildly, but the dream is already
fading in my mind's eye. A dark figure tears the door open
and steps into the moonlight. I don't recognize the man;
he must be from the night watch. We've set up camp in a
deserted town and occupied a few houses. Our room is
above a pub.

The man calls in a low, clear voice: "The Russians—"

At that instant, the window above me shatters. Instinc-
tively, I throw my arms over my head to shield myself from
the rain of glass.

"Take cover!" yells Blöm, our platoon leader. "Grab
your weapons!"

"Those bastards. In the middle of the night!" Wilhelm growls.

I put on my helmet and crouch to the right of the window, straining to listen out into the night. There—more shots. Where are they coming from? How many are there? Will they attack right away and overrun the town? Or is it just a couple of snipers, trying to scare us?

Blöm consults quietly with the watchman. "Do we have a sharpshooter here?" he asks the group.

"Me," I hear myself say. Then I freeze.

He measures me with his gaze. "You're stationed by the window. Keep an eye out. If the enemy approaches—shoot on sight."

I swallow hard, reaching for my weapon. Why couldn't I keep my stupid mouth shut? Outside, a few shots still sound. Mechanically, I load the rifle.

Blöm waves Gerhard over, shoving a hastily-scribbled note in his face. "Take this to the commander and return immediately with new orders. Your buddy here's got your back." He points at me.

I don't even have a chance to catch Gerhard's eye; he's already hurrying out of the room. They've set up the command post in a house across the street, a few yards away. The moon illuminates the entire path. How's Gerhard supposed to make it over there? My veins feel like they're filled with ice.

I kneel to one side of the window, trying to position myself so that I can aim without being seen. Then I wait.

Where are they hiding? I can still hear shots, but there are no shooters in sight. I concentrate on a grove of trees behind the houses. The trees' dark shadows sway gently in the wind, and I think I glimpse someone moving between them—but I can't be sure. There's no trace of Gerhard, either. He probably used the back door and is sneaking through the shadows. At least, I hope that's what he did. I'm clutching my rifle so tightly that my hand hurts.

A scream echoes from the house across the street. Maybe someone was hit.

Blöm curses softly. "They must have snipers, too."

He crawls over to the window. With the butt of his weapon, he knocks the rest of the broken glass from the frame. "Do you see anything?" he asks.

I shake my head. But then a shadow scurries across the street, crouched low, quick as a rabbit. That must be Gerhard. Another shot rings out. The figure falls to the ground.

"Go on, boy. I thought you were a sharpshooter," growls Blöm.

I can't seem to move. Then Gerhard jumps up and runs on. Trembling, I let out the breath I've been holding. Looks like he was only playing dead.

Blöm peers out the window, his rifle pointing into the night. "Little red bastards!" he murmurs. "Where are you hiding? Come out, come out, wherever you are."

My gaze is still riveted on the figure sprinting across the street. He tears open the door to the farmhouse and disappears inside. Gerhard's safe—for now. Blöm shoots once and ducks back down.

"They fight like animals, the Russians," he says. "Wouldn't surprise me if they're nocturnal too."

A shot echoes. Blöm stops mid-sentence and collapses to the floor. He lies there on his stomach, head turned unnaturally to the side. His features go blank as if they're frozen. A dark spot forms on the wooden floor under his head and begins spreading outwards. I can't move, can't even tell if I'm still breathing. My ribs feel like they're being squeezed, like a great weight is pressing them inwards.

Wilhelm creeps over. Slowly, he turns Blöm on his back. Blöm must be heavy, but Wilhelm flips him over effortlessly.

"He's dead," he says, a slight tremor in his voice.

A foot to the right and the bullet could have hit me instead. I gasp for air. Calm down, Anton. Breathe in—and out. In and out. Concentrate on the task at hand.

I look around the room; the whole unit is made up of boys my age. Most of them are cowering in the corners, distraught. I'd really like to join them, but I can't. Gerhard is still outside. He'll be headed back soon with our orders.

Now everything has gone silent. I watch and listen. An owl screeches, and the enemy is lurking…the *enemy*. I turn the word over in my mind. It seems so meaningless. We're shooting at them; they're shooting at us. We're defending our homeland; but they're doing the same thing, aren't they? I remember Uncle Emil's words: *If the Russians pay us back just half of what we've done to them—then Lord have mercy.*

The door to the house across the street opens again. Its squeaking echoes eerily in the silence. I clutch my weapon tighter and concentrate on peering out into the moonlit night.

Gerhard sprints across the street. Another shot sounds. This time, I think I spot the flash of a gun barrel. Over there, between two tall pines.

"Shoot already," Wilhelm hisses beside me. He's crouching on the other side of the window. Turning around quickly, he fires off a shot.

I squint and aim at the trees. Gerhard is still running across the street, unprotected. I should just fire, shoot at the spot where I saw the rifle flash. But my hand feels paralyzed. That's a person between the trees…but it's an emergency, isn't it? You're a soldier, you're just doing your duty; that's what you were trained for…your best friend or a faceless enemy?… Uncle Emil's voice: *It's a sin to use children as instruments of death*…the crumpled bodies in the striped prison uniforms…

My gun drops from my hands. I lean back against the wall and slide towards the floor. Sweat streaks my forehead.

"Coward," Wilhelm snaps contemptuously. He shoots again. I can't tell if he hits anyone.

A second—or maybe a lifetime—later, Gerhard bursts into the room. I'm so relieved, I almost faint.

"The commander says to hold our position. Shoot anything that moves. There aren't many of them out there; otherwise, they would have taken us already."

I spend the rest of the night in a haze. We exchange a few more salvos with the Russians, but eventually, they leave us in peace. Maybe it was only a diversion, meant to scare us.

I sit against the wall and avoid looking at Blöm's lifeless form, which still lies under the window, half hidden in shadow.

"What's up?" Gerhard asks finally, as the first light creeps over the horizon and shines through the broken glass. It's been a while since we've heard shots. He crawls over and sits down next to me.

"Nothing." I stare silently at the floor. Still, I can sense his skeptical expression.

"Are you okay?"

I nod, but I can't look Gerhard in the eye. I let him down. Wilhelm is right—I'm a coward.

"He's been sitting there all night," Wilhelm adds.

At his words, a shiver runs up my spine. Gerhard ignores him, but Braun doesn't give up so easily. He's like a hunting dog who catches his prey and then shakes it between his teeth until it's limp and weak.

"He didn't lift a finger when you were outside. He would've let you die."

"Shut up," says Gerhard.

"Ask him yourself," replies Wilhelm. "Blöm stationed him at the window because he's a sharpshooter. And now Blöm is dead. Köhler didn't fire a single shot. And he calls himself a soldier."

I never wanted to be a soldier, you moron I think, but my cheeks grow hot.

Wilhelm doesn't let up. "He just stared into space— even when they started shooting at you."

I feel like I'm sinking deeper and deeper into the floor.

"So what happened?" Gerhard asks. In his voice, I hear the certainty that something beyond my control kept me from shooting. He trusts me. He trusts me with his life. And I failed him, miserably.

I shrug. "I couldn't...see." The lie makes my throat tighten.

"Bullshit!" Wilhelm cries. "Even I saw where the shots were coming from. You're a coward, that's all. Too weak to shoot. You could've taken at least one of them out."

Gerhard frowns. "Stop with the speeches, Braun," he says. "You're the biggest coward of all of us."

Wilhelm dismisses him scornfully and stalks off to another corner of the room. Then he pulls his helmet down over his eyes and goes to sleep. Who knows how long the quiet will last.

"Thank you," I murmur.

Gerhard is playing with his weapon, cleaning it even though no one ordered us to. "What really happened?" he asks softly.

I continue to avoid his gaze. "No idea. It was…just a difficult situation."

"Don't let Braun rattle you. You know how he is."

"Yes," I whisper. "Except…this time he's right."

Gerhard stops cleaning and looks at me. "What do you mean?"

I don't know why I keep talking. Maybe I want to punish myself. "I had him right in my sights. I saw the gun barrel flash in the bushes. All I had to do was pull the trigger. But I couldn't do it."

I throw him a sidelong glance. The breaking dawn casts a red shimmer across his face. His brow is slightly wrinkled, and his lips form a thin line. He shakes his head. "Whatever. You've saved my ass so many times…" he murmurs. "Maybe I couldn't have done it, either."

I know he doesn't believe it.

My stomach churns, though there's nothing in it. We vowed to stick together, to look out for each other. I made a promise. Tears of anger prick my eyes. I quickly blink them away.

"I couldn't do it…" Again, I try to explain myself, explain it *to* myself.

Gerhard takes a deep breath, then lets it out. "It was just a Russian. I mean—you don't even know him. They're the enemy. It's a war."

"I know."

"I'm your best friend."

"I know."

"It's not like they would hesitate to shoot us."

I nod.

Gerhard opens his mouth to say something more, then closes it again.

We stare silently at our feet. So much goes unspoken between us that the air feels thick as porridge.

Chapter 33

Rushing and gurgling, the dirty brown waters of the Elbe River sluice through the floodplains. Plunging my shovel into the earth, I loosen the top layer of sod with old, dead grass from the previous year and toss it off to the side. It's somewhat easier to dig trenches now that the ground isn't frozen, but at the same time, it's harder, because now we're exhausted and hungry, while back then we were relatively well-rested and fed.

The Russians have supposedly arrived in Dessau, in the middle of Germany, where the Mulde flows into the Elbe. We've been ordered to halt their advance by digging trenches along the bank.

Gerhard, Wilhelm, and the other soldiers in our company are shoveling next to me: a long row of silent figures in field-gray, swinging their shovels in synch like a grotesque, monotonous symphony.

We're doing our best to tamp down the soil with our boots. At the edge of the trench, toward the riverbank, we build makeshift fortifications out of sandbags and sod. Immediately to our left, some soldiers are setting up a machine gun, piling ammunition next to it.

When we're finished, I spread my tarp out in the trench so I don't have to sit on the cold ground. Gerhard sits down next to me, drawing his long legs against his chest;

the ditch is too narrow for him to stretch them out. He wraps his arms around his knees and tries to find a comfortable position for his head. We're in for another long night under the sky, sleeping on the wet, frigid earth, with empty stomachs, uncertain whether and when the Russians will attack.

Bored, and to distract myself from how hungry I am, I load and unload my carbine a few times. As I do, I notice the grime under my fingernails. My uniform is stiff with dirt, my boots caked with dried mud. I don't even notice the rancid smell we give off, anymore. If Luise could see me now...or Mother. They probably wouldn't recognize me.

Despite the tarp, the damp chill creeps through the seat of my pants and spreads through my whole body. I'm shivering. "What I wouldn't give for a hot bath..." I murmur.

Gerhard lifts his head. His eyes light up a little. "And fresh rolls. And cheese, and ham..." He stares dreamily into space. "How can they expect us to fight on empty stomachs?"

"You don't really think we're going to fight, do you, boy?" interjects an older private, crouched down next to the machine gun. He speaks with an unmistakable Berlin dialect.

"What do you mean? Do you think they're not coming?" I ask hopefully.

The man snorts. He's just as filthy as the rest of us. Gray stubble covers his chin, and enormous ears jut out from underneath his cap.

"No, they're coming. You can bet on it. But there won't be much time to fight. We'll be too busy dying." He spits. His tone is contemptuous, like he doesn't give a damn about death.

Wilhelm, who unfortunately is squatting nearby decides to butt in. "That's treason! They'll shoot you for talking like that."

The private gazes at him, calmly, from deep-set eyes. "Be quiet, boy. They won't shoot an old man like me—bullets are far too precious."

"You can't say that either!" insists Wilhelm.

"Don't get your panties in a twist. You young'uns are way too eager to die like heroes. They've sure beat it into you."

Wilhelm opens and closes his mouth a few times, like a fish gasping for air. Finally, he says, "I'm ready to die for the Fatherland."

I'm not buying it anymore.

"I've been on the front for three years, boy. You couldn't even begin to count the number of people I've seen die. But heroes' death—" He holds up a hand, making a circle with his thumb and index finger. "That's how many I've seen of those. Zero. Zip. Zilch." He shrugs, then continues. "Don't misunderstand. Better to die on the battlefield than old and sick at home. But don't think for a moment there's anything heroic about it."

I shiver, and it's not because of the creeping cold of the night. I'm haunted by the faces of our comrades killed in the first air attack...by the countless dead bodies with their empty gazes...by the people burned beyond recognition...when will it all end?

Slowly, darkness falls. Wilhelm has sunk into morose silence. Maybe he's too tired to fight; his willingness to argue has decreased significantly in recent days. Now I can barely remember why I used to hate him. It's all meaningless, anyway.

I rearrange my body to fit the narrow space, using my duffel bag as a pillow. I feel Gerhard's warmth at my side. Though I'm exhausted, it's hard to fall asleep; I'm too anxious about what's to come. But that's nothing new: every evening, I go out like a light, exhausted, but I've never once slept through the night.

If I could only talk to someone about my fear, which clenches at my insides with an iron fist. It's a fear they never warned us about, a fear they never write about in those books about heroes and epic battles. They never told me that fear can make you vomit, or tremble all over, that it can make your heart pound so hard that you think it'll stop beating from sheer exhaustion. I never knew that fear can make you wet yourself, or turn you into an animal, always running away, driven only by instinct. Or it can do the opposite, and make you attack instead, like a berserker.

But I can't talk about it. Not even to Gerhard.

If I survive this, I can survive anything. This thought is the only thing that keeps me going—besides the memory of Luise and my family. I try to recall their faces. I lost their photos somewhere on the run, and I'm afraid I'll forget what they look like if I don't think about them every single day.

When I open my eyes, gray light announces the new day. My stomach tingles nervously, and I bolt upright. Are they going to attack today?

My limbs are stiff from the cold and from my strange sleeping position. Gerhard, whose head rested on my shoulder, is jolted awake when I jerk upright. I shake my legs, which fell asleep at some point. They tingle as the blood flows back into them. Around me, everyone else has begun to stir.

I put on my helmet and make sure I have my weapon on hand. The Russians didn't make their move last night, so now the waiting begins all over again. I peer over the edge of the trench across the floodplain. I can't see much; it's cloudy, and the morning fog still hangs over the meadows. Wilhelm is stacking some hand grenades near him, and the private from Berlin is manning the machine gun.

The waiting is the worst part. I remember what Willi told me about the trenches during the Great War. Back then, soldiers had to live for weeks, even months in these filthy holes.

Then—finally—someone cries, "Heads up! They're coming!"

"Theoretically, we have the advantage," Wilhelm mutters nervously. "They have to come to us. We can pick them off from a safe distance. Plus they have to cross the bridge, which is open, and we have cover."

My weapon weighs a ton. *I'll shoot,* I tell myself. *This time I will shoot. If I have to. If I can save my own life that way, and Gerhard's.* I look over at Gerhard, who's staring fiercely over the edge of the trench. He notices my gaze and thumps me on the shoulder encouragingly.

A rushing noise, barely audible, reaches my ears. Is it the river? It swells, louder and louder. Then I realize it's a roar—a hoard of voices bellowing *"uraaaaaaaaay."* The cry rumbles like thunder over the landscape.

Then, a dark mass emerges out of the fog; it's only just possible to make out individual soldiers. They come rolling toward us like a tsunami, thousands upon thousands of boots thumping dully against the soft ground. They're storming the bridge.

"Fire!"

The machine gun clatters. They're hurtling toward us like a force of nature...and us, with only a few shells...we don't have a chance.

Gerhard gets off a couple of shots, randomly. Wilhelm hurls his grenades as far as he can. A couple of our attackers fall, but it's not enough; instantly, they're replaced with others.

They'll trample us. We'll be crushed. We have to get out of here...

I scream something into Gerhard's ear, but he doesn't hear me, or doesn't understand. He keeps shooting. I try to drag him away by his arm, but it's like he's grown roots. "Let's get out of here!" I yell. "They're going to be here soon."

"Shoot already!" I can hear Wilhelm to my other side. "What the hell's the matter with you? Shoot!"

My heart is racing, and my hands are slick with sweat. Again, I tug at Gerhard's arm. "We've got to go!"

Around us, the first soldiers are making a break for it. They drop their weapons, jump out of the trench, and dash away from the rapidly approaching army. I want to join them, but I can't leave Gerhard behind. "Come on! We don't have a chance in hell!"

Then, suddenly, the machine gun next to us falls silent. We all turn our heads at the same time. The private with the Berlin accent has sunk down onto himself. His head rests almost peacefully on his arms.

"Somebody get to the machine gun!" cries Wilhelm. But the soldier who was responsible for reloading now takes to his heels and flees as well.

"Let's go!" I scream desperately.

Finally, Gerhard snaps out of it. The Russians have stormed the bridge. He lets me pull him up and away.

"Damn it, what are you doing? That's desertion!" bellows Wilhelm as we start running, but I don't let him faze me. He can die there if he wants to.

We climb up over the edge of the trench. Behind us, there's the roar of voices and cracks of gunfire…around us are the other fleeing soldiers. I don't look back.

I've never run so fast in my life. It doesn't matter where as long as it's away from the Russians. We cross fields, meadows, forests, more fields, dash across a road. Eventually, I begin to wonder if the cramp in my side will kill me. How far have we run? I've lost all sense of space and time and only look around to make sure that Gerhard is still with me.

Finally, we slow to a walk. Wheezing, snorting, we drag ourselves, doubled over, through the heath. I'm holding my sides, which burn as though somebody has stabbed me with a red-hot knife. At last, we stop.

Once I'm standing still my legs buckle beneath me like twigs in a storm. I sink down onto the soft marshy ground. Gerhard lands next to me. For a few long minutes, neither of us can do anything but gasp for air. My tongue is glued to my gums. I wipe dry white gunk from my mouth, trembling and retching. But we made it. We're still alive.

When I finally feel like I'm not going to suffocate, I greedily gulp down some water from my canteen and look around. The sun has climbed higher, a gloomy disk in an overcast sky. To our left, soldiers with bowed heads and slumped shoulders are trudging down the road toward a nearby town.

"Man, I can't believe we made it out of there alive," gasps Gerhard. "If you hadn't dragged me with you…"

"Like I would've left you behind." I stare at the ground. Gerhard must really think I'm a coward now. I've run away *again*.

"I don't know what came over me…I shot like…" He takes off his helmet and wipes his eyes.

I hand him a cracker to help him regain some strength.

"The way they ran at us—like barbarians. I totally lost it."

He stares at the cracker for a moment before stuffing it in his mouth. Immediately he looks queasy.

"I don't know if I hit anyone. Did I hit anyone?" He looks at me pleadingly.

"It's hard to say. With the crowd and all," I respond, choking my own cracker down my dry throat.

"The guys in front dropped like flies."

"Yeah."

"What if I did hit one of them…"

"Well, there's nothing you can do about it now." Maybe it's harsh, but I can't think of anything to say to comfort him. I don't want to either. "It's war—you said so yourself."

Gerhard looks like he's going to be sick.

Groaning, I stand up. "Come on, let's keep going."

We drag ourselves to a town a few hundred yards away. I pause in front of the town sign.

"Hundeluft," I say, astonished. "That must be like, what, ten miles from Dessau? Did we really run that far?"

Gerhard shakes his head in disbelief. "Nothing like a little fear of death to get you moving." He seems back to his usual self. "At least we weren't the only ones. Who ran, I mean. They can't court-martial half the company. They still need us."

The residents of Hundeluft are giving out food to fleeing soldiers. We each get a serving of potato soup. As we're looking around for a quiet place to eat, we nearly bump into Wilhelm Braun. He stares at us with a mix of shame, relief, and anger.

"What happened to a soldier fights down to the last cartridge?" I can't help but ask.

Wilhelm shoots me a dark look. "The *Führer* doesn't want to spill precious German blood unless it's absolutely necessary. Under the circumstances, it was clear that we were in an inferior position…and it wasn't wise tactically to…" He trails off.

"It's okay. We all made it out in one piece," says Gerhard. "Come back and sit with us when you've got your soup."

Wilhelm and I gape at Gerhard, both equally astonished. Wilhelm's jaw tightens, but then he nods curtly and heads to the pub for his soup.

I shake my head. "Why so friendly all of a sudden?"

Gerhard shrugs. "He's almost like family, isn't he? The only one from our old troop who's still with us."

I don't think we were ever really in the same troop as Wilhelm, but I don't say anything. He's not so bad, now that he can't act like a bigshot. We'll never be best friends, but he doesn't bother me so much anymore.

Chapter 34

It never ends. Over and over, we join forces with other decimated units. We march until our feet are sore, rest, and clean our weapons…that's important, always cleaning our weapons. Then comes an air raid and we're once again scattered in all directions. We lose our provisions because we're fleeing across rough terrain, across fields and forests, while the supply trucks stay on the road. Our only option is to look for food in abandoned houses and factories. We've become plunderers in our own country.

We're always hungry and always tired. So, so tired. Several times I come close to falling asleep while marching, then my head snaps up, and I realize that my legs are still moving in lockstep. When we do sleep, it's never for long, and it's interrupted by frequent alarms.

I've grown numb. Only one thing matters: staying alive from one day to the next.

Gerhard is just as apathetic as I am. His eyes, once dark and twinkling, have become dull. There's no escaping the cycle. But nobody talks about it, because there's nothing we can do. We can't escape our fate.

Every time there's a lull, we hear rumors. Apparently, the Red Army has started its full-scale attack and is now advancing on Berlin from the south and east. We were ordered to help defend our capital. *How* we're supposed to do that—

without tanks or ammunition, with only our hand-held weapons and limited artillery—is never discussed.

We've just finished another long march. Our platoon trails down the road in a long line of bobbing helmets and shuffling feet. Then a message makes its way down the column: we're going to take a break. There's a town a few miles along the way, with a pub that will give us something to eat. In the distance, I can already make out red-shingled roofs.

Next to me, Gerhard sniffs the air. "Does my nose deceive me, or does it smell like goulash?"

"You're dreaming. The wind is blowing in the wrong direction."

Gerhard sighs. "I don't care what they give us; I could eat anything. Dry bread, cold potatoes…or a knockwurst. A big, fat one…"

If I weren't so thirsty, I'd be drooling by now.

In front of us, the road climbs up a small hill.

"That's it. Up that hill and no further," gasps Gerhard.

"Wimps." Wilhelm has to get his jibes in.

"You keep going by yourself then—all the way to Berlin, for all I care," Gerhard replies testily. That's his stomach talking.

When we round the top of the hill, I can finally see the little town with its inviting houses, not much more than a handful of them lining a single main street. To the right side of the road is a large paddock where the officers' horses are grazing. They arrived long before us in their cars, of course, together with the provisions.

The first members of our platoon have reached the edge of the town and are already dispersing among the houses. Some soldiers are taking off their helmets and dropping down in the grass at the roadside, desperate to rest their feet.

But most are streaming into one of the houses like they get something for free there. Food! My feet speed up by themselves. Now I can smell the soup, too.

"Damn it. We'll never get in there," Gerhard grumbles, spotting the long line in front of the pub.

"We'll be waiting there all night," I mutter. "Come on, let's let them go first. No point in standing around."

Gerhard agrees, reluctantly.

"At least the weather's good." I try to cheer him up. "We can sit and enjoy the sun awhile."

I look for a place that will give us a good view of our surroundings. Call me superstitious, but I don't trust peace and quiet. Not anymore. But I don't mention that to Gerhard. I head toward the west side of town, near the paddock. There's a little embankment on the side of the road that we can lean against and keep the houses and the pub in clear sight.

I sink down in the grass and stretch out my legs. The ground is still cool and damp. Though it's been shining all day, the spring sun isn't at full strength, yet. I take off my helmet and close my eyes.

"I could live with this," says Gerhard. He sounds sleepy. "If I weren't so hungry…"

I sigh. Gerhard folds his arms behind his head and gazes up into the sky. An image appears in my mind of Gerhard last summer, lying in a field, chewing on a straw instead of mucking out the farmer's stalls. How long ago was that? Forever.

He blinks lazily at me, but his eyes are serious.

"Anton," he says softly.

"What?"

"I just…I'm sorry. I don't think you're a coward."

He must see that I'm confused because he continues: "Our argument, a couple of days ago. When the snipers attacked us."

I don't know how long ago that was, anymore. "It's no big deal," I reply.

Still, I feel my ribcage loosen like it was unconsciously clenched.

A fly buzzes around his head, and he waves it away. "Anyway, you're not a coward," he says, trying to sound casual. "Actually, you're the bravest of us all."

I snort. His earnestness worries me—it's unusual for Gerhard. The last couple of weeks since we were drafted must have really affected him.

"Seriously," he assures me. "I've been thinking about it, and...maybe," he licks his cracked lips, "maybe the important thing isn't just getting out of here in one piece; maybe we've also got to..." He trails off, searching for the right words, then shrugs in resignation.

Still, I think I know what he's trying to say.

"What do you want to do when the war's over?" I ask to change the subject. The sun's warmth on my skin is making me sleepy.

"Eat," he responds promptly. "As much as humanly possible. That would be *fan*-tastic."

Food—that's all we ever think about nowadays. "And after that? I mean, what do you want to do with your life?"

Gerhard picks a blade of grass and puts it in his mouth. The end bobs up and down as he talks. "I won't go back to Moltke's farm. If he's still there...if our whole town is still there... Otherwise, no idea. Why are you asking?"

"Once upon a time you wanted to be an aerospace engineer," I say. "Remember?"

"Of course I remember."

"Do you still want to? Be an engineer?"

He considers a moment. "As long as I don't have to build airplanes that drop bombs…"

I watch wisps of cloud float through the clear sky. They're gathering on the horizon, piling into white-gray heaps. I wonder what it's like to fly up there, in the clouds.

"Yeah, that's what I'll do." Gerhard's voice is dreamy. "I'll go back to school and get my *Abitur*…as soon as the war is over."

"But then you'd actually have to work…"

He grins. "You don't think I can work? Granted, I didn't do much on the farm. But that's because I didn't really care for mucking out stalls and milking cows. How 'bout you? Do you want to be a watchmaker?"

"Well…" I say, indecisive.

"If you could do anything—anything you wanted—what would it be?"

"I want to play the violin." The thought pops out before I can stop myself. My ears are hot, and I feel like an idiot. "I know it's crazy. I can't even read music. And I should've started much earlier. I don't even know if I could learn, this late… Even if I started tomorrow—"

"Let's try," Gerhard interrupts.

"Hmm?" I ask.

Gerhard props himself up on his elbows. "As soon as this damn war is over and we're back home, we'll do whatever we want. Nobody'll order us around. And you'll be a famous violinist and I'll be an engineer like von Braun. And I'll design a new plane: a big passenger plane, one that can fly across the whole ocean…" he continues theatrically. Then he stretches a hand out to me. "Deal?"

"Alright," I say, hesitantly, without really believing it, "when the war's over…" I take his hand and shake.

Gerhard lies down and stretches with satisfaction. "And if that doesn't work," he says drowsily, his eyes closed, "we'll both become professional soccer players. That was always my plan B. Sound good?"

I smile and sink back against the embankment, trying to stay awake so I can rouse Gerhard as soon as the line in front of the pub has shrunk.

My eyes open wide and I glance around, confused. Did I doze off? The air seems to crackle with electricity, like a storm is brewing. Clouds have gathered in front of the sun.

Gerhard is awake, too. "The line's shorter now."

My stomach grumbles loudly and contracts painfully around the emptiness inside. I put on my helmet. Gerhard starts to get up, but I place a hand on his arm. "Wait."

I glance back over the edge of the embankment, toward the horses in the paddock. Some of them are lifting their heads. They must be sensing the change in the air as well. Their ears prick up like they heard something.

Gerhard looks at me questioningly. I point back over my shoulder with my thumb, now staring in the direction we came from.

"The horses…", I mutter.

"So?" Gerhard asks after a moment. "Come on! Another few minutes and I'm going to starve to death. No joke."

He extends a hand. I reach for it, hesitantly, letting him pull me to my feet. My whole body tingles weirdly. I look at the horses again and—

A deafening crash splits the noonday silence. The next instant, a pressure wave cuts my legs out from under me.

Chapter 35

The pressure wave throws me to the ground. Gerhard falls down next to me. Dazed, I try to reorient myself.

A shell has torn the roof off the pub and buried the people standing in front of it under an avalanche of debris. For a second, there's an uncanny silence, as if the world has come to a complete stop. Then all hell breaks loose. Soldiers scream and scatter in all directions; the whole town is in an uproar. Shots ring out, and explosions resound.

Gerhard and I climb to the other side of the embankment, which gives us a little cover. I glance around frantically. Where are they coming from? Where should we go?

Then Wilhelm comes running toward us.

"Tanks…hundreds of them," he gasps, leaping over the embankment and landing beside us.

Is he exaggerating as usual? But then I hear the jangling of chains and the slowly-swelling hum of engines. Another shell explodes against a nearby barn, sending splinters flying through the air. I dive to the ground, throwing my arms over my head for protection. The second the dust has settled, I jump up again.

"They're coming at us from all sides," Gerhard bellows in my ear.

"Damn Russians. They snuck up on us," Wilhelm yells, his face contorted with fear.

Some of the tanks are racing over the hilltop and rumbling along the road toward the town. Their turrets are spitting fire. Others are cutting across country at terrifying speed. We can't escape through the town where one explosion follows the next. There's only one way out. "The paddock!" I shout. "Across the paddock!"

I sprint away. With one effortless leap, I'm over the fence. Gerhard follows close behind, but Wilhelm is hesitating. The horses are panicking, galloping across the paddock like they're being pursued by furies. Eyes wide with fear, nostrils flaring, they're trying to escape the chaos and the noise. Their hooves throw dust and sod through the air.

"They won't trample you," I call to Wilhelm. I know something about horses from the times I helped out our local farmer—or at least, I hope I do.

He peers at me skeptically, but then his dread of what's following us seems to outweigh his unease, and he jumps the fence.

I dash through the galloping herd, caught up in a flurry of bullets, dust, and hooves. But the horses are avoiding us like I thought, and they offer a little cover from the machine guns. We head toward the grove of birches on the other side of the paddock, though I can tell it's barely thick enough to hide in. I've almost reached it when I hear a cry behind me.

I turn around and see Gerhard stumble. He falls onto all fours. The horses race past him in a blind panic, obscuring my view.

"Gerhard!" Frantically, I search for a gap in the galloping herd, trying to get to him.

Wilhelm rushes past me, finally reaching the trees, but I run back toward Gerhard, slithering the last stretch on my knees. Gerhard is trying to stand up. He looks pale, his face a grimace of pain.

"What is it?" I ask breathlessly.

Then I notice he's clamping his hands around his left thigh. A dark spot is spreading quickly across the fabric of his uniform. I fight my growing nausea and grab him by the arm, trying to pull him up.

"Let's get to the trees. I can help you there."

Gerhard stands up, putting all his weight on his right leg. The machine guns continue to hammer out shots behind us. Grenades detonate with a deafening crack like they're right at our side.

I place Gerhard's arm around my shoulder and hold him as tightly as I can. His weight pulls me down. Step by step he limps forward, sweat running down his face. The trees are just a few yards in front of us. But then Gerhard puts too much weight on his injured leg. He cries out in pain, falls, and threatens to slide out of my arms. I lose my balance.

Suddenly, Wilhelm appears between the trees. He seems to be wrestling with himself. His eyes dart back and forth, and he's biting his lip—though whether in fear or frustration, I can't tell. Finally, he runs toward us with powerful strides, grabs Gerhard's other arm and effortlessly pulls him up.

Gerhard between us, we hurry toward the forest. A few yards in, his strength gives out and he sinks down. I stop and help him slide to the ground so he can lean back against a birch trunk and rest.

He has his injured leg stretched out, the right one bent. His forehead's damp with sweat, his cheeks paper-white, and his eyes are rolling back in his head. I'm afraid he's slipping away from me.

Wilhelm slaps him across the face with the back of his hand. Gerhard gasps and his gaze clears. Any other time, I would have beat Braun up for that, but right now I'm grateful.

I kneel down in front of Gerhard and force myself to examine his shot-up leg. There's an ugly hole in the fabric of his uniform, scorched around the edges and soaked with blood. Underneath, more blood is gushing out, flowing onto the soft, mossy forest floor.

"Shot clean through," murmurs Wilhelm, as I fight another wave of nausea. "He got lucky."

"Lucky?" Gerhard's voice is weak. "Do you know how much this hurts?"

"It could have hit you anywhere. And at least this way it's not stuck in your flesh."

I try to search my pockets for gauze, but my fingers are trembling so violently that I can hardly undo the button. Finally, I succeed and tear out a pressure bandage. All at once, my thoughts go quiet. *Just concentrate on the next task. Bind the wound, get Gerhard out of here, look for an orderly.* I lift Gerhard's leg to wrap it. Though I handle him as gently as possible, he digs his fingers into the ground, wincing with pain. I place the bandage over the wound and tighten it to stop the bleeding.

Wilhelm's peering out from behind a tree, keeping a look-out. "More tanks," he croaks. "Coming at us from all sides. We've got to get out of here!"

Gerhard tries to stand up again. I grip him under one arm while Wilhelm takes his other side. As we carry him, Gerhard attempts to keep the weight off his bandaged leg. We stumble and slide across the forest floor, which is covered in leaf litter from the previous fall.

Other soldiers in German uniforms are running past us, scattering madly before the Russian attack. I can hear the humming of the tanks catching up to us. They're faster than we are, with Gerhard between us.

Directly in front of us, an explosion tears the earth open and sends the thin trunk of a young birch flying through the air. The pressure wave knocks Gerhard over, and we're pulled down with him.

They're firing into the grove. On all sides, trees are falling like matchsticks. Wood explodes, and men are screaming. Behind us, somebody falls, probably wounded. But when he sees a tank rolling toward him, beating a path through the forest, his eyes grow wide. He drags himself forward with his arms and crawls across the ground, pulling his legs behind him. He's using all his strength, but I can see he won't make it.

I crouch on the ground, numb, staring at the crawling man behind us: a snail trying to escape an approaching car. I can't help him. With horror, I watch as the tank closes and the man realizes he won't escape.

"Let's go," cries Wilhelm, but I can't move. "They'll crush us!" His voice is hysterical. He drops Gerhard's arm and bolts away.

The tank has reached the soldier. It continues on like nothing's there—right over the man's legs. There's a crack and a crunching sound. The soldier unleashes a bloodcurdling scream that eats into my soul like rot. I want to scream, too, but I can't make a sound.

"Anton, run. I can't…I'm just holding you back." Gerhard can hardly breathe from the pain.

My head is spinning and it takes a while for the meaning of Gerhard's words to sink in.

"Don't even think about it," I say, tugging at his arm.

"I'm too slow," he mutters, gritting his teeth.

The tank rolls on, searching for its next victim. Its machine guns pound; shots tear up the soft ground in front of us, narrowly missing me. I drag Gerhard forward, cursing Wilhelm for leaving us in the lurch.

Gerhard stumbles again, his good leg catching on a tree root. I try to load him onto my back. He's not that heavy because he's so thin. Still, he's taller than I am and his long legs drag along the ground. After a few steps, I trip and lose my grip.

"Run, Anton!" Gerhard cries again.

"Never!"

I feel the blood pounding in my ears. But I'm not leaving without him. I swore I wouldn't.

"Never," I repeat. I don't even recognize my own voice.

I duck as the next blast sprays us with clumps of earth and leaves. With effort, I force myself to turn around. The tank is close. So close.

Then I notice the *Panzerfaust*, just an arm's length away. A soldier must have dropped it as he fled. I grab it and point the heavy weapon at the approaching monster.

I have to save Gerhard's life. I can't fail again...I promised myself to protect him.

I launch the warhead towards the tank. The kickback sends me flying and I hurtle backward into Gerhard's leg. He cries out, but the tank comes to an abrupt halt. The missile is stuck between the chains. In my excitement, I didn't manage to hit the turret or another weak point.

The next moment, the warhead detonates, throwing the enormous vehicle onto its side. The hatch pops open and Russians stream out, yelling at the top of their lungs.

I grab Gerhard by the shoulders and shove him roughly behind a thick tree.

He's breathing heavily, trying to suppress a groan. I don't dare to peer out from behind the trunk and see which way our enemies are running. Another explosion nearly shatters my eardrums. Seems like the whole tank has blown up now. Metal pieces rain down from the sky.

I place my hand on Gerhard's shoulder. "I'm not leaving you, got it? Not even if it's ten miles to the next town and I have to carry you the whole way."

He's too weak to protest.

I try to hoist him onto my back again, even though my legs are trembling and can barely support my own weight. Then, all at once, a Russian soldier is looming in front of us.

Chapter 36

I hold my breath. The Russian has emerged from the bushes to our right. His face is soot-blackened, but I can tell that he's still young, not much older than we are. He freezes when he sees us, staring at us fearfully. The carbine he carries is not pointing at us. My own gun is also hanging on my shoulder, unused.

For a few seemingly endless moments we stare into each other's eyes. His gaze travels from me to Gerhard, who is holding his bandaged leg and wheezing. Then he says something in a language I can't understand: guttural, choppy sounds.

Very slowly, I raise my hands. I hardly dare to breathe, and my heart is beating fast. "We won't hurt you if you don't hurt us," I say, trying to keep my voice level.

The Russian utters something else incomprehensible. Then he retreats in the direction he came from, without lifting his carbine, but not taking his eyes off us. I don't move. He has almost disappeared into the bushes when a shot rings out. Almost instantaneously, the soldier collapses like a discarded marionette, an ugly little hole in his forehead.

"No!" I scream, looking around for the shooter.

But I can't worry about the Russian; we have to keep moving. And I know that I can't help him anyway.

I load Gerhard onto my back again and trudge on. One foot in front of the other. Bullets whistle around us, pounding against tree trunks and the ground, but I keep moving, hoping for a miracle. I have no idea where I'm going. I've lost all sense of direction, but it doesn't matter. Just away from the noise, away from this hell.

Gerhard's arms are wrapped tightly around my chest. I struggle to breathe. My load gets heavier and heavier with each step until I can barely lift my feet off the ground. Still, I drag myself onward.

"Anton," whispers Gerhard, close to my ear. "You won't get anywhere...not like this... Let me down."

I ignore him. Even if I'd wanted to answer, I couldn't have: I need all of my air just to breathe.

"You won't make it...."

"Stop!" I exclaim, so angry now that I find my second wind.

My grip keeps loosening. Some German soldiers are running toward us. Did I run the wrong way? Wilhelm is with them. He sees us and dashes over.

"They're coming—from the west. We're surrounded!" he bellows.

Finally, my legs give way. There's nothing I can do but make sure that Gerhard slides to the ground as gently as possible. I don't even have the strength left to call Wilhelm a cowardly dog.

"There's no choice," says Gerhard. "You have to go on...without me. Then you can survive, at least."

His words cause my anger to flare again.

"Help me!" I yell at Wilhelm. He hesitates noticeably, glancing around and looking like he'd rather run away. But then he nods curtly.

Ignoring his protests, we support Gerhard between us by making a seat with our hands. We edge around a dead soldier, whose eyes seem to stare right at us, and run toward the east, where I hope the tanks haven't gotten to, yet.

My hands keep slipping and my arms are slowly going numb. Yet, I struggle forward. Another shot sounds but there's no time to turn around. Suddenly, Gerhard's arm falls from my shoulders. He tumbles backward. Shit! I sink to the ground and crawl toward him. As I bend over him, his right hand jerks upward, clutching my shirt.

"Anton." I can barely hear him—it's more a gurgle than a word.

"Gerhard?" I gaze into his wide, horror-stricken eyes. Bile rises in my throat. "What is it? We —"

Then I see the dark, wet spot spreading across his chest.

"Anton," wheezes Gerhard. "What…happened…?" I can hardly make out the words.

I loosen his hand from my collar and stare at the spot. "It's…not so bad," I lie.

"Help, he's been shot!" I bellow at Wilhelm, though I have no idea if he's still with us. "I need bandages! Now!"

I press my hands on the wound, trying to stop the bleeding. Gerhard's face is getting paler by the second as if all the color is being sucked out of it.

"Come on! Bandages!" I scream again, so loudly that I'm sure my voice echoes throughout the entire forest.

I turn back to Gerhard. "Hold on. We'll fix you up." My fingers trembling, I try to unbutton his uniform jacket.

From far away, I can still hear the screams of the battle raging around us. I don't care. Finally, I manage to get the jacket off. I feel around for my own bandages. Damn it! I left them back where I first patched up his leg.

Gerhard shakes his head weakly. His eyes have lost their spark. "Anton…don't leave me here…"

"No," I whisper, feeling completely helpless.

Now I can see the full extent of his wound: a shot through the chest. I don't know what to do. I'm not a medic. I don't even have any bandages. My lungs feel as if an iron fist is squeezing every ounce of air from them. I'm dizzy.

"Anton," Gerhard whispers again. His voice is so weak that I have to put my ear close to his mouth to understand him.

"I'm not going anywhere without you," I promise, clasping his hand, which is smeared with his blood.

Then, suddenly, Gerhard smiles. It's a peaceful smile, undistorted by pain. His eyes focus on something beyond my head, something only he can see. He seems…happy…like he used to be, before the war.

"Don't forget…our deal," he breathes.

I read the words from his lips. Something drips into my eye and I blink. It's hot like hell beneath my helmet.

Gerhard, I want to say, but no sound comes out. His smile droops. He coughs. A thin trickle of blood runs out of the corner of his mouth.

I push myself off the ground, looking around. Wilhelm is standing nearby. "Help me," I croak, though I feel like screaming.

Wilhelm's mouth is hanging open. He stares down at Gerhard with a mixture of fear and revulsion. Then, slowly, he shakes his head. "There's no point." His voice is just as hoarse as mine.

I stare at him blankly. His gaze is hard as he nods at Gerhard.

I look down at my best friend. His eyes are closed. The trickle of blood on his pale skin looks like a thin red hair, which I want to pull from his mouth.

"He's dead, Anton." Wilhelm's voice sounds as if it's coming from a great distance.

"Don't say that!" I shake Gerhard by the shoulder. "Wake up! Come on, we're almost there…we'll find a medic," I plead.

"We have to keep going. They'll be here soon." Wilhelm lays a hand on my shoulder. I wheel around as if he's bitten me.

A stabbing pain shoots through my right fist, and I realize I've punched Wilhelm in the face. He tumbles backward, holding his nose, which is gushing blood.

I stare at my throbbing fist. It seems to belong to someone else, like I have no control over it. Then I feel a completely different kind of pain, deep in my chest, like something in there is tearing. *Gerhard.* Dazed, I bend over him. His ribcage isn't moving. I put my ear up to his nose. He isn't…no. It can't be.

"Gerhard!" The word comes out in an almost sob.

Suddenly, Wilhelm is behind me, pulling me up by the arm. "We have to go. You heard what he said. We have to save ourselves."

"We can't just leave him here," I say, my voice breaking.

Wilhelm bends over Gerhard and tears the dog tag from his neck. When he breaks it in half to take one of the two identical pieces with him, something deep inside me breaks as well. No! What's he doing? Gerhard still needs his identification! I want to throw myself at Wilhelm, but there's no strength left in my body

"Come on!" Wilhelm yells.

I can't tear my eyes from the shot wound on Gerhard's chest. The bleeding has stopped.

The woods around me start spinning until I get nauseous. Wilhelm yanks me to my feet and drags me along behind him. I feel like I'm being pulled by a higher power that I can't resist. A bitter taste stings the back of my throat. I look back over my shoulder as we're running.

Gerhard's still lying there.

No, it's not Gerhard anymore. It's a lifeless shell that once held my friend. My friend, who just a few moments ago was moving, speaking, smiling at me. Now he disappears between the tree trunks.

The world blurs before my eyes, but this scene is edged into my mind forever. I've left him behind.

Chapter 37

Finally, Wilhelm stops in front of a gravel quarry several hundred yards across. Up till now, I've let myself be dragged along without any sense of what's around us or where we're running, seeing nothing but Gerhard's lifeless body.

As soon as Wilhelm lets go of me, I bend forwards, hands on my knees, gasping for air. Then my whole body starts shaking and everything inside of me contracts, like my stomach wants to force its way out of my body. I vomit on the gravel, wishing I could rid myself of the image this way, and of this feeling of emptiness inside.

Once the fit is over, I feel completely drained. I sink to my knees, staring at my hands. The right one is still smeared with blood. Gerhard's blood.

"Better?" asks Wilhelm.

I'd almost forgotten that Braun is here.

"Better?" I whisper hoarsely, my throat burning. "How could I possibly be better? How can things ever get *better*? He's dead."

"Alright," says Wilhelm. He sounds tired.

But I can't leave it alone.

"What do you mean, 'alright'? Nothing's alright. It's never going to be alright again. Everything is shit!"

With wobbly knees, I haul myself upright and pace madly up and down the edge of the gravel pit, screaming incomprehensibly. My feet kick at everything they can reach. Pebbles go flying through the air. Whole avalanches of stones loosen under my feet and slide down the edge of the pit, plummeting into the puddle of water that has formed at the bottom.

"It's all your fault!" I bellow at Wilhelm, who watches me warily. "You cowardly maggot! You should be lying there, not him. If you hadn't run away…"

Even through the red veil of my fury and anguish, I know what I'm saying doesn't make sense. If I'm going to blame someone, it should be myself. I wasn't able to protect my best friend.

Wilhelm just looks at me, his jaw clenched. It's like I'm running against a stone wall. That makes me even angrier. I storm toward him until I'm no more than half an arm's length away. We stare into each other's eyes, his gaze just as fixed and penetrating as mine. He still doesn't say anything. His face is covered in dirt and scratches, and blood is drying under his nose where I hit him.

All at once, I feel the air go out of me, like a popped balloon. Nothing's left of me but an empty shell. Trying to push down another wave of nausea, I turn back to the pit and gaze across it. It must be almost a quarter mile wide. We're alone in the middle of nowhere, far away from where we were attacked.

What happened to Gerhard? To his…remains? Just thinking about it makes me sick again.

I can feel the weight of the carbine on my shoulder. Suddenly, I want to be rid of it. I can't do this anymore. It's insanity, and it's all for nothing. I tear the gun from my shoulder and start stuffing it with cartridges. Stupid fucking thing; it couldn't save my friend. I need to get rid of it, right now, and erase the memory of everything it's brought with it.

My first shot flies, unaimed, into the gravel pit. The butt of the gun slams backward into my shoulder, but I barely notice.

I shoot again, this time into the water below. It makes a satisfying splash. And again. The shots ring out in the empty quarry. You can probably hear them a long ways off, but I don't care.

"What are you doing?" I feel Wilhelm's hand on my shoulder and turn around, my gun still poised to shoot.

He jumps back like there's a lion in front of him and throws up his hands. "I just asked what you were doing," he repeats nervously.

"I can't do this anymore!" I scream. "I won't! I won't do it! They can come and get me. I'm outta here. I'm quitting!"

I aim the weapon back at the pit so I can fire off the last shots and reload.

"At least keep the noise down," pleads Wilhelm between shots. But I notice that he no longer dares approach me.

My only answer is to fire off another clip. Then I remove the hand grenade from my belt and pull out the pin. I glance back at Wilhelm, who's staring at me wide-eyed. "I don't need these stupid things anymore."

He takes another step backward, pointing to the grenade in my hand, which I've almost forgotten. Forcefully, I hurl it away from us; it explodes mid-flight. Another grenade follows. I aim for the water at the bottom of the pit, wanting to see it splash.

This is great, some tiny, hidden part of me thinks, the last part that can still enjoy this—enjoy anything at all.

"Oh, what the hell," I hear Wilhelm sigh after another minute has passed. To my surprise, he moves up next to me and hurls one of his own grenades into the pit, loosening an avalanche of stones.

"Let's see who can throw the farthest," he says. He grits his teeth and pulls another pin out. As he does so, I notice he's still carrying a *Panzerfaust*. When he's finished throwing, I point to it.

"Do you still need that?"

He stares at me, trying to determine whether I've gone completely insane. Then he shrugs and hands me the weapon.

I place the heavy tube against my shoulder. Wilhelm just watches, shaking his head.

"That's crazy, Köhler." But I can hear the slightest trace of admiration in his voice.

When the anti-tank warhead hits the quarry, a huge fountain of water, sand, and rocks shoots up into the air.

"Awesome," I murmur with grim satisfaction. Fireworks. For Gerhard.

Wilhelm and I fire off his remaining ammo. As I reach for the last grenade, I hear the cracks of shots behind us, four times in quick succession.

I freeze, glancing around. About fifty yards away three figures have emerged from the same grove of trees we came from: men in German uniforms wearing the sickle-shaped tag around their necks. MPs. One of them has raised his pistol and must have fired into the air to attract our attention.

"Shit," Wilhelm mutters.

Chapter 38

"Stop! Put your hands up!" cries the MP who fired the shots. He lowers his weapon and points it straight at us.

I'm surprised to find that I'm completely calm. So what if they caught us and court-martial us? It doesn't matter anymore.

The three watchdogs approach. We don't move a muscle until they're standing directly in front of us. The heaviest one, who seems to be the leader of the bunch, squints at us through narrow eyes.

"What were you scamps doing?" he demands.

I remain silent. There's no point in denying. Wilhelm doesn't say anything either, but I think it's because he's terrified.

"I asked you a question, soldiers!" bellows the MP.

By now I'm tired of all the yelling, so I say, "We were disposing of our ammunition."

"I can see that. And may I ask why?" he snarls.

I fall silent again. The doughy face of the MP reddens. "Don't you know what's at stake here? Execution. I could shoot you on the spot."

I try to suppress a petulant shrug.

"How old are you?" he snaps.

"Sixteen."

"Which unit?"

Not waiting for an answer, he grabs the dog tag hanging from my neck and checks the inscription.

"Our company was…decimated," Wilhelm grits out, as another one of the watchdogs inspects his tag. "The Russians…they took us by surprise. Tanks, infantry. We—"

"So you turned on your heels and ran for it?" the MP interrupts. "You wasted your ammunition here, instead of using it to fight?"

Nice try, Wilhelm, I think, still feeling detached.

"Come on! Let's go!" The MP grabs us each by the arm and drags us forward.

"Aren't we going to shoot them?" one of his henchmen, a tall, thin man, asks. "They're standing in front of a pit and everything." He grins, flashing crooked teeth.

"We have to take them to the commander first," growls the leader.

"Why?" the other man asks.

"Because they're minors. Are you questioning my orders?"

I don't get it. The MPs have the right to shoot defectors anywhere, on the spot, no questions asked. But the thought disappears from my mind as rapidly as it came. I still don't feel like any of this is really happening. As if I were in a dream, where nothing I say or do is important. They can do with us whatever they want.

We stumble across a field and toward a small forest, driven by the MPs. The soldiers take large strides, and we're so exhausted that we can barely keep up. Luckily we don't have to go far—these cowardly dogs wouldn't have been able to hear us if they hadn't been close in the first place. It's not as if MPs are ever in the thick of battle.

They lead us into their camp, where a provisional command post has been set up. It's here that the commander makes decisions and communicates them with the individual battalions. I'm surprised that they even still have that kind of organization. We stop in front of a hastily assembled wooden shed. It has a flat roof made of heavy beams and camouflaged with a mat of branches and military tarp. The MP knocks on the door, and an officer opens. He's unshaven, and his eyes are weary.

"*Herr Hauptmann*, we detained two deserters as they were disposing of their ammunition in a quarry. I'm here to turn them over to you."

The *Hauptmann* shoots the MP a surprised glance, then looks at Wilhelm and me. "What? Alright, I'll take down minutes. Then you can state your charges." He sounds disinterested, distracted.

"Remove their tags and take them away," the MP calls to his lackeys.

One of them grabs me by the scruff and shoves me behind the shed, where he pushes me to the ground. Wilhelm lands heavily next to me. Our guards stand in front of us, legs splayed, pistols drawn. The one who grabbed me scowls. He was probably excited at the prospect of shooting me. But maybe he'll still get his chance. Not even this thought can jostle me from my stupor.

Sitting up so I can lean against the wooden wall of the shelter, I stare straight ahead, with an empty gaze and an empty mind, hardly noticing the cold and damp of the forest floor, even as it seeps through my pants. I listen to the melancholy song of a single blackbird, the tapping of a lone woodpecker. Most of the birds still haven't come back from their migrations. I might never hear them again.

In the silence and inactivity, I can't ignore that emptiness inside me anymore. It's as if a tank grenade blasted right through my chest and left a gaping hole. I'm like a watch without gears: a useless housing. Is Father's watch still running? I don't have the strength left to pull it out. My heartbeat and breathing speed up as pain overwhelms me again. I try to fight it, clenching my fists in my lap. Why am I still alive when Gerhard…? *Maybe not for much longer.* The thought is almost comforting.

"None of this would have happened if…" Wilhelm hisses next to me.

I flinch.

"We ran for miles to escape the Russians, and now…" His voice breaks.

Wearily, I turn toward him. His eyes are red, and I see the fear in them.

I don't answer but stare away into the distance. I don't know how much time passes. The sun has sunk low in the sky, nearly reaching the top of the trees. Its blinding rays stab my eyes. The MP steps out of the officer's shed and confers with the other two. I can't make out what they're saying, but I'm not really trying to, either. It doesn't surprise me when the MP snaps at us to get up and follow him.

"Where are we going?" Wilhelm dares to ask.

One of the watchdogs drives a fist into his lower back, prodding him on. "Shut up and stop asking questions."

"Save it for your last words," says the other.

I stare at my feet.

"I demand a hearing!" cries Wilhelm. "My father—"

"I said, *shut—up*." Wilhelm stumbles again as the MP kicks him.

"There already was a hearing. The verdict has been passed, and now we're going to carry it out," their leader drawls, sounding almost bored.

"My father is *Hauptsturmführer* in the SS. If he hears that you—"

A right hook to the cheek cuts off Wilhelm's protest. He stumbles sideways.

"Move! Backs against the trees!" commands the MP. A rough hand shoves me so my back and head crash against the trunk of a young pine. The resulting numbness is a welcome feeling. Everything is happening in a daze.

Wilhelm is shouting something that sounds like, "You can't do this! They'll get you! My father—"

He starts howling without control as the two MPs stand in front of us, bracing their weapons against their shoulders. "It was his idea…" the words fade away in a sob.

"Are those your last words?" asks the MP sharply. "Or do you want to say a prayer?" His voice cuts through the fog in my brain.

A sharp click echoes through the forest as the guards release their safeties. They aim directly at us.

Chapter 39

"Last chance," says the MP, exchanging a glance with his men, who have their guns at the ready. "Do you want to say anything else?"

"Yes," I pipe up. It's the first thing I've said since I arrived in camp. All eyes swivel in my direction; even Wilhelm stops his hysterical sobbing.

"Okay, but make it quick," snarls the MP, hooking his thumb in his belt loops and looking around impatiently, as if something might interfere with his plan.

My head is empty. Now I'm wondering why I spoke up at all. An ancient survival instinct? Or maybe I was playing for time—but to what end? So I could prolong this torment even more?

Hesitantly, I begin to speak. My tongue feels like it doesn't belong to me. "I just wanted to say…he's right. Wilhelm is right. It was all my idea. I took his gun so I could waste his ammunition. And his father really is in the SS. *Hauptsturmführer* Braun. You should let him go, if you…"

"That's enough," interrupts the MP, but he's frowning. Maybe I've confused him—it's the best I can hope for.

When he hesitates, I continue, "I made him do it. Wilhelm was always a loyal soldier. He loves the Fatherland more than anybody—" The MP cuts me off with a wave of his hand. In the twilight between the trees, I can't see his face, but the gesture seems to mean something to the other watchdogs, who point their guns at us once more, having lowered them during my speech.

I swallow. Wilhelm has fallen silent next to me. So we'll die together. Who would've thought I'd be spending my last moments with Wilhelm Braun.

"Ready!" calls the leader of the MPs.

I squeeze my eyes shut tightly and imagine Gerhard… Luise's smile…Mother's sad eyes when she learns about my death…

"Stop!" cries a sonorous voice, which carries perfectly to us, though I can't see the owner of it yet. "Don't shoot. Anyone who disobeys will answer to me."

My eyes snap open. I know that voice!

"*Herr Major*?" The MP gives a signal, and the others lower their guns. One of them looks almost relieved.

A man steps out from between two tree trunks across from us, into the clearing. Darkness is falling, but even in the twilight, I can see that his hair is white as snow.

"*Hauptmann* Segeler showed me the report," says *Major* Schirmer. "And I have some questions that need answering. These two are coming with me."

"But, *Herr Major*…"

"Now." He says it calmly, but with such firmness that it's impossible to argue.

The MP wavers for a moment. In the field, he would have had the right to shoot us right then and there. Here, he answers to the commander.

He motions to his lackeys to grab us again, but the major waves him off. "I'll take it from here. Thank you!" He gives the watchdogs a sharp look..

The major orders us to follow him. Confused, I stumble along behind Wilhelm. I never would have expected to meet *Major* Schirmer here, or that he would swoop in and save us at the last second. I'm amazed at how relieved I feel, the way my knees are trembling. Maybe I cared more than I thought…

We reach the command post. The major holds open the door so we can enter his shed. The inside is lit by a single gas lamp on a crate in the corner; next to it is a field telephone.

The slapdash wooden building isn't even tall enough for Wilhelm to stand up straight. He has to bow his head slightly. The major sits down behind a folding table and pushes aside a map. On the table are two metal dog tags, mine and Wilhelm's.

"So, you're the deserters." He peers up at us—at me in particular—as if he were looking over a pair of non-existent glasses.

"*Major* Schirmer," I stutter. My voice is hoarse, and I have to clear my throat twice.

"You're Anton Köhler and Wilhelm Braun, correct?"

Wilhelm clicks his heels. "Yes, *Herr Major.*"

Does he recognize me? He could have forgotten; there were so many recruits in the barracks.

The major nods to himself and pulls out a sheet of paper. With a pen, he traces along the lines as he reads them, then measures us with another long glance.

"You were detained while AWOL, for firing your weapons in the absence of the enemy. Is that correct?"

"Yes, *Herr Major,*" replies Wilhelm, less enthusiastically. I can tell that he's itching to explain himself. But he doesn't want to incur the major's wrath by speaking out of turn.

The major pauses, then looks directly at me. I see recognition in his eyes. "Surely those were just shooting exercises, right boys?" he asks softly.

"Well…" I stammer. He raises his eyebrows expectantly. "Y-yes, *Herr Major*…"

He turns to Wilhelm. "Yes, *Herr Major*," Wilhelm replies. By now he has pulled himself together. "We were…trying to improve our accuracy."

"I thought so." The major's face remains completely impassive. "It's a good thought, boys, but we have to conserve ammunition. That should be clear to you by now."

"Yes, *Herr Major*," responds Wilhelm eagerly.

The major picks up our dog tags and tosses them to us. I catch mine, clutching the cold metal plate in my fist. That reminds me of Gerhard's half-tag. Wilhelm must still have it. Should we give it to the major?

Schirmer gets up from his seat and walks around the table until he's standing right in front of us. "Effective immediately, you're both assigned to a new unit. Your previous one seems to have been obliterated. They tell me that's been happening a lot lately. Nobody will be asking any questions…"

I nod with mixed feelings. I thought it was over. Now I have to put that little metal thing around my neck once more, have to keep going…but I won't fight anymore. All I want is to get through this, somehow. The war has to end at some point.

"*Herr Major*?" I have to clear my throat again. "I need…to make a report…" I find myself unable to continue and shoot Wilhelm a helpless glance.

He seems to understand and begins fishing around in his breast pocket. When I see him clenching something in his fist, my throat closes up. But Wilhelm relieves me of the need to explain myself. He opens his hand and shows the major the half-tag.

"*Herr Major*, sir, I regret to inform you that Gerhard Engler has fallen in battle against the Red Army. We were unable to remove his body from the combat area."

Major Schirmer takes a long look at the semicircular piece of metal. Then he places a hand on my shoulder. I'm trembling. The major doesn't say anything, and I'm grateful. I don't want to hear the usual empty phrases, that Gerhard died a hero's death, that he's sorry. Words can't change anything. Only after a few moments do I summon the strength to meet the major's bright blue eyes. There, I see everything that remains unspoken.

"Is there someone I should notify?" he asks.

I shake my head. "He was an orphan," I whisper.

Major Schirmer nods sympathetically. He squeezes my shoulder once more before letting me go.

"Boys," he says. "I don't want to see you here again, understand? Go on now, and don't let yourselves get caught." His face is grave.

Wilhelm salutes. "*Jawohl, Herr Major*. Thank you, sir."

I nod. Then I turn on my heels and leave.

Chapter 40

The night in camp stretches out endlessly. Some soldiers sit in front of their tents, drinking. I remain off to the side, unable to sleep. This day feels like it's lasted for years, even though it's only been a few hours—hours in which everything changed, hours that left me no time to reflect. I can't believe that Gerhard was still with me this morning, and now he's not.

Finally, I head into the forest, claiming I need to pee. I want to be alone, away from the noise of the camp, away from the much-too-happy voices. Though the faint moonlight is my only illumination, my feet find their way across the stones and roots of the forest floor almost on their own. Slowly, the voices fade away until only the sounds of the nighttime forest remain. The rushing of trees in the wind, a soft cracking of underbrush as some nocturnal animal scurries away, the hoot of a small owl.

In front of me, the moonlight illuminates a small stream, a shimmering silver ribbon threading its way through the wood. I kneel down on the bank, dangling my right hand into the clear, cold water. I can still feel Gerhard's blood on it. I scrub it with my left hand until it grows numb in the icy water. Not enough! I drag my hand across the pebbles in the streambed, but they've been washed smooth and it's not painful enough either. Finally, I scrape the back of my hand across a rough stone on the bank until my knuckles burn and little strips of skin are hanging off them.

"What are you doing?"

I jump and whirl around. Wilhelm is standing behind me; I didn't even hear him coming. He's the last person I want to see right now.

"Go away, Braun." My voice is so detached that even I can't take myself seriously. Neither does Wilhelm, apparently. He looks down at me, arms crossed.

"What are you doing?" he repeats.

"Washing my hands. They're all bloody," I mumble.

"Well, what did you expect, washing them like that?"

I examine my sore knuckles. "Go away," I say again.

"Make me," replies Wilhelm, crouching down on a rock beside me. "I have just as much right to sit here as you do."

I feel the anger flaring up in me again. At first, I want to get up and chase him away, but then I stop caring, my anger evaporating as quickly as it came. I place my left hand on my shredded knuckles and press my fists against my chest.

"You always were a windbag," I say, but without much feeling.

"And you were always a wimp."

I don't even have enough energy left to be provoked by him. "What do you want, Braun? Why do you keep trailing me like a stray dog?"

"Me? Following you?" Wilhelm sputters. "I got you out of there, didn't I? Maybe I should've just let you die like…?"

"Shut up!" I scream. "It should've been you lying there! You just went along with it. With this whole stupid war…you were the one who was so eager to fight for the Fatherland. You couldn't wait to sign up."

Wilhelm is silent. In the moonlight, reflected off the water, I can see his nostrils flaring. I stare at the stream again, plunging my wounded hand into it. It doesn't help—no physical pain can erase the pain of loss.

"It was my father who wanted that." Wilhelm's soft, almost defiant voice interrupts my thoughts again.

"Your father! He's one of the..." I bite my tongue.

"One of the what?" Wilhelm snaps.

I hesitate for only a second. I shouldn't say this, but then again, who cares if he gives me away at this point? "One of the ones who started all of this," I say bitterly. "It's his fault we're in this mess. And that Gerhard—"

"What the hell do you know about my father?" growls Wilhelm.

I stare at him fearlessly. "You think I don't know exactly what he's doing? Have you forgotten the trek of prisoners?"

Wilhelm presses his lips together tightly.

"Do you think it's any different in his camp?" I press on.

"I know what my father is doing. I don't need you to tell me that. I know he makes them work. Hard labor—"

"Hard labor?"

"Otherwise they won't obey! Suffering builds character—that's what he always said. He treated me the same way. That's why I'm not weak like you."

"Oh, really? Did he starve you too? You don't look like a skeleton to me. But who knows...a man who beats dogs is probably capable of anything."

Wilhelm gapes at me. Maybe he'd repressed the memory, of that time when I went to repair the big grandfather clock in Braun's study and witnessed *Herr* Braun *building character*. Lots of parents beat their children, but Braun...he really thrashed him good. He tried to hit

Wilhelm's dog too, a large German shepherd, but Wilhelm got in between them, which surprised me. I ran across Wilhelm in the foyer after that. He had red eyes and a big, purplish mark on his chin.

Now, as he's sitting on the rock, his face frozen, I almost feel sorry for him. To have a father like that...

"So my father's a pig! Is that what you're saying?" he speaks up at last. His voice sounds hollow, not angry as I expected.

I meet his gaze and hold it. "You have to decide that for yourself."

Wilhelm breaks off a branch of a nearby hazel bush and scratches random patterns in the sandy bank. When he speaks again, he seems to be deeply immersed in what he's doing.

"I don't know anymore."

I swallow hard, suddenly unable to look at him. The soft, sad cry of an owl echoes overhead.

Wilhelm throws the branch into the water. "The thing with Engler," he says with a husky voice, "I mean, Gerhard..." His jaws move as if he's chewing.

I wave him off, tears welling in my eyes again.

But I can just make out his whisper, nearly lost in the rushing of the stream. It sounds like, "I'm sorry."

The military situation becomes less clear by the day. The Allies are storming Berlin from all directions, and we're caught in between. I couldn't care less. For days, I've hardly been able to eat, though our new company is relatively well-supplied. In a twilight state, somewhere between waking and sleeping, I march onwards, sometimes allowing myself to believe that Gerhard's still beside me. Then

I start and realize it's Wilhelm, not Gerhard, and I feel like a dagger has been plunged into my chest.

At least Gerhard is beyond it all: the dangers, the fear, the stresses and strains…again and again, I ask myself how long this can possibly go on. The constant Allied air raids send my heart pounding each time. Its rhythm proves to me that I'm still alive, that at least I have the will to survive.

Head toward the Elbe; that's the unspoken rule. That's where the Americans are, they say, and nobody wants to be taken prisoner by the Russians.

A stream of German soldiers retreats across the hilly countryside toward that river—dirty, worn, defeated figures. That's how I must look, too. Sometimes we hear shots, and then there's another skirmish with enemy troops…the enemy is everywhere now.

I have no idea what day it is, or even what month. Only the subtle changes in my surroundings signal the progress of spring. The air is still cool, especially at night, but I welcome the first, pale green buds and the pussy willows, which remind me that life, like everything in nature, goes on.

One murky, overcast morning, we finally reach the banks of the Elbe that we were supposed to defend against the Russians, an eternity ago. The river is still full of snowmelt, and its muddy waters have flooded the banks. In the middle channel, the waters gurgle and bubble, sweeping branches and shrubs downstream.

We follow the line of German soldiers until we come to a massive reception camp near Tangermünde, where the Americans are waiting on the other side of the river for us to cross.

I pause to survey the scene in front of me: thousands of soldiers waiting to cross a narrow pontoon bridge—no more than several rickety boards fastened to floating barrels—or to be taken across the river on one of the few boats. The line seems endless, and more soldiers keep arriving by the minute.

You can only cross the bridge single-file, ten feet behind the man in front of you. And the tiny boats can only shuttle a handful of people at a time. It will take forever until it's our turn. Days, even weeks…the Russians will have surrounded us by then.

Exhausted, I collapse into the dewy grass. What's the point of having survived for so long? I don't want to go on anymore. I just want to sit here and wait. This is the end, one way or the other. Either the Russians will take me prisoner, or the Americans will. Or else…I don't care. Gerhard is still lying somewhere far away. He didn't make it here, and more than anything else, I wish I were lying down next to him.

Chapter 41

Wilhelm sinks down in the grass beside me. Even though he doesn't bother me as much anymore, I'd rather have my peace and quiet right now. But I'm too tired to drive him away, or even to talk. For a while, we watch the goings-on in the encampment. The lines for the pontoon bridges aren't getting any shorter. Many soldiers have given up waiting; they're cutting down the trees near the riverbank and building their own rafts. All around us, more and more people are streaming toward the river.

"What do you think? How long will it take us to get across?" asks Wilhelm.

"Too long."

Wilhelm gives me a sidelong glance. "So, what now?"

"Why are you asking me?" Since when does Wilhelm want my advice?

"We could try to help the raft-builders," he says, ignoring my petulance.

"That's useless."

"Sitting around here won't help either," Wilhelm snaps.

I stare in front of me, arms wrapped around my knees and chin resting on my forearms. Down on the riverbank, several soldiers are taking off their gear and throwing themselves into the current. The waters are lead-gray, like the sky. Heads, no bigger than the heads of pins, bob across the river, dragged and swirled by the current. Some of them disappear before reaching the other bank, swallowed by the rushing floods.

"We have to do something," insists Wilhelm.

"So go down to the rafts," I say. "Go and ask if they'll take you across."

"What about you?"

I shrug.

"Are you just going to sit here until the Russians come?"

"What do you care?"

"I don't," he says contemptuously. "I just thought you weren't such a coward anymore..."

"Coward?"

"Anyone can just sit here," he says. "It's much easier than finding a way across the river."

I frown. Can't he just leave me alone?

Wilhelm glares into the distance. "You know what? I'm sick of you wallowing. Pull yourself together! You're not the only one who's lost a friend. That's the way it is. Men have always died in wars. You get over it and move on."

"How do you know how it feels? You don't have any friends!"

"And what kind of a friend are you, if you pay him back like this?" he asks quietly.

I clench my fists and tear up some wilted blades of grass. I shouldn't let him get to me, but I can't help it. "What's that supposed to mean?"

"Who are you helping by falling apart? That won't bring him back. He'd want you to survive."

I grit my teeth and throw away the grass. I don't care what he says. What does he know about Gerhard, or me, or anyone? *I can't go home without him.*

Wilhelm lets out a snort of annoyance, and I realize I've said this out loud. "What else were you supposed to do?"

"I…"

"You carried him for as long as you could. Hell, I carried him myself, and he wasn't exactly light," he rails. "You can't save everyone."

His words awaken a vague memory: Willi, sitting at August's sickbed and telling me about the Great War. I can't believe it's Wilhelm, of all people, who's using those same words.

Wilhelm jumps to his feet. "Well, I guess there's nothing else I can do for you, Köhler. I'm going to go talk to the raft-builders." He throws me one last glance, turns away, and dashes off down the meadow toward the river.

I watch him go. He can be a real asshole, but he's not a liar. Which doesn't mean he's right. Or does it? Damn it, why do I let him get to me? Wilhelm has no right to speak to me like that. He's always showing off. If Gerhard were here…what would he do? The image of him lying on the ground, a big wet spot on his chest, jumps at me without warning. *Don't forget our deal.* Up till now, I always thought he meant our agreement to look after each other—the promise I didn't keep. Only now do I remember the conversation we had just before the attack, about what we'd do after the war.

My hand reaches into my coat, clutching at the pocket watch. I've protected it throughout all the fighting and fleeing. In the last couple of days, since…since *it* happened, I haven't taken it out. The hands have stopped.

What should I do?

Luise made me promise that I would bring the watch back in one piece. And my family needs me. I hate to admit that Braun is right, but sitting here waiting for the end doesn't do anyone any good. Gerhard wouldn't have wanted that either. If I do nothing, then I've really lost.

At that very moment, a shell explodes in the midst of the crowd of waiting soldiers. At first, I'm deafened by the crash. Then, slowly, muffled cries reach my ears. Everyone in the camp is running around wildly. The barrage from the east has begun; the Russians are coming...

I put the watch away, leave my weapons lying in the grass—no need to worry about MPs anymore—and sprint down the slope to the riverbank, where everything is chaos. Cries, bellows, and curses fill the air. A stampede on the bridge has begun. Everyone is desperately trying to escape the Russian's artillery fire. As I look for the raft builders, I try to assess the state of the Elbe, the direction and speed of its currents, its width, and the condition of its banks. I remember the spots where swimmers went under; there must be whirlpools beneath the surface there.

I know it will be hard, but I can do it. I've always been a strong swimmer. Even when I was little, there wasn't a river or lake that scared me. The only thing I'm worried about is the cold: with the snow-melt, the water will be frigid. I can't help but think of my brother Frank, but I quickly suppress the memory.

Finally, I see Wilhelm, who's chopping away at a tree on the bank, his strength amplified by panic and desperation.

"Drop that; it'll take too long," I call to him.

He stops, looking faintly relieved, but then resumes chopping at the trunk.

I tear the ax from his hand as he's adjusting his grip.

"Hey! What the hell?" The aggression has returned to his tone. He's still a head taller than me, but I'm not scared of him anymore.

I toss the ax into the wet grass and shout to make myself heard over the roar, "By the time we build a raft, the Russians will be on top of us."

"And how else are we supposed to get out of here?" He throws an arm out, pointing at the shaky, overfilled boats and the long lines of men desperately trying to cross the bridge.

Then another shell explodes right next to the pontoon bridge. A giant plume of water sprays up, and the bridge shakes dangerously. Everyone nearby is thrown into the water and either borne away by the currents or pulled under.

Wilhelm's eyes go wide. "Did you see that?"

I nod with determination. "We only have one option. We've got to swim."

He stares at me. "You saw what happened to those people!"

"They didn't all drown. You just have to use the proper technique. You can't swim against the current—you have to let yourself be dragged to save energy, even if you come out a few hundred yards downstream."

"It's still crazy. If the whirlpools don't get you, the cold will. All those guys who got in earlier thought they'd make it, too."

"They took their clothes off. And their coats. We have to leave everything on so we can retain our body heat for longer."

"And the coat will get soaked and become heavy as a rock."

I look steadily into Wilhelm's eyes. "Scared, Braun?" I sound much more confident than I am.

But my words have the desired effect. Wilhelm squints at me. His nostrils flare with his rapid breathing.

Then he snarls, "Okay, Köhler. Someone's got to fish you out."

I quash my reply, heading up the bank to look for a good starting point.

"We should go further upriver," I say when I spot Wilhelm following me. "If we drift too far, the Yanks won't be able to haul us out."

The Americans have spread out on the other bank and set up cable winches, but only in a certain area. When we're far enough away from our camp, I stop and take off my equipment.

Once again, Wilhelm looks hesitantly at the river, toward the opposite bank. I'd guess it's about five hundred feet across—not far as the crow flies, but our path will be longer since we will have to go diagonally. It's going to be exhausting.

Wilhelm shakes his head, muttering, "You're nuts, Köhler. Absolutely insane. And I must be crazy for listening to you."

Chapter 42

We aren't the only ones who have had this idea, though; a lot of soldiers seem to think it's better to swim than to fall prisoner to the Russians. I note where the others are headed, where the current is swiftest, where the dangerous whirlpools are lurking. My stomach flips each time I see a head that doesn't resurface.

To protect the watch and my ID from the water, I wrap them in a tarp, which I place inside the otherwise empty duffel bag. As I'm tightening the straps, I have an idea. I sort through the equipment I've left lying on the ground, looking for a rope. A sturdy hemp rope should do it. I throw one end to Wilhelm, fastening the other to my bag.

"What am I supposed to do with this?" Wilhelm asks.

"Tie it to your pack. That way we can't lose each other. And we can stop each other from drifting."

Wilhelm hesitates, rope in hand. "So if one of us goes under, the other goes down with him."

I glare at him. "You have a knife." *Coward!*

Wilhelm relents, tying the rope to his belt. It's about fifteen feet long—enough that we won't get in each other's way. Then I take another deep breath and turn to the Elbe.

I approach the river slowly, picking my way across the gently rolling floodplain. I'm still wearing my uniform, boots, and coat. It feels strange, going swimming with my clothes on, but I'm sure we're better off this way.

The muddy grass squelches under my feet. Puddles of dirty water have collected in small depressions, giving off a rancid smell. When I reach the edge of the gurgling floods, I turn to look at Wilhelm again. His face is white as chalk, but it shows the same grim determination that I'm feeling.

I wade into the river. The murky water, full of branches and moldering grass, laps at my ankles, and I inhale sharply as the frigid water soaks into my boots. It gets deeper quickly. Behind me, I hear Wilhelm's splashing footsteps. Already, I can feel the strong pull of the current.

I urge myself on. The longer I hesitate, the more likely my courage will desert me. But the distant thunder of artillery reinforces my decision. Now the water is lapping at my knees, my hips. I hold my breath and throw myself belly-first into the floods. My thick woolen coat dampens the shock of the cold water ever so slightly.

The moment I leave the shallows, where I could still stand, I feel the current pulling me downriver. I let myself be carried along, concentrating on keeping my head above water, and nudging myself in the right direction with strong, calm strokes. The other bank seems miles away. I hear the rushing of the water and Wilhelm's wheezing behind or next to me. Every now and then there's a tug on the rope when we've drifted too far apart.

Something yanks at my feet, so firmly it feels like an invisible hand is grabbing me. I have just enough time to fill my lungs before my head gets pulled under water. I kick out desperately, trying to suppress my rising panic. All around me there's only murky darkness. I have no idea which way is up.

Stay calm. Don't panic—it will only sap your strength. Controlling my strokes the best I can, I propel myself through the water in the direction I think is up. A sharp tug on the rope shows me the way.

Finally, my head resurfaces, and I gasp for air. Wilhelm's swimming in front of me. His pull on the rope helped get me out of the whirlpool I was caught in. Now we're in the middle of the river, where the Elbe is deepest and the current swiftest. I can see the Americans from here, in their dark green uniforms. They're running up and down the bank, looking for swimmers, their trucks with rope winches ready to pull us out. We just have to get within range.

Slowly, the cold begins to creep through my coat and down into my skin. I can't feel my toes anymore. My heart is beating more and more slowly despite the fear and the physical exertion. I feel a sweet exhaustion, a lethargy beginning to lull me.

I blink furiously to keep myself awake and take a gulp of cool air. Just a few more minutes and we'll be across. The other bank appears before my eyes for a second, then my head goes halfway under. I push forward, taking slow, steadying breaths.

Glancing to the side, I spot a tree trunk rushing toward me like a battering ram. I swim faster, trying to move out of the way. The trunk turns, its broad side now toward us. Before I can shift course, it's caught up with us. I watch it strike Wilhelm full on the shoulder. Then I feel a hard tug on the rope and find myself going under again. Damn it. The log must have knocked him out.

My head plunges into the icy water, which comes streaming into my ears and nose. The river bubbles and froths all around me. Even with my eyes wide open, I can't see anything but water, dirty and brown with tiny specks in it.

I stroke rapidly with my arms, but it doesn't help. It's like there's a weight pulling me down; I can't get back to the surface. *Help!* What with the panic and lack of oxygen, my vision is rapidly narrowing.

Then I remember what I told Wilhelm: *You've got a knife.* I have to cut myself loose. Confused and disoriented, I feel around for the rope that's tied to my duffel bag.

But I can't just let him drown, not even if he's Wilhelm Braun. Though my lungs are burning and I can barely feel my limbs, I pull myself along the rope, hoping it will lead me to Wilhelm.

The current is slower near the bottom. Groping around, my hand comes across something soft—a body. By now I'm aching for a breath of fresh air. It goes against my every instinct not to swim to the surface, but I can't—not without him. I reach under his arms, trying to pull him upwards, but I'm met with resistance. We're stuck.

He won't make it, whispers a voice in my head. You have to leave him behind. You can't save everyone.

No! My fingers, which barely feel like my own anymore, move along the rope; it seems to have tangled around something. A sharp branch scratches against my skin, but I hardly notice. Each second brings us closer to death.

The knife! Wilhelm put it in his belt. It must still be there. Yes, I've got it. I pull it out and hack blindly at the rope, feeling my arms weaken.

Finally, the last fiber snaps. The knife slides out of my hand and I grab Wilhelm by the collar. With every last ounce of my strength, I drag us both to the surface.

My mouth opens of its own accord as my lungs gasp for air. Bubbles form, everything goes dark. No, wait, it's not dark here. It's full of light.

Gerhard, surrounded by a halo of bright light, is standing on a golden wheat field the same color as Luise's hair. He waves at me, laughing. Then he gestures for me to follow. I'm trying, but my legs and arms won't obey. I can't even move an inch. Smiling, he points to something lying in the grass in front of me. A rope. I grab it and hold on tight. I don't know why that's important, but I trust my friend.

I feel a sharp burning in my lungs. As I open my eyes wide, I catch a glimpse of sky. It's overcast, nothing like the brilliantly blue sky over the field I just visited.

My chest feels like it's about to explode. With deep, rattling breaths, I gulp in the air. The fog before my eyes slowly clears. One of my hands is still clutching Wilhelm's collar, the other a thick rope that the Americans have thrown me from the opposite bank.

Somebody is standing on the grass and waving, but it's not Gerhard. Of course not.

I let the rope pull me along while I try to keep Wilhelm's head above water. But my strength deserts me. Just as I'm starting to think I can't do it anymore, I feel gravel under the soles of my boots. Then everything really goes dark.

Chapter 43

The next few days pass in a seemingly endless cycle of waking and sleeping, daydreams and nightmares. Often, I startle awake, drenched in sweat. During one of my rare moments of alertness, I learn that I'm in a Yankee field hospital with other German soldiers. Wilhelm has recovered quickly from our ordeal. They released him after just a day. But my fever just won't go away.

Once, I have the hazy impression that a German doctor is standing over me, talking about some sort of infection. Sometimes my teeth chatter so violently I think they'll shatter. The next instant, I'm sweating so hard that I wish I could take off all my clothes. My head is buzzing, my lips are chapped and raw, and even my eyes ache in their sockets. Every now and again, it feels like somebody is applying a hot iron to my molars and I cry out in agony.

Something cool presses against my forehead; it feels good. Then somebody drips water on my chapped lips. When I open my eyes, I see a familiar, blurry figure sitting in front of me. *Gerhard*, I think, and fall back asleep, exhausted but happy.

At last, I regain consciousness and glance around, confused. Rows of cots with grayish-white sheets surround me, full of gaunt figures in gauze. And standing by my bed is…Wilhelm Braun.

I can't help but feel disappointed. So it wasn't Gerhard taking care of me. But why would Wilhelm do that?

Once again, a hot iron seems to touch my molars, and I cringe. I feel my cheeks with one hand; they're swollen.

Wilhelm leaves and comes back with a doctor, who examines me.

"You were hypothermic. Your molars have gone septic," he says, opening my mouth carefully with his fingers and peering in. Even this tiny movement causes the pain to flare up.

"I have to pull them. Otherwise, the pus will enter your bloodstream and you could get blood poisoning. I'll prep everything for surgery."

He leaves and I stare at the ceiling. Every muscle in my body aches, but the pain in my jaw eclipses it all. Though I'm not crazy about having my teeth pulled, I can't wait until they're gone.

Only now do I notice that Wilhelm is still standing at my bedside, looking down at me uncertainly.

"Morning, Köhler. You sure slept long enough," he mutters.

I try to respond, but everything in my mouth is swollen, even my tongue. I can't get a word out.

Wilhelm kneads his cap in his hands. "I bet the operation will be quick. You were lucky; the cold just got your teeth. The other guys...half of them can't even pull up their pants."

I wrinkle my brow and painstakingly form syllables with my lips: *Dys-en-tery?* Wilhelm nods.

I'm not so sure I'm lucky. The pain radiating from my jaw is so intense I can barely think, though the morphine the doctor gave me is starting to take effect. Still, diarrhea can't be fun either. And a lot of the soldiers around me are missing limbs. I didn't so much as lose my little finger…

"The whole damn camp smells like a latrine," Wilhelm says. "Anyway, I'll leave you alone."

He kneads his cap again as if hesitating. The gesture looks silly in a boy of his size, and it irritates me because I've never seen Wilhelm like this, so…sheepish. I nod weakly.

He puts his cap on and turns away, but doesn't leave. Not yet. I watch, confused, as he turns back around and takes a step toward the bed. He squares his shoulders. "By the way…thanks."

I blink.

It's clearly an effort for him to continue. "You pulled me out, didn't you?"

I don't reply—because my mouth won't let me, but also because I'm so surprised at his words.

"The last thing I remember is that tree coming toward me," he goes on. "I didn't even have time to duck. Next thing I know, I'm waking up in the hospital. I still don't know how I got here."

He looks steadily at me, and for a moment I glimpse a grudging respect in his gray eyes.

"I owe you."

After the operation, they wheel my bed outside every day so the warm sunshine can help heal my jaw. The light, plus the hearty broth they're feeding me, lifts my spirits.

Wilhelm comes to keep me company every day while I'm sitting outside. We don't say a lot, sometimes nothing at all. Still, I can tell that he's changed. If someone had told me a year ago that Wilhelm Braun could be a decent guy, I would have laughed them out of the room.

When we do talk, the conversation usually turns to our plans for the future. The war is over. Hitler died a few days ago; or at least, that's what they're saying. Rumor has it he killed himself, which wouldn't surprise me. And now it's just a matter of time until Germany surrenders. But what will become of us then, of all the prisoners in this massive, temporary camp, those men without a future?

"I don't know what to do," says Wilhelm. "When we get out of here, everything's going to be different. And my family…I don't even know what happened to them."

I remain silent, wondering if I should feel sorry for Braun if they've caught his father. As an SS officer, he'd stick out even without his uniform, because of the tattoo on his upper arm. I've heard that the Allies shot a lot of the SS guys on the spot. Wilhelm has almost certainly heard the same thing. And even though his father was a criminal and probably deserved it…the war has killed so many fathers already.

I gaze out the window as the train rattles merrily down the tracks, past fields covered with a thin layer of snow and a few scattered farmhouses, their chimneys trailing smoke.

It's hard to believe that a whole year has passed. 1945 is coming to an end, and everything has changed.

I grow more and more restless the closer we come to Leipzig and keep asking myself if I actually recognize my surroundings, or if I'm just imagining it. I'm equal parts excited and afraid. Excited to see my family again; afraid they won't recognize me after all these months—months that have definitely changed me. And afraid that something happened to them while I was gone.

When they gave me my discharge papers, they offered me the opportunity to train as a policeman. Since so many men died in the war, there are labor shortages everywhere. But I refused. I swore I would never touch a weapon again.

Wilhelm took them up on it. "I don't know what else to do. What else I *can* do," he said, the last time we saw each other.

I'm not sure if I'm glad to be rid of him, or if I'll miss him. Maybe a little of both. He was the last link to my old life in Silesia, which isn't even part of Germany anymore. The Allies gave it to Poland. During my last few months as a prisoner of war, I got used to Braun. When we said goodbye, I realized I didn't feel any of my old resentment toward him. We parted with a handshake.

Now I'm walking across Leipzig, wearing my heavy backpack. The city feels changed, yet still oddly familiar. Burned-out buildings and bomb craters still scar the streets, but the rubble has been removed. Every house that survived the bombings must be crammed full of people who lost their homes. Children in tattered coats and worn shoes play on the sidewalk; a young woman wearing a scarf bustles by, pushing a stroller full of coal. When a Russian army patrol passes, I quickly lower my eyes.

I cross the park where I said goodbye to Luise. The last time I was in Leipzig, Gerhard was with me. Every time I think of him I still feel a stabbing pain in my chest.

Then my heart skips a beat: I've turned into the street where Luise and Aunt Martha live. But where Luise's house used to be, now there's just an empty space. The walls have been reduced to a few scattered stones, and even the basement has caved in. Only the old apple tree in the garden remains intact, stretching out its bare, knotty branches.

Suddenly terrified, I speed up my pace and knock on Aunt Martha's door.

It's Lieschen who opens it. Her mouth hangs open and her eyes are big as saucers when she sees me. Then she flings her thin arms around my waist.

"Anton's here!" she yells after letting go. She dashes down the hall, her pigtails bobbing. "Anton's here!"

At her cry, all of the doors along the hall fly open, and Mother emerges from the kitchen. We stare at each other for a long moment. I can't find the words to speak. The smile in Mother's eyes makes her look much younger; her whole face shines. Aunt Martha, standing behind her, bursts into tears. I barely manage to set down my backpack before Mother crushes me in a bear hug.

"My boy," she murmurs. "My boy."

I'm home. My siblings' rejoicing is music to my ears as I clutch tightly at Mother, feeling her warmth, the coarse material of her cardigan under my hands. Here, I can forget everything that's happened.

After a long, long while, Mother lets me go, and Aunt Martha and Uncle Emil pull me into their embrace.

"What's in the big bag?" chirps Lotta, meanwhile. "Looks like the sack from Father Christmas. But Christmas Eve isn't until the day after tomorrow."

"Anton, wanna see what I carved with your knife?" Fritz bellows in my ear.

It feels like I'm dreaming; everything seems so unreal— until I remember what I saw outside. I touch Uncle Emil's arm so he knows I'm trying to get his attention. "Uncle, Mother, where…" I have to steel myself to finish the question. "Where are the Hofmanns?"

"Ah, yes. That happened during the last few weeks of the war," Uncle Emil begins, softly.

I swallow.

"But don't you worry," Mother interrupts, seeing my expression. "Luise and her family are fine. They're in Markranstädt, with her grandparents."

I'm dizzy with relief, and she pulls me into her arms again, wiping tears from her eyes.

"And Helmut? Any news?" I ask next. I never really got along with my oldest brother, but he's still my brother.

"Still in the Yankee camp. We got a telegram from him a little while after you were drafted. He's doing okay, all things considered. But he's not a minor, so they're not going to release him anytime soon. He doesn't know when he can come home."

I look down at the little ones, still crowding excitedly around my backpack. Erich is getting so big!

"We took care of everyone while you were gone, Anton," Max says proudly, sticking his thumbs into his waistband.

I take my bag into the kitchen and begin laying its contents out on the table. My family watches, astonished, as packs of flour, sugar, salt, barley, dried peas, butter, cheese, bread, and chocolate appear before them.

"Oh Anton, it's just like in a fairy tale," sighs Aunt Martha, smelling an especially large sausage. "Where did you get all this?"

"In the West. I traded my cigarette coupons before I got on the train," I reply, passing out chocolate to my siblings. Their beaming eyes are large and luminous in their thin faces. "I know this stuff is hard to come by here."

"And they just let you take it over the border?" Uncle Emil asks.

I grin sheepishly. "Well, it was kind of a close call. One of the Soviet border guards made me empty the bag near Erfurt." I remember how I sweated as, piece by piece, I unpacked the food that I had stacked so neatly, wondering if it would ever reach my family.

"I'd taken about half of the stuff out, my train was leaving in just a few minutes, and then suddenly he waved me on and said—" I imitate the growling voice with its thick Russian accent. "Pack it up!"

The children squeal with laughter at my impression. I don't mention that I was crying and that it may have been my tears that persuaded him to show mercy.

"And then you made it to the train?"

I smile. "Yeah, I had to repack everything, but I made it—just barely. Or else I wouldn't be here."

Mother puts her arm around my waist and rests her head on my shoulder. "But you are. You're finally home."

Chapter 44

I shift nervously from one foot to the other as I wait for the door to open. I'm wound as tightly as a violin string. Will she be happy to see me? Is she even home? I wish I could have called ahead, told her I was coming. But I don't even know if Luise's grandparents have a telephone. The door opens, and I hold my breath.

Luise stares at me like I'm a ghost, one hand still on the latch. Her silence gives me time to take her in. She's changed; she looks…grown-up. Her soft, white-blond hair, which always hung in two braids over her shoulders, has been cropped short. She's wearing it chin-length now, an unfamiliar sight, but it looks good on her.

"Anton," she whispers finally.

"Hi," is all I can say.

"How did you—when—why," she stammers and lifts her hand tentatively from the latch. She stretches it toward me as if to make sure I'm really there. But before her hand touches my arm, she stops.

Our eyes meet and time stands still. Her cornflower-blue irises are shining, just like they always have. She lets her hand fall down to her side.

The hero's return…shouldn't she be throwing her arms around my neck? What was I expecting?

"I'm back," I say stupidly.

"I didn't know if… Why didn't you write?" The question sounds helpless, not accusatory.

"I sent a telegram, but…"

"Oh…right. Our house."

I nod. "I'm sorry."

She nods too, then we fall silent again. There's so much to say. Where are we supposed to begin?

"How long have you been home?" she asks, glancing around the hall as if someone might be watching us.

"A couple of days. I came over as soon as I could."

She fixes me with an inscrutable look. Then she reaches for the scarf that's lying on a side table and throws it around her neck. "Want to go for a walk?"

We walk side-by-side through snowy Markranstädt, its streets unmarred by bombs. We're only inches apart, but we're not touching.

"Where's Gerhard?" Luise asks timidly.

I stare at my feet. This is the hardest part. Even when I told Mother, I only said that he'd died, no details. I can't relive that scene again. "He didn't…" I murmur.

She stops abruptly. "You mean…?"

My silence is all the confirmation she needs. Her eyes grow moist and she covers her mouth with her hands. "I'm so sorry," she whispers.

"Me too."

"He was always so cheerful. So…optimistic." Her voice breaks.

"Yeah," I say, swallowing hard. "And your father?"

She sighs. "No news. They're still not saying when they're going to release adult prisoners. And even then, we don't know…" I hear both hope and resignation in her voice.

The war has left all of us with ugly wounds—scars that will take a long time to heal.

A raven croaks, perched in a nearby tree. It inspects us with wise eyes as we pass. Pedestrians bustle by, and we make way for them, separating briefly.

"What was it like for you?" Luise starts again after we've walked a while in silence. "After the war ended?"

I take a moment to piece together my thoughts, trying to suppress the grief and concentrate on our conversation.

"I was a POW. When the Yankees learned I was a watchmaker, they made me appraise the value of all of the things they'd looted: watches, gems, gold jewelry…anything they put in front of me. But they treated me okay. Fed me properly. At some point, they sent us to a different camp, near Hamburg. I lived there with a couple of other boys at a miller's house. We were all minors, so they let us roam free as long as we didn't go far from the mill. I could have stayed there…in the West. But I just wanted to come home. Even if it meant going back under Russian control."

"Yeah, the Russians. They have everything so under control," she says sarcastically. "So what now? What's the plan?"

"First I need to earn some money," I say. "Help my family. Maybe I can get a job taking apart the munitions factories in Leuna."

"And then?" asks Luise.

"I'm not sure yet. When I've saved a bit, maybe I could…" I gather all my courage and look at her. "Do you think you could teach me to read music?"

A smile flits across her face, half questioning, half surprised. "Really?"

I smile back and nod.

"Of course I'll teach you. Anything you want," she says and gives me a look that almost makes me choke.

We walk for a while through the near-empty streets as the winter sun sinks lower and lower. Luise tells me how she made it through the last weeks of the war, before the Yankees took Leipzig, and how her house was destroyed.

"Two of our neighbors went out of the cellar just two minutes before the bomb dropped, to get a shovel and other tools. They never made it back...but they'd left the door slightly ajar—that was the only reason we got out at all, with all the rubble that was piled up in front of the door. We could never have moved it otherwise..."

She falls silent as if reliving what must have been a traumatic night for her and her family. I can't say how glad I am that she got out unharmed.

"I'm sorry you lost everything," I say.

"Yeah, well...seeing my piano all in pieces hurt a lot. But at least I've still got the letters and diaries from my father. We should start heading back," she says, though she sounds regretful. "There's a curfew at sunset. Only for Germans, of course."

I was so absorbed in our conversation that I didn't even notice the fading light.

"We'll take a shortcut," says Luise, cutting across the marketplace and heading past the church.

As we round the corner, I hear rough voices. A crowd of Russian soldiers has gathered in front of the movie theater, some of them wearing the unmistakable fur caps. There's no one else left in the streets. From the way they're slurring their words, they're obviously drunk, even if I can't understand what they're saying. Suddenly, a girl's scream sounds from among them.

"Come here!" A harsh male voice with a thick Russian accent commands.

The group parts slightly. Now we can see that they've surrounded two young girls. One of the girls spots us and cries, "Help, please!"

Acting on instinct, I shove Luise into a shadowy alley right next to us. "Hide," I whisper to her.

She hesitates for a moment, but my determined expression seems to persuade her.

The Russians have turned toward me now, their faces dark. They're not much older than I am but seem much larger and stronger, and they're only a few feet away. I feel the familiar prickling of fear. But I survived worse in the war.

"Leave them alone!" I yell.

Don't show them you're afraid, I say to myself. Always look the lion in the eye.

The Russian soldiers aren't used to having Germans stand up to them. They abandon the girls and turn their attention toward me. A bullish young man with a pock-marked face rolls up his sleeves and lumbers toward me. The others follow. The girls wisely take advantage of the distraction to run away.

I want to turn on my heels and run as well, but suddenly I'm surrounded. They are standing in a circle around me, legs splayed, arms crossed, their faces hardly visible in the gathering gloom. When one of them tries to grab me by the scruff, I react without thinking. Instantly, I drop to the ground and skitter on my hands and knees across the cobblestones, straight through one of the soldiers' legs. I leap to my feet on his other side and dash off, as fast as my legs can carry me. If the war's taught me one thing, it's how to run away.

I head away from Luise and the girls. At first, the soldiers are too dumbfounded to react, and I have a slight head start. But by the time I turn onto the next side street, I can hear their angry shouts and the ringing of their footsteps on the cobblestones.

They catch up quickly, even though they're drunk. The footsteps sound directly behind me as I reach a fork in the road, trying to decide which way to turn. I know I can't hold them off for long. At least one of them must be faster than I am, and I don't know my way around this town.

I turn into the marketplace that Luise and I just came from. My eyes settle on a pub, The Old Boar. The front door is open wide, and a dim light glows inside. The innkeeper must be airing it out. Before I can think about whether there's an exit on the other side, I burst in.

The innkeeper, a plump man with broad shoulders, is putting chairs on top of the tables so he can sweep. He looks at me wearily and without surprise as if boys stormed into his pub every day.

"We're closed," he growls.

"Is there a back door?" I manage to wheeze between two gasping breaths, dashing toward the back of the room.

He studies me silently. Then he hears the curses and cries of the Russians outside. He gestures behind him with his thumb.

I sprint around the tables toward the door, well-hidden in the dark hallway behind the pub.

"But it's a dead-end," the innkeeper calls as I'm turning the knob.

Still, I keep running; I can already hear the Russians bursting into the inn. Now I find myself in a small courtyard garden. The innkeeper was right—there's no way out. The whole place is surrounded by a ten-foot stone wall.

A ten-foot wall…

Something clicks. I can see Müller's wall in front of me again, the one he forced me to climb so many times.

Run toward it, you sissy! I hear Müller's voice screeching in my head. *Don't crawl like a snail.* And Gerhard saying: *Just close your eyes and go!*

I can do this, I think.

I run straight at the wall like it will dissolve into thin air. With the force of my leap, my legs carry me up the face of the wall. I grip the edge, pull myself up the last yard, and drop down onto the other side, then pause to take a breath.

Back in the garden, I can hear astonished cries and angry yells. I jump quickly to my feet in case they've had the same training I have and drag myself into the park behind the pub. There, I lean back against the thick trunk of a linden tree, listening. The night is clear and calm. It's starting to snow. The flakes melt on my hot face. I hope Luise got home okay.

Then I hear the Russians' voices again. They've come around the back of the pub to look for me. Stubborn bastards. They're probably just sore that a pipsqueak like me led them around by the nose.

After a while, they disappear. And now I hear different noises—loud banging and crashing. It sounds like they're wrecking the poor innkeeper's pub. I come out from behind the tree and trot cautiously back toward the front of The Old Boar. Should I help him? It's my fault they're blowing off their steam in his pub, after all.

Just then, a car pulls up in front of the inn, and four uniformed soldiers with nightsticks and pistols jump out. They charge into the pub. I watch from a safe distance as melee erupts. Finally, the seven drunken soldiers are dragged away by the officers. Maybe the innkeeper called the Soviet command post; they're responsible for keeping the troops in line.

Once they're all gone and I can breathe easy again, I take off toward the movie theater, thinking I should go back to Luise's and see if she made it home. I try to remember which way we took on our walk. Then, as I pass the narrow alley, a figure emerges from the darkness and into the light of a streetlamp. I stop, rooted to the spot.

In the milky glow, I can just make out Luise's slender silhouette. Big, feathery snowflakes are falling all around her. She looks angelic.

Then she steps completely into the light, and our eyes meet. My heart is beating fast. Must be from all the running. Without a word, she flies into my arms and presses her face against my shoulder. As I wrap my arms around her gingerly, I'm reminded of the day of the bomb attack, but this time feels different. *I* feel different. We stand like this for a long time. I breathe in her sweet flowery scent and hardly dare to move.

Finally, she pulls back so she can look up at me, her eyes shining in the lamplight. Her hair is capped with a layer of snow.

"Are you okay?" she asks, her voice hardly more than a whisper.

I nod, pausing a moment to search for the right words. "You…waited for me." It's a statement and a question at the same time.

A slight smile plays on her lips. "Of course I did," she says.

I reach down and take her hand—not hesitantly and shyly, but like I've never done anything else in my entire life.

I smile at her. "I'll take you home," I say.

Hand in hand, we walk back through the glistening snow.

Epilogue

New Year's Eve is quiet and clear. My youngest siblings have already gone to bed, though it's not midnight yet. The new year has yet to begin.

I step out into the garden. The icy air envelops me, but even though I'm not wearing a jacket, I'm not cold, so long as I keep my hands buried in my pockets. I lean against the garden fence and tilt my head back, looking up at the twinkling stars. My gaze is lost in the endless expanse of the Milky Way, which curls like a silk ribbon across the sky.

Maybe, I think suddenly, *people become stars after they die*. It's a silly thought. Still, I search for a star that reminds me of Gerhard. I find him under Cassiopeia. He glimmers impishly at me and has a warm, yellow-orange color. I take note of the star's position and its brightness.

The clock in the nearby church steeple chimes twelve: 1946 has begun. There are no fireworks—people have experienced enough explosions in recent years.

A year ago, on New Year's Eve, all of this began…back then I was still in Silesia, miles away. Then they separated me from my family, locked me in the barracks and made me a slave of their damned war…those people who are no longer in power, of whom nothing remains besides a black mark on Germany's history. They're the people responsible for Gerhard's death, and August's, and so many more.

I think about the letter from August's mother. I was surprised when Mother gave it to me on Christmas Eve. Surprised and nervous. Did she hate me? Did she blame me for what had happened? But the letter was nothing like I'd expected. She wrote,

> *Dear Anton,*
>
> *Thank you so much for your lovely letter. We can hardly express how much it means to us, to know that August didn't die alone, that you were there for him when we couldn't be. I know that August always looked up to you and wanted to be like you—and I can see why. Don't feel guilty. Maybe God took August so that he didn't have to experience these last, horrible months of the war. It's such a comfort to know that you will remember him fondly.*
>
> *We wish you all the best.*

I swallow hard. A great weight has been lifted from my shoulders—a weight I didn't even know was there, until it was gone.

This year, my life begins anew.

I owe it to Gerhard and myself to make the best of it, of this new life. The path forward feels unfamiliar and strange; I'm still not sure how I'm going to pull it off. But if I don't follow my dreams now, then when?

I survived. I survived the war; I swam across the Elbe. After that, I can do anything.

I pull out the pocket watch and flip open the cover. The filigree hands tick tirelessly along, displaying the time: five minutes after twelve. As the cool metal rests in my palm, a plan solidifies in my mind.

I'm going to work to earn money, like I told Luise. But I'll save some of what I earn so I can buy a violin and take music lessons. I'll practice for as long as it takes to be good—all night long if I have to. And I'll go to night school to earn my *Abitur*; Luise will help me with that.

These are grand plans. But when I look up into the sky, full of twinkling stars, a feeling of freedom, of infinity overcomes me. As if anything were possible. For an instant, I almost believe that I can leap up into the sky.

Gerhard's star blinks down at me, amicably. He seems to be saying, *Yep, that's it, buddy. Now you've finally figured it all out.*

Afterword

Much has already been written about the Nazi era and World War II. After decades of silence, Germans have begun to come to terms with their past. Given the abundance of stories, reports, documentaries, and novels, it's difficult to create something entirely original. But that wasn't my intent; every story matters because it helps us to "never forget" what transpired.

The initial purpose of this book was to record my grandfather's experiences. But in the end, these experiences came to stand for the fate of many people—that's why all of the characters are fictional, and why I only borrowed from his stories. Most of the events actually happened; the others could just as easily have happened.

Born in 1929 in Silesia, my grandfather, Hubert Stych, was ten years old when the war began. He had the bad fortune to be drafted during the final months of the war and served as a sixteen-year-old 'soldier'. When I was little, I often asked him to recount his experiences, and he told me freely. Back then, I thought his stories were great, exciting adventures; only later did I realize that my grandfather had gone through things that no fifteen- or sixteen-year-old should go through. I began to think of him as living history. The most astonishing thing about his stories was that he was able to tell them to me, his granddaughter. He survived—often by sheer luck.

For me (and perhaps for other Germans my age), it's difficult to imagine that what's happening today in other parts of the world happened here not that long ago—and that it could happen again at any time. The sorrow and hardship of war is something that no reader should have to go through. But experiencing it through a character in a book may help us better understand our past and gain a different perspective on the problems of today's world.

Anja May

About the Author

Anja May is a German author, born in Leipzig. After her dissertation in Astrobiology, where she studied the survival of extremophilic bacteria under Martian conditions, she followed her passion for writing and became a freelance author and translator. Her first novel, *When the War is Over*, was originally published in German in 2016.

Anja loves books, walks during sunset, and the United States, where she has lived for two years.

To learn more about Anja and her books, visit her website: www.anjamay.de/english-books.

Ranks of the German *Wehrmacht* compared to the US Army

German *Wehrmacht*	US Army
General Ranks	
Generalfeldmarschall	General of the Army
Generaloberst	General
General der ...	Lieutenant General (" ...")
Generalleutnant	Major General
Generalmajor	Brigadier General
Officer Ranks	
Oberst	Colonel
Oberstleutnant	Lieutenant Colonel
Major	Major
Hauptmann	Captain
Oberleutnant	1st Lieutenant
Leutnant	2nd Lieutenant
Enlisted Ranks	
Stabsfeldwebel	Command Sergeant Major
Oberfeldwebel	Sergeant Major
Feldwebel	First Sergeant
Unterfeldwebel	Staff Sergeant
Unteroffizier	Sergeant
Obergefreiter	Corporal
Gefreiter	Private First Class
Ober-... (Obergrenadier, Oberkanonier...)	Private ("Infantry", "Artillery", "Gunner"...)
Soldat (Grenadier, Kanonier, Schütze, Pionier...)	Private ("Infantry", "Artillery", "Gunner", "Pioneer"...)

Map

Map of the German Reich in 1944 with the dashed line
marking Anton's journey from Silesia to Leipzig, and finally
to Tangermünde.

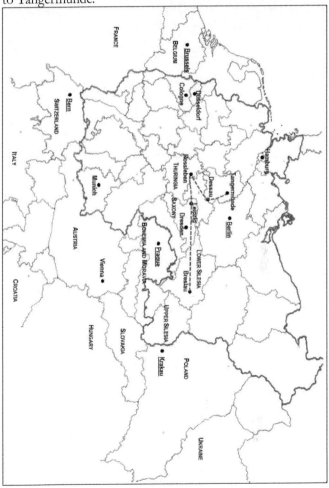

38664449R00192

Made in the USA
San Bernardino, CA
13 June 2019